She Knew She Was Right

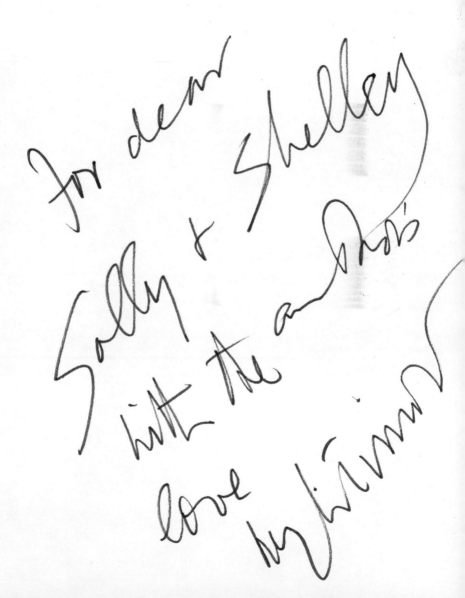

She Knew
She Was Right

STORIES BY

Ivy Litvinov

THE VIKING PRESS

New York

Of the stories in this collection the following nine appeared originally in *The New Yorker*: "Sowing Asphodel" (1966), "Farewell to the Dacha" (1967), "Babushka," and "She Knew She Was Right" (1968), "Call It Love" (1969), and "Bright Shores," "Apartheid," "The Boy Who Laughed," and "Holiday Home" (1970); and were copyrighted © in the respective years shown by The New Yorker Magazine, Inc.

First published in 1971 by The Viking Press, Inc.

625 Madison Avenue, New York, N.Y. 10022

Published simultaneously in Canada by

The Macmillan Company of Canada Limited

SBN 670-63947-8

Library of Congress catalog card number: 75-104135

Printed in U.S.A.

ACKNOWLEDGMENT: The lyrics from "Always" by Irving Berlin, Copyright 1925 Irving Berlin, Copyright renewed 1952 Irving Berlin. Reprinted by permission of Irving Berlin Music Corporation.

To Rachel MacKenzie with love

Contents

She Knew She Was Right

Any Day Now

CAMBRIDGE WAS A NAME, it was a name with names in it. At first there were only Mummie and Dadda and Eliza; then there was Doris, and Eileen had to walk beside the pram. When Doris could sit up there was room for Eileen in the pram too, but Eliza said she hardly liked to lift her in, the children did look at each other so queer across the coverlet. "How d'you mean queer?" Mummie asked, and Eliza said, "As if they'd be glad of the opportunity to do one another bodily arm." And there were streets with houses in them and some of them had very high walls so Eliza walked in the road and Eileen walked on the top of the road, and one day she fell on the wheel of the pram where the rubber was worn away and ever after there was a nick in Eileen's left eyebrow because Eliza said air never grows on a scar. Long, long after, even when Eileen was grown-up, people who looked at her face quite near sometimes said, "Where did you get that scar, darling?" but most people never noticed.

Then Bee came. Bee was partly for Baby, but it was her name too, short for Beatrice, and Eileen and Doris had to walk one each side of the pram. And Eliza pushed the pram with her right hand and let one of the children hold her left hand. And Eileen and Doris didn't really want to hold Eliza's hand at all, but neither of them wanted to let the other hold it, because then she could jig up and down and say, "You've lost your situation you little botheration."

The children heard Mummie tell Dadda about it in the evening. She said, "You wouldn't think a grown-up person would *teach* children to be spiteful, would you?" And Dadda sighed and said we ought to do something about it, and Mummie sighed and said, "Yes, but what?" And afterward Doris said to Eileen, "How did she know?" And Eileen said, "How do I know how she knew?" But she did because she was the one who told Mummie.

Eileen remembered three things about Dadda in Cambridge, and why she knew they happened in Cambridge was because Cambridge was the only time she had slept in Mummie's and Dadda's room; when they went away from Cambridge she had to sleep in the night nursery. They were all awful things, but they were different kinds of awful.

One was waking up early in the morning and crying for the chamber and Mummie jumped right across the room where she slept with Dadda in a great enormous bed with little bells on it that sometimes rang in the night but when you went to look for them in the daytime there weren't any, only little knobs, and Dadda said, "I tighten those blasted things every day and still they jingle." And Mummie sat Eileen on the chamber and gave her a rusk and put her to bed again and went back herself and the rusk crumbled while Eileen was munching it and she tried to pick the bits up and eat them but the littlest bits stayed and they hurt Eileen's bottom and she cried and Mummie came and picked her up and sat her at the end of the bed while she brushed the crumbs away and put her back and said, "Now you go to sleep and let Mummie have a tiny bit of peace." And two crumbs stayed on the sheet and they pricked Eileen's heel and she began to cry again. This time Mummie didn't get up and Eileen heard her say to Dadda, "What shall we do to a little girl who won't let poor Mummie go to sleep?" And Dadda said in a thin sleepy voice, "Smack her little bo-bo." After this it was very very quiet in the room. Eileen couldn't even cry, she felt as if she had been squeezed into a tight ball. That was the awfulest thing that ever happened to her because up till then she had been quite sure Dadda was hers, and he said smack her.

The next awfulest thing hurt very much at first but it ended up not awful a bit but very sweet. Eileen had been put down for her afternoon nap but when Eliza went out of the room she stood up on the mattress to look closer at the picture of a kitten playing with a ball of wool and the picture fell onto the eiderdown and Eileen sat down and tried to put the little nail at the loose end of the string back into the hole in the frame, but it wouldn't stay so she began winding the string round and round her middle finger and it got tighter and tighter and she couldn't unwind it because the nail had wedged itself into the coil. Her finger then her whole hand got icy cold and she began to scream and Dadda came bursting in and uncoiled the string and kissed her finger and took her icy hand into his enormous warm hands and held it and rubbed it till it got warm too.

The third awful thing was when Eliza took her away from Doris where they had been playing with picture blocks on the nursery floor one afternoon, and washed her face and put her white silk dress with the blue sash on her, and Dadda took her in a fly till the horse stopped and they got out and went into a house and upstairs into a dark room full of lots of children and some uncles and aunts with no faces. Everybody seemed to be trying to get closer to the window and Dadda and Eileen tried too. There was a noise like woosh and weeoo outside the window

and when Eileen looked up she saw the whole of out of doors
had broken into tiny colored bits, dark red and dark blue and
orange and green. Eileen shrieked and clung to Dadda's trouser
leg. It was quite quite dark outside now and the sharp pain of fear
inside Eileen went away, but soon there was more wooshing and
weeooing, and again the darkness broke up into millions of
colored bits. Eileen screamed so hard that Dadda had to push his
way back through the people and take Eileen downstairs and get
into the waiting fly with her.

And now there was nothing outside the window but lovely
thin almost darkness, and white houses, and shafts of pale light
from street lamps. Eileen stopped sobbing and leaned against
Dadda, who only said, "Poor girlie, she was frightened" and
wiped her face with his handkerchief which smelled consolingly
of pipe.

Back home Eileen stood guiltily between Mummie and Dadda
while he told all about it. Mummie lifted Eileen's face between
her long cool hands and said, "I hope she isn't going to be a
coward."

And there was one other thing to remember about Dadda in
Cambridge but it wasn't awful at all it was lovely. Another afternoon when Eliza had put her down for her nap and she was
sitting up in bed someone came softly into the room before she
had time to lie down again. Sitting up in bed was naughty and
Eileen wasn't *just* sitting up, she had the eiderdown pulled over
her head and was looking through its tiny stitched holes. Then
someone sat on the edge of the bed, another thing you must Never
Do, and a head poked in beside Eileen's under the slant of the
eiderdown and it smelled of Dadda and a cheek that was a weeny
bit prickly but never mind it was lovely, rested against Eileen's.
"What are you doing, Tomkins?" he asked. Eileen put the tip of
her finger against a point of light and took it away and said,

"Tinku Littu" rather hoarsely because it was hot and smoky under the eiderdown now. "Oh," said Dadda, "a star!" And oh Dadda and oh stars! And oh Eileen and Dadda in the warm smoky dark with stars all round them and all over them.

Another thing at Cambridge was Follow. Follow was an enormous dog outside the butcher's shop who allowed Dadda to sit Eileen on his back close up to his heavy head and waited for her to dig both hands into his thick ruff before he lumbered to his strong short legs and walked along the front of the shop and back again. And Eileen said, "Don't hold me. I won't fall." But Dadda always walked beside them with his hand open over her back. And Dadda took Eileen for a ride on Follow's back every single day. And once when Eileen had measles the butcher allowed Dadda to take Follow to see her and he put his chin on the quilt and Eliza was cross because he dribbled ever such a little dribble on the quilt she had especially washed and starched for the doctor. But Doris was afraid of Follow.

One day a fly with a very thin horse with a drooping head came to the door. Dadda put a Gladstone bag under the seat and a small trunk on the floor of the fly for Eileen and Doris to put their feet on; he lifted them in and then helped Mummie in and got in himself and the fly jerked and rumbled and they knew they were going to the station to live in London, and when the fly was properly started and had turned round the corner of the road, Eileen and Doris exchanged meaningful glances. No Bee. But when they got to the station the fly stopped, Dadda got out and jumped Eileen and Doris onto the pavement and there was Eliza smiling into the pram. And Mummie said, "Give her to me" and held Bee in her arms all the way to London. Eileen and Doris looked at one another again and looked away.

Doris could remember nothing about Cambridge except going away from it. She was sure there had always been a baby and of course she didn't believe there had once been no Doris. She didn't even remember Follow but that was because she had been afraid of Follow.

In London the night nursery was at the top of the house where there wasn't any carpet on the stairs only linoleum, and the day nursery was at the very bottom and the children could see out into the road and there was a pavement on the other side too and houses with iron railings and you opened a little iron gate and went down iron steps to the back door and that was the area. Errand boys went up and down the pavement and down the iron steps to the area. A man with a barrel organ came on Saturdays and played "Home Sweet Home" and "Nazareth," only the tunes, but there was a book on the top of the drawing-room piano with the words of all the songs in the world in it, and Mummie played the tunes and taught Eileen and Doris the words. But when Mummie wanted to teach the children nicer songs more for children, like "Pussycat, pussycat, where have you been?" and "Where do fairies hide their heads when snow is on the ground?" she sent Eileen downstairs to give the man a penny to go into the next street and a lump of sugar for his monkey. Sometimes two men, one with a harp, came and the children loved to watch the one with the harp take the leather cover off and hand it to the other one who held it over his arm and sang "The Minstrel Boy to the War Has Gone," and "The Wearing of the Green," while the man with the harp played the tunes on the harp, but the children liked the organ-grinder best because of the monkey and once a boy on a bicycle, balancing a little boat with meat on it over his shoulder, fell, bicycle and all, into the gutter just in front of their area, and Annie came up the steps and took a leg of mutton and helped him to pick up a bunch of sausages and two lamb chops and told him never trust yourself on a bicycle with a trencher of meat again, she had a good mind to complain to the butcher. "Did she say trencher?" Mummie asked when the children told her and she was so pleased when they called out together, "Trencher! Trencher!" that she never said a word to Annie about taking meat straight out of the filthy gutter. And when Dadda came in they heard her tell him, "She called it a trencher."

One of the nicest things they ever saw from the nursery window was a move. The people opposite put a card in their window with C.P. in blue letters on it, and that very same day a van as big as a house, drawn by two enormous broad-chested horses with hairy hoofs, stopped at the door and backed till the wheels were right against the curb. The horses faced the children, tossing their heads and stamping their great hoofs, and Eileen and Doris could hear the end wall of the van being let down with a rattle of chains till it rested on the pavement, and see the driver and a thick-looking man run into the house and come back with sideboards and closets and ferns and chambers. It wasn't so interesting when people moved in because you could only see the men's backs, but afterward it was lovely to see the horses arch their necks and rattle the empty van away as lightly as if it were a cab.

Sometimes a cab jingled round the corner and stopped in front of their own house, and a gentleman got out and stretched up his hand to pay the driver and then walked up steps and tugged at the handle of the bell. Then Eliza would have to brush Eileen's hair and change her dress and take her up to the drawing room, always Eileen because she could shake hands and answer when she was spoken to but Doris would hang her head to one side and stick out her underlip and if people asked her too many questions she sometimes cried. And one day there was a gentleman sitting beside the fire opposite Mummie and he was drinking a cup of tea but when he saw Eileen he put the cup on the saucer on the tea tray and said, "D'you mean to say this is Eileen! How she's grown!" And Mummie said, "Don't you remember Mr. Clarke?" And Eileen didn't and Mummie said, "The only thing Eileen remembers about Cambridge is Follow." Mr. Clarke said, "Follow has fallen on evil days. The old man died and the son married a woman who does not like dogs." Eileen thought of the time she fell on the wheel of the pram and when she got back to the nursery she said to Doris, "Poor Follow fell down." But Doris couldn't remember Follow.

Never in their wildest dreams had the children expected to see a Carter Paterson van come up to their own front steps, but one day this happened. The horses came spanking round the corner into the road and while the children crowded to the window to see where it was going to stop, the driver turned the horses and ran round and let the back of the van rattle on its chains till it touched the curb. And in the enormous opening stood a great tawny beast with brown drooping ears and a white chest. It stood very still for a moment and then raised its head and barked once, a single toll of a great bell, and walked down the slanting boards to the pavement and up the steps where Eliza and Eileen stood waiting, with Doris hovering behind in the hall. Follow had come to London.

Everybody who had been in Cambridge was in London now but they were all in Cambridge too and whenever Eileen liked she could see them there and she was there herself, standing in London and looking into Cambridge, and Doris wasn't afraid of Follow any more, but in the night in his kennel in the area he came out and stood away from it the length of his chain and moaned to break a person's heart, and Dadda had to get out of bed and go out into the street and down the back steps (because Annie always kept the front-door key under her pillow) and take one of Follow's thick crusty-underneath paws in his hand and say, "What's the matter, old man? Follow, old fellow, what's the matter?" and show him his pan of water, and at last Follow would lap some water and lick Dadda's hand and turn back into his kennel. The children never waked up when Follow moaned but they heard Mummie and Dadda talk about it at breakfast. Mummie thought Follow could never forget the bitter time he must have been through when the butcher died and his son married a woman who didn't like dogs and kept him chained up in the back yard day and night. "Why do people keep dogs?" Dadda asked. "Haven't we got enough bitterness of our own?" Mummie said, "Oh, Walter, don't say that!" and the children burst out crying and said, "Oh, Dadda, don't say that!" But Annie wouldn't have him in her kitchen, she said he smelled. And when Auntie Gracie and Auntie Florrie came they wouldn't let him come near them and Auntie Florrie said, "The poor old tyke's a bit high, isn't he?" And Auntie Gracie said, "You shouldn't have let Walter send for him, an old dog like that. You have your children to think of, Wyn."

Some people said the winter of 1895 was the coldest winter there had been in England for a hundred years; others said seventy-five or fifty. The children couldn't go out for ten days and there were no cabs on the stands, and the buses could hardly run; horses sometimes fell dead in the street and the horses that had to carry food in vans and coffins in hearses had long needles of ice inside their noses and hanging from their chins. There were bonfires on the Thames and Follow had to be allowed into the house, and Dadda came back from the office with a bad cold and went to bed and the doctor came every day and one morning very early the children were buttoned into their coats with their arms left out of the sleeves, and had a blanket put over their heads and were carried one at a time into the house opposite where a

dressmaker lived who had a darling mother cat with three
kittens and thick bundles of patterns for the children to play with
till Eliza came for them, and when she had taken off their coats
she took off her own shawl and they saw she had a black bow
in her cap and it was her best cap and she said, "That's for your
father." And Mummie came into the nursery and said, "Dadda's
dead." And the very next day the sun came out and the snow
melted and people said it was like spring. But Mummie said
Dadda would never come back any more. But whenever Eileen
remembered Cambridge Dadda was there just as much as everyone else was. But he wasn't in London any more and now he
would always stay in Before-London, that was Cambridge, you
couldn't be in two places when you were dead, that was what
being dead meant. Now there was Sandy. He was Mr. Hart at
first and Eileen used to be sent up to the drawing room when
he came and he took her on his knee and read her the story of the
Frog Prince. But very soon he went out with Mummie and came
back when the children were in bed and they must be sure always
to call him Sandy. He taught Eileen a song "The Mill Belongs to
Sandy Still" and read her the Frog Prince, always the Frog
Prince, but Doris always cried and hid behind the curtain when
he wanted to play with her. And he said Follow was a splendid
creature, only "not to put too fine a point on it, Mem" (he called
Mummie "Mem")—"the old chap stinks."

There came a day out of a mist of days when Bee who was
consumptive was sent to a sanatorium at the seaside and Eileen
and Doris were buttoned into white frocks, and leghorn hats
wreathed with long-stemmed daisies were jammed onto their
heads ("Go out and buy them lagorn hats" the children heard
Mummie tell Auntie Gracie and Auntie Florrie). Each had a
coral necklace fastened at the back of her neck and a bunch of
bachelor's-buttons and ivy leaves and now they were bridesmaids.

As soon as Eliza finished hooking her powder-blue Sunday dress they were all going to St. Andrew's to see Mummie get married to Sandy. Follow padded up the area steps and lumbered after them hopefully. "Who took *you* off the chain?" Eliza muttered. The great dog retreated before her stamping foot, but was back in a moment at their heels, wagging his tail apologetically. Auntie Gracie was waiting for them outside the church. She told Eliza to take Follow home this instant because the vet would be coming for him any moment.

Eileen and Doris were guided into the church and told to walk behind Mummie only try not to tread on her skirt. They all went up the aisle to a clergyman in a white surplice who talked to Mummie and Sandy a few moments in a rather booming voice. He called them Winifred and John and they said "I do." Then everybody went into a little room, chattering and laughing as if they weren't in church any more, though there was a picture of the Virgin Mary holding the Infant Jesus over a big desk, and an enlarged photograph of a clergyman on the opposite wall. When Mummie and Sandy and Auntie Gracie and a gentleman the children didn't know had written something in a book, everyone went back into the church and down the aisle out into the street and there was Eliza waiting outside the door for them. Auntie Gracie looked at her and raised her eyebrows and Eliza nodded and took Eileen and Doris by the hand and walked off with them. A carriage overtook them on the way home and somebody put out a hand in a white glove and waved a bunch of tumbled violets. *Mummie.* When they got to the front door the carriage was waiting at the curb. The driver had a white bow on the handle of his whip and the children called to Eliza to look at the horse's darling face. Eliza took them upstairs to the open door of the drawing room and went away. There were lots of strange ladies and gentlemen in the drawing room, all talking and laughing, but they stopped when somebody said, "Here come the bridesmaids!" Glasses of lemonade and wedges of cake were held out to them but they would not take anything till Mummie came up and took the flowers out of their hands. Everybody asked them their names and how old they were and Doris looked as if she were going to burst into tears, so Mummie called Eliza to take them to the nursery. She said it was time for her to change into her traveling clothes anyhow. The children stayed in their brides-maids' dresses till it was time for them to say good-by to Mummie and see her go away with Sandy in the carriage. Mummie who now had on a purple dress with a hat all made of pretend-violets, kissed them on the doorstep and said she would be back very soon and they would all go and live in a darling little house in the country.

When the carriage turned out of sight round the corner of the street Eileen and Doris clambered down the area steps to say goodnight to Follow, but the kennel was empty and the chain hung from its staple and lay dreadfully still and snaky on the flagstones.

The children were as good as gold with Auntie Gracie. They never asked when Mummie was coming back. "They don't miss her one bit," Auntie Florrie said. "And they haven't once asked about Bee." "It's out of sight out of mind with these little people, I'm afraid," said Auntie Gracie cheerfully. "You'd think they'd want to know where Follow was, at least." Auntie Gracie *did* think that was a little strange, but then she had never thought they were particularly affectionate children. "You always have to tell them to kiss one." A few days later Eliza wasn't there when Eileen and Doris woke up, and even then the children said not a word.

The days went on and on with nothing happening and the

children all the time as good as gold, except when they were alone in the nursery and the grownups could hear them quarreling fiercely. But at last a ring came at the front door which made the aunts rush out of the dining room, where they were all having dinner. Eileen felt a funny sort of inside flying when she heard Mummie's voice in the hall and she saw that Doris's cheeks were waxy white. Neither of them got up to rush into Mummie's outstretched arms when she appeared in the dining-room doorway, they only raised their heads and stared at her over the table. Mummie said, "They don't seem to know I've been away." "Oh, we've got along famously," said Auntie Gracie. "Perhaps I'd better go away again," Mummie said, but Doris let her spoon fall into her plate and raised her voice in a dismal howl. Mummie stood her reticule on the floor and darted across the room. She gathered the weeping Doris into her arms and promised wildly never never to go away from her girlies any more. She said Doris must finish her dinner like a good girl and Auntie Gracie would dress her and they would all go and live in a darling little house in the country. Then she turned to Eileen, sitting at the table with drooping head and upward glance. "Eat up your fish, darling, Auntie Florrie will dress you and we'll go the moment you're ready." And Eileen said, rather uncertainly, "Me too?" When she saw Auntie Gracie bustle Doris out of the room she spooned up the scraps of fish on her plate and was ready in a minute.

Before they went Auntie Gracie put the C.P. card in the window and Eileen understood that the furniture from the upstairs room that had been brought down into the hall would be taken to the country by Carter Paterson. They had noticed their own beds being taken down the stairs by Auntie Gracie and Auntie Florrie that very morning, and never asked why.

The first thing the children saw when they got out of the train was an advertisement for coal exactly like the ones Eileen thought had been left behind forever in the Fulham Road. "Is this the country?" she wailed. But Mummie told her not to be so impatient, station yards were always hideous, and after she had steered them out into the road and round the tip of a vacant lot choked with nettles, it really did begin to look a little bit more like the country. Gardens full of homely flowers stretched from a row of cottages right down to the sidewalk, and there was no sidewalk on the other side, only a hedge and glimpses of cows slowly crossing a tilted field. The children halted at each wicket with glad cries "Is this it?" but Mummie hurried them on till cottages and front gardens came to an end in a high tarred fence. Puffings, snortings, grindings, and an occasional piercing whistle came from behind the fence and when the children put an eye to a crack they could see stumpy engines vanishing round curves and speeding back again. Their hearts sank—was *this* the country? But Mummie took them across the road to the top of shaky wooden steps and they climbed down to a sunken lane between high walls with flowering branches hanging over their tops. It was dark in the lane, but the glare of daylight waited for them at the other end, and Mummie let go of their hands and told them to run on in front till they got to a little red gate with Hillside on it in golden letters. The street they were now in was itself the side of a hill and the children panted as they trotted past gates dark green, purple, brown, even a faded crimson, but never anything that looked like red to their eyes. The houses went in pairs and Eileen spelled out the name on each wicket gate: "The Laurels," "Jesmond Dene," "Sunny View," and "The Nook," were easy enough for Eileen but there were some—"Auchinleck," "Notre Nid," "Beau Lieu," and "Sans Souci"—which she could not take into her mouth. They passed "Hillside" without noticing it and had to be called back. Its front garden was just like the others, dark bushes and a lone laburnum at the gate. The children trundled dejectedly up the path behind Mummie. But the front door opened and in the opening was Eliza, in a white apron and blue cotton dress, and they flew into her arms with joyous cries. They had never thought to see Eliza again. Mummie pushed them into the hall past a stand without a single hat or coat on its waiting pegs, into a dim passage along the side of a staircase where banisters soared out of sight. She stopped to throw open a door in the wall opposite the staircase: "This is your room." A rocking horse stood in the middle of the floor as if it had been waiting a long time for this moment, but before they could take any notice of it Doris crossed her thighs and had to be led out shambling. Left alone in the room Eileen sidled past the horse, trying not to see up its flaring crimson nostrils. The window looked out on a yard closed on one side by a fence, on the other by a low wall with a roof over it and a window and a door in it, and at the end by a trellised screen overgrown with leaves; a pencil of light at the outer edge of the trellis showed that it didn't go right up to the fence and movements behind it suggested waving branches. But Eileen didn't understand that this was a way out and she was ready to cry with disappointment. Was this the country, this meager yard, the overflowing dustbin in the corner, the black shed under the window where she stood, the black fence? Her eyes filled with tears and she didn't notice that Eliza had come into the nursery till she was close behind her, touching her elbow. "Well, Misery, do you think you're going to be happy here?" Eliza said.

Still holding Eileen's elbow, Eliza steered her into the passage, where light filtered through the banisters from a window on the first landing, through a bright kitchen two steps down from the end of the passage and into a stone-floored scullery. "Go on out into the garden," she said, and almost pushed Eileen through the door into the yard. Now Eileen could see there was plenty of room to pass between the leafy screen and the fence, and in a moment she was standing on a gravel path at the edge of a shaggy lawn. A great tree from the next-door garden drooped its branches over this lawn, which came to an end at a long turfy mound planted with apple trees. Swaying movements and flashes of color seen through the branches of the trees invited to the real garden behind. But Eileen liked pink-tipped daisies and dandelions more than flower beds and went no farther across the lawn than a sawed-off tree stump at its edge with an iron scraper sticking out at the bottom. Just as she arrived for a closer look at it (somehow it was a very interesting stump) a small bird dropped out of the wide sky on to the rim of the scraper. Its head was inky black, its wings chestnut brown, its breast a lovable fluff of gray and pale yellow. Eileen hoped the iron rim wasn't hurting its pink claws. It looked straight at her before opening its snub beak for a loud chirp, bounced along the scraper and gave another chirp, and back to the end again for one more chirp, loud and liquid; then it hopped back to the middle of the scraper, sang three piercing notes, raised and lowered tiny wings, and soared out of sight.

Eileen and Doris, accustomed to Bee's sudden disappearances and reappearances, were not surprised on returning from a morning walk to find her lying on the sofa in the dining room. It was the discovery of an abandoned kennel in a nettle-grown spot at the bottom of the garden that made their hearts beat: *Could it be that Follow would come back? Would they meet him any day now in the garden path, heavy tail swinging, red tongue lolling?* Together they examined every nook and corner of yard and garden, but no beloved bulky form lumbered to its feet at their approach. Once they caught sight of something brown through the tangled boughs of a rhododendron bush, but it was only a bit of wrapping paper blown from the dustbin borne through the gateway on a powerful shoulder to a waiting cart. Sometimes they thought they heard a snuffle and a low whine in the night, and once Eileen crept downstairs in her nightgown and stood on the scratchy door mat to listen at the keyhole, but it was only the wind sighing in the trees. One day a distinct sound of whining came from the top of the house; Eileen and Doris tiptoed up the last steep flight of stairs till they came to an open door. But it was only Annie and Mrs. Owen, the weekly charwoman, pushing a dilapidated armchair on three squealing casters into the box room, where it joined a pile of trunks, a chest of drawers with one drawer missing, and a sewing machine with a prolapsed treadle. The signs never led to Follow, and Mummie told them Carter Paterson would bring a kitten any day now.

She Knew She Was Right

W HEN WYN HAD BEGUN looking about for another husband, a few months after her first husband's death at thirty, nobody blamed her; what was she to do when the insurance money ran out?

Wyn was a well-grown, upstanding young woman, but she was pigeon-breasted and flat-buttocked. She tried to counter these defects by stuffing stockings or a towel in the top of her stays and sewing bustles into the skirts of her dresses. But it was all no good, and her fiancé's sister had written to a school friend, "Walter is going to marry a girl with no bottom and no bust." An unidentified illness at boarding school had depleted her eyelashes, and she picked her nose when she thought herself unobserved. But men were crazy about Wyn, even when she was a widow with three little girls and a mouthful of false teeth, lamentable result of three births. This was a bitter pill for Gracie and Florrie, her two spinster sisters, who had almost all their teeth intact and no distressing habits. Wyn had several admirers, and two bona fide suitors: John Hart and John Hedley, her John and her Other John.

John Hedley, hereinafter to be referred to as Mac, was in the Foreign Office, which Wyn and her sisters learned to call, with reverent familiarity, the F.O. John Hart —Sandy—was only in the British Museum, vaguely associated in the minds of Wyn's sisters and their friends with outsize statues and uniformed attendants. He was small, had a squeaky voice, and told unfunny stories, choking with laughter, to grave faces, compelling attention with the bore's uplifted finger.

The only present John Hart ever brought his ladylove was *The Scottish Student's Songbook*, and *his* evenings (the Johns never came together) were almost entirely spent at the piano. Wyn vamped accompaniments courageously, following a singer through all modulations and shuffling instinctively between tonic and dominant till her fingers fell into the right key. She was careful not to drown Sandy's tenor moo, and he thought no one had ever before understood the music in his soul. Gracie and Florrie stayed in their bedroom till it was time to climb the uncarpeted stairs to the nursery and see to the children. On their way down again they would pause a moment to listen outside the drawing-room door, trip down the last flight into the hall, and clatter down the back steps to the basement kitchen. The singing overhead told them when to begin getting the supper tray ready: they put the kettle on the spirit lamp at the opening of "Shall I Wasting in Despair," and took it off to mix the cocoa in a pottery jug at the end of "Blow, Blow, Thou Winter Wind." The triumphant refrain of "The Mill Belongs to Sandy Still" was the sign for them to toil up the kitchen stairs with the loaded tray.

On Mac's evenings there was never any music, but he could be counted on to leave a long-necked bottle or a basket of fruit from Fortnum & Mason's on the hall stand before mounting the stairs to the drawing room. Gracie and Florrie told each other that there could be no comparison, which, of course, they meant any comparison was entirely in Mac's favor. That Wyn could hesitate for a moment was more than they could understand. "By their fruits ye shall know them!" cried Florrie, biting into the flushed cheek of a hothouse peach. "It isn't only that, it's the whole style of the man," Gracie said reprovingly, digging into the skin of a tangerine with her thumbnail.

Each John had his alternate Sunday. Sandy always arrived bright and early and conducted Wyn on foot by exhausting short cuts to Paddington Station, where they took the train to Leafy Bucks. They tramped across meadows and through copses, with frequent pauses for Sandy to consult his map, till darkness fell, stopping only once at a wayside pub to eat bread and cheese washed down with stone ginger. Wyn, always the good sport, pecked along at his side on her French heels, but she arrived home faint and hungry from these excursions.

One fine day in June, a whistling boy paused outside the railings of No. 9 Fairholme Road, attracted by the unusual sight of a hansom drawn up in front of a house on a Sunday morning. The boy watched a swell in a gray sack coat and black trousers carry a little party in a bonnet and pelisse of white piqué down the steps, followed by a lady with a tiny hat slanted over her forehead and her skirt gathered to one side in the palm of her left hand. In the doorway stood two ladies with Princess Alexandra fringes, each holding a hand of an anxious-looking little party in a white pinafore and ankle-strap shoes. From a window in the basement kitchen, a servant lifted the curtain to peep out, and a St. Bernard dog stood with its front paws as far up the area steps as its chain would allow. The gentleman put the child into the cab, next to the window, then turned to help the lady in and climb up after her. The ladies on the doorstep waved their hands and tried to make the little girl between them wave hers. The driver whipped up his horse for a sharp turn, and the eyes of the child in the cab swooped in their sockets, twin black comets trailing a flash of white. The ladies on the doorstep caught their breath and exchanged smiling glances, the servant watching from the kitchen window clutched unconsciously at her heart, and the boy on the pavement detached himself from the railings and went on his way whistling. He thought he would never forget those eyes as long as he lived; he didn't know that generals in Whitehall were even now plotting the deaths in the Veldt of thousands of whistling boys, and that, in fact, he had only four more years to live.

"Sandy would rather die than keep a cab waiting twenty minutes," Florrie mumbled over the fat chocolate she had popped into her mouth the moment the hall door closed behind them. Gracie reminded her tartly that Mac did not have to live on his salary; he had a little money of his own. Florrie knew that very well; it was what was so nice about him.

The cab carried Mac, Wyn, and Eileen smartly to Paddington Station, and the train drew them out of town as fast as it could puff. So far, but how much less strenuously, Mac followed in the footsteps of Sandy. Everybody who wanted a day in the country went to Bucks, Leafy Bucks, because it was so easy to get at. They left the train at High Wyncombe and made straight for the White Hart, where Wyn put Eileen down for a nap, and left her in charge of a smiling chambermaid so that she could go for a stroll in the woods with Mac while the special lunch he had ordered was cooking. Mac treated her with exaggerated respect, only brushing the back of her hand for a moment as he freed her skirt from brambles. In the dining room of the White Hart, Wyn settled herself on the crimson plush seat of a corner divan and unfolded a cool, shiny napkin. Looking round, she saw that there were mere cornflowers and dog daisies in britannia-metal vases on the other tables, and her glance came back exultantly to the heavy cut-glass bowl of apricot-tinted roses (real *gloire de Dijon!*) on their own table. The headwaiter himself, leaving underlings to serve the table-d'hôte mutton to less exclusive customers, set a still bigger glass bowl, erupting crisp whity-green lettuce leaves, in front of Mac; ivory salad servers turned up slices of tomatoes and crescents of hard-boiled eggs as, with pontifical solemnity, the headwaiter mixed in the dressing. Just as a roast chicken came rolling up for Mac's approval, swing doors at the end of the room opened and Eileen was delivered by a still-smiling chambermaid into the hands of a smiling waiter, and led across the floor to her mother. Diners lifted their heads from their plates for a peep at the interesting trio, and Wyn saw in every face that the loveliness of the child flattered her own looks. When she glanced across the table at Mac, the slavish adoration in his eyes almost oppressed her. She asked herself if even Walter had ever looked at her like that, forgetting that Walter had not had to plead for love that had never been denied him.

When the table was cleared for dessert, Mac placed a closed fist on the table, and then lifted it to give a sudden twitch with thumb and forefinger to a hidden object. One flashing gyration, and a gold hoop lay on the cloth in front of the wondering child. She pounced on it with a chubby paw, but dropped the shining thing when it pricked her finger. "Don't be afraid," Mac said. "It won't bite you." But Eileen *was* afraid, could not be persuaded to touch it again; there was something sharp and frightening in the middle of it. Mac leaned over to give another spin to the hoop, but this time he was clumsy and it rolled off the edge of the table. A waitress hastened up and stooped over, close to Wyn's skirts, coming back with the ring in her fingers. She seemed uncertain whether to hand it to the lady or the gentleman.

"Is it pretty?" Mac asked.

"Very pretty, sir," said the girl. "Lovely, I should say."

The sight of pale gums and uneven, discolored teeth so in-genuously displayed embarrassed Wyn, and she turned aside, but Mac looked unflinching into the blurred sallow face. "Keep it," he said banteringly. "Nobody else wants it." He leaned his head with the tiniest gesture in the direction of Wyn, now busy tucking a napkin under the bush of curls on Eileen's neck.

"Oh, sir!" The girl giggled. Her hand closed involuntarily over the ring, but the next moment she put it on the tablecloth, well away from the edge, and hurried off at the approach of the watchful headwaiter.

Mac scooped up the ring with a blind motion of his fingers and slipped it into a vest pocket.

Mac found an empty first-class compartment for the homeward journey, and Eileen was soon fast asleep in her mother's arms. For a moment, the thought flashed through Wyn's head that not even for the sake of being alone with her would Sandy have taken first-class tickets, spoony little man though he was, but she dismissed it as unworthy. Mac, who had been gazing at her in silence for some time, suddenly got up and let down the window to lean over the top for a smoke. After two whiffs, he threw the cigarette out with a muffled groan and sat down beside Wyn, drawing her toward him and kissing her over the head of the sleeping child. She had forgotten the feel of lips against her own. How fragrant Mac's breath was! What was he whispering? *"Winifred! Winifred! Winifred!"* over and over again. He was the first to draw away, but it was only to pick up the sleeping child and lay her on the opposite seat. Then he came back to Wyn with assurance, like a bailiff who has managed to get his foot in the door. But the moment of illusion had passed. Mac's breath smelled like any other man's after dinner, and the burning of his lips no longer thrilled Wyn. Still, she felt pledged. She had let him feel her moment of response; to go back on it now would be cruel.

The train entered a tunnel, everything was one great confused roar. When it came out, the roaring inside and out suddenly subsided. Mac got to his feet and blundered to the window, smoothing his hair and wiping his face with his handkerchief. Then, bracing himself in the swaying carriage, he felt in his vest pocket again. Eileen was back on her mother's lap, blinking sleepily. Mac bent over to open her fist. "Give it to Mummie," he said, closing the warm baby fingers over the ring. Wyn took it herself and examined the diamond in its delicate clawed setting. "Tell Mummie to put it on."

"Put it on, Mummie," the child piped obediently.

Neither of the grownups smiled. Wyn began pushing the ring over her knuckle, all the time looking sad-eyed out the window at the flying telegraph poles. But Mac broke into a great cry of triumph that rolled up to the low roof like the roar of a caged lion and frightened Eileen into a burst of tears. With weeping and exultation, with words of consolation and hurried tying of bonnet strings, they were drawn into the resounding cave of the terminus.

Gracie and Florrie were enraptured by the ring, could hardly leave it to get Eileen her supper. But black depression had clamped down on Wyn. She threatened to send the ring back if her sisters said another word about it, and really did tug it off and fling it into a corner. Florrie retrieved it with squeals of horror; she tried to put it on her own finger but couldn't get it over the second joint, and Gracie snatched it from her and handed it to Wyn, who put it in her reticule.

The next morning her sisters found Wyn in tears. "It'll kill Sandy," she sobbed. "He'll never get over it, never." Gracie hummed the tune of "Fiddle-dee-dee, fiddle-dee-dee, the Mouse has married the Bumblebee."

Gracie and Florrie went to their room early that evening. When the silence of the house was shattered by the pealing of the front doorbell, they clutched at one another, listening through its diminishing clamor for Wyn's light step on the stairs. Five minutes later, they heard the muted thud of the front door being gently closed, and knew John Hart had been dismissed. "You'd think she'd have asked the poor fellow into the drawing room," Florrie said.

"She was quite right," snapped Gracie. "Least said soonest mended in such cases."

The day after, Mac arrived with a bottle of champagne and a bunch of roses. Gracie and Florrie would have received him with enthusiasm if Wyn had not been so grave and aloof; it would not do, they felt, to appear happier than the bride-elect. So there was something almost funereal in the solemnity of the first greetings, and the older sisters were glad to hurry out for glasses and a vase. When Florrie came back with the roses, the lovers were seated at opposite sides of the hearthrug, *both smoking.*

"She was leaning over lighting her cigarette from his," Florrie reported. "Wouldn't you think she'd be afraid of forfeiting his respect?" "She's probably a great deal more afraid of him finding out about Bee," Gracie said.

Every evening was John Hedley's evening now, but Wyn did not behave in the least like a bride-to-be. She got up late, spent most of the day in her dressing gown, refused to hear a word about wedding clothes, and forbade her sisters to spread the news of the engagement. They noticed that she only put on the ring when her fiancé was expected. Florrie was distressed; Gracie did not like the look of things at all. By imperceptible degrees, the

emotional barometer slipped from the high point in John Hedley's favor. Once he had gained his end, he turned out to be as
selfish and inconsiderate as most men. Annie complained that he
pushed past her without a word when she opened the door,
whereas Mr. Hart always used to say, with a pleasant smile,
"Good morning, Annie. Are the ladies at home?" Mr. Hart had
greeted Gracie and Florrie with an old-fashioned chivalry which
they remembered regretfully now that Mac's party manners
had degenerated into the hollowest of jocular exclamations and
an obvious impatience to get them out of the room and be alone
with Wyn. Eileen was accustomed to her share in the courtship
of her mother, but now if Wyn had her sent up to the drawing room in her gray frock and black sash, it was never long
before Mac thrust a packet of butterscotch or a tangerine into
her hand and told her to run away and share it with her little
sister Doris. Once, having come unprovided, he insinuated a
threepenny bit into Eileen's clenched fist, and led her to the
door. "She doesn't know what it is," Wyn said fondly, but she
felt vaguely affronted, and the next time Mac came Gracie gave
him back the coin. "Our children are brought up not to take
money from visitors."

When a letter with a Newcastle postmark came for Wyn,
Gracie turned it over and over in her hands; the address was in
John Hart's neat handwriting, and she would have opened it if
she dared. She even considered throwing it on the kitchen fire.
They all knew that John Hart had gone north to seek consolation
in the bosom of his family; why should he be allowed to remind
Wyn of himself? In the end, traditions of decency prevailed and
Gracie put the letter back on the hall stand. She knew Wyn
would leave it on her dressing table. Investigating a few hours
later, Gracie found nothing in the torn envelope but a few snap-
shots nestling in the folds of a half-sheet of note paper. A single

sentence in small, very black letters (John Hart's civil-service calligraphy) was neatly centered under the embossed address: "Sandy is always yours." Gracie cast a condescending glance at the photographs—the Pier, the Collingwood Monument, and the Venerable Bede's Hermitage.

That same evening, Wyn told Mac she had heard from Sandy.

"How's he bearing up under the blow?" Mac asked.

Wyn did not quite like his manner. "He says he's always mine."

"Well, you're not always his, I hope."

"John Hart is a very good man."

"But I'm the one you're going to marry."

"Yes, Mac, but there's something I keep meaning to tell you."

"Speak, lady, for thy servant heareth."

"It's about the children. I never told you—"

Mac fidgeted impatiently in his chair. "Your children shall be my children. What more is there to say about them?" Mac supposed she was going over old ground, and he did not care to waste the precious moments in idle talk.

When Wyn let her lover out in the small gray hours of the morning, the distant policeman pacing the pavement seemed to be the only other person awake in the whole of London. Far away in the King's Road, the wheels of market carts rumbled drowsily on their way to Covent Garden. Wyn shut the door behind Mac and crept up the stairs to her room, chilled to the bone. She awoke in the morning to profound, inexplicable depression, and after Annie had brought up her morning cup of tea none of her household saw her till she appeared for the children's dinner at half past one, still in her dressing gown. But a few days later she got up as soon as she had drunk her morning tea in bed, and dressed herself for company—stays, camisole, and frilled taffeta petticoat beneath the gray cashmere dress that had replaced her deep mourning. She put on her close bonnet and short cape and went straight

out of the house without a word to anybody. Gracie called down
the kitchen stairs for Annie to come and take the children for a
walk, so that she and Florrie could discuss the extraordinary situation over breakfast. Never before had Wyn gone out so early. They
were still at their tea and toast when she came back and stood in
the doorway pulling off her gloves to deliver her bomb.

"I've done it!" she said defiantly. "I've sent for John Hart."

"I knew it!" Gracie cried shrilly. "I knew you would."

"What did you write?" asked the ever-practical and inquisitive
Florrie. "How could you put it in a wire?"

"I put it in six words," Wyn said proudly. "I didn't even put
the signature." Pressed by her sisters, she at last told them what
the six words had been: "The mill belongs to Sandy still."

"Barmy!" said Gracie scornfully. "Barmy on the crumpet."

"Will he understand?" Florrie asked.

The course of the day showed them how well John Hart had
understood. Every few hours came a telegram, three in all, but
it was always the same telegram: "SANDY IS COMING." And there
was one more at nine-thirty the next morning: "SANDY IS HERE."

"He must have sent one every time the train stopped," Florrie
said in awed tones and began calculating the total cost.

Wyn's friends were astonished to hear that she had thrown
over the brilliant John Hedley for a prosy and penurious little
man like John Hart. Wyn explained that Sandy was really very
distinguished in his own line—an authority, *the* authority on
illuminated manuscripts, a scholar with a European reputation.
Wyn would gladly have come out firmly with "savant" if she had
been quite sure of the pronunciation.

John Hart's friends (bores have friends, too) were no better
pleased. He was cranky and tiresome, but he was one of them-

selves, learned, virtuous, clean, with an assured position, a welcome guest in academic groves where a daughter lingered under the parental roof or a sister had been too long entrenched in a married brother's home. Why, then, did John Hart have to take a bride from the semiliterate daughters of Belial who lived in West Kensington and Bayswater but aped the manners and customs of Mayfair ("My dear, have you seen the sisters?"), a widow with no money, and a little girl to support; two, some said, though this was not generally believed, for she was never seen with more than one. To keep Wyn out of their homes became an obsession with Museum wives, but they urged husbands to "speak" to Mr. Hart—in a friendly way.

So little Hill of Printed Books, passing John Hart at a table in the Express Dairy next door to Mudie's on the corner of Museum Street and Holborn, congratulated him jocosely on the acquisition of a ready-made family. The other lifted a thoughtful chewing visage, put down his knife and fork, swallowed. "Thanks, Hill," he said simply. Mr. Hill, more than half-ashamed, made his way to a table as far away as possible, discouraging with glum looks two ladies who showed signs of taking chairs opposite him. Opening his *Morning Post*, he read, not without satisfaction, that the Earl of Galloway had been fined five shillings at Marlborough Street for driving to the danger of pedestrians in Park Lane and resisting a policemen in the performance of his duties. Mr. Hill did not dislike earls—in fact, he was rather fond of them than otherwise (a learned nobleman is the savant's delight) —but his feelings as a commoner were gratified. Reading further, he was distressed to learn that "only the pick of Oxford undergraduates knew who wrote *Ivanhoe* or what the *Pickwick Papers* were, and any allusion to Mrs. Proudie, Becky Sharp, or Mr. Micawber was likely to fall on deaf ears." It perturbed him rather less that there were three hundred and forty-two patients in the smallpox wards of London hospitals; the authorities probably had the situation well in hand, whereas nobody could force undergraduates to read Trollope.

Looking up furtively from his paper, he caught sight of Mr. Hart, a folded copy of the *Times* clenched in his armpit, the bill for his lunch in one hand, a cup of coffee slopping over into the saucer in the other, bearing down upon him over the congested floor. Oh, how Mr. Hill wished he had not frightened away those harmless ladies! How he dreaded "speaking" to Mr. Hart! He need not have been afraid. Hart, too, had been reading the paper, and his thoughts were of his country. As soon as he was seated with his coffee cup on the table beside him, he liberated the *Times*. "What do you suppose this signifies?" he asked, tapping with one knuckle at a Reuter dispatch: FURTHER GRANTS TO RUSSIA IN MANCHURIA.

"Nothing good," said Mr. Hill, who was as much addicted to viewing with alarm as the next man, and for a quarter of an hour the only names mentioned were Mr. Gladstone, Lord Rosebery, Manchuria, and Armenia.

John Hart had been the only bachelor in Illuminated Manuscripts for a number of years, and now he too was going to be domesticated. Secret triumph craved to show itself in public rejoicings, and one morning John Hart was carried off to a room at the end of a passage to which men from several departments repaired on occasion for a smoke and a chat. Grave Bulletins and Transactions had been swept off the table to make room for a small battalion of bottles and tumblers, and John Hart's health was drunk amidst the jocund popping of corks. "And 'here's to the widow of—thirty!'" cried a bold spirit. All drank deep and joined in the chorus. Thursfield of Greek Antiquities proposed a still more daring toast: "And here's to the Widow's Mite!"

"She has two mites, hasn't she, Hart?" The question came from Scholes of Printed Books, a newcomer to the Museum (he had only been on the staff eight years and had not caught the tone of the establishment yet).

"What did you say to that?" Wyn asked him.

"I said it was quite true and I'd marry you if you had three."

"I have," said Wyn.

John Hart gulped once, but took it like a little gentleman. He loved Wyn and he would love her children. When Wyn told him in a breaking voice that Bee's leg would never bend at the knee, owing to a bungled operation, Sandy's pity and indignation drove out all selfish considerations. His sister Mary was matron of the surgical ward in St. Thomas's Westminster, and knew all the great surgeons personally; nothing should be left untried. Wyn put her head on his shoulder and wept. The dreaded moment of confession had brought comfort. It was the happiest hour they had ever spent, or ever would spend together. When Sandy said jocosely, "My brother Edward is Senior Classical Master at Eton. Sure you haven't got a promising little chap in his teens hidden away somewhere?" Wyn almost wished she had.

After the wedding, Wyn's sisters went straight to a cozy little flat off Marylebone Road, and the newlyweds moved to a house at Harrow-on-the-Hill for the sake of the children and because Sandy must have a garden.

Wyn had not wanted visitors till the house was thoroughly presentable, but Sandy soon began to receive intimations that his colleagues and their wives wished to call on the bride. Strange rumors, starting from kitchens and staid clubrooms, had been circulating for some time, and Museum wives who had been loudest in their determination to boycott Mrs. Hart had flocked to the wedding but had come away with their curiosity sharpened rather than satisfied. Now they pestered their husbands to take them to call, and Wyn, fuming, found herself obliged to entertain a succession of couples at afternoon tea on two consecutive Sundays, though she was still not nearly ready.

The ladies were charmed with the house. The children were darlings, and anyone could see what a lovely garden there would be when the roses were out. It was while their host was conducting them on a tour of slippery paths and naked flower beds that the discovery was made. The rumors, the whispers at the wedding, had been perfectly true: there she was, the third little girl whose existence had been so carefully concealed, stretched out on a high-wheeled couch under a tree.

When Eileen and Doris entered upon their teens, their mother began to take them about with her. Eileen's beautiful manners must be allowed full scope, and something must be done to combat Doris's morbid shyness. "I think I'll take the girls to see poor old Mac," Wyn said one day at lunch. "I'm sure he'll be pleased, and he lives next door to Madame Tussaud's."

Sandy's "Oh, yes" had been particularly narky, and the children glanced at one another over the table. They remembered very well who Poor Old Mac was. "Is the gentleman aware of the honor in store for him?" asked Sandy.

Mac did his best to make his unexpected visitors at home in his cramped bed-sitter. He opened a bottle of wine, brought almonds and raisins in a paper bag from a cupboard in the sideboard, and showed the girls how to slide the handle of his stereoscope so as to get the Falls of Lodore and the Leaning Tower of Pisa in focus. Worn out by the hideous tedium of Madame Tussaud's, Eileen and Doris crammed peeled almonds into their mouths and examined the views in the stereoscope with languid curiosity; there was not one that they had not seen dozens of times in Grand-papa's stereoscope. Mac had another set, which he held out in an ungummed envelope for Wyn to look at. "Not for the young, I'm afraid you'll say."

Wyn half pulled two cards out of the envelope and glanced at them before letting them slip back and returning the lot to Mac. "Not for the young, and you know, Mac, nakedness was never any treat to me."

It was time to go. Sandy would be clamoring for his wife and his dinner. "And how is His Holiness?" asked Mac, closing and unclosing the lid of a cigar box on a small carved table.

"As ever, infallible," Wyn returned lightly, and there was something in her manner the children didn't like. They did not love Sandy, but home still held their loyalties.

Mac bent over Wyn's hand and kissed the arched wrist. "It's not often you deign to disturb my stagnant pool," he murmured. "And when I look into this charming countenance—" He broke off with an ineffable glance at Eileen, who was hovering behind her mother. "The image of you, Wyn, when I first knew you." He seemed to have forgotten that Wyn had been going on for thirty when he first knew her.

"How did you find His Excellency?" Sandy asked over his first forkful of meat and potatoes.

"Same as ever," replied Wyn. "He sits smoking his cigars and reading French novels all day, and spends the night in mysterious haunts."

"That legacy was Hedley's undoing."

"It could have been the making of him," Wyn said warmly.

"He should never have left the F.O. I would never have let him. He might have been an ambassador by now."

"And you would have been an ambassadress. You backed the wrong horse that time, Mem." This was ungenerous, considering that Wyn had given up Mac, with his good position and brilliant prospects, for the impecunious Sandy. But when was jealousy generous?

Sandy withdrew his gleaming gaze from Wyn's face to the bewildered countenances of the children. "How would you have liked being a little Excellency, Eileen? I don't think it would have suited Doris, she's too stout a fella."

Both children scowled, and Wyn asked herself wearily why he must be forever pitting Eileen's beauty and brilliance against Doris's solidity of character.

"What a good thing she chose Sandy!" Eileen said to Doris that night across the table between their beds. Doris couldn't have agreed more. What? A revolting old funny with dewlaps and a tasseled skullcap might have been their stepfather! Sandy was bad enough, goodness knew, but habit had overgrown antagonism, creating the tolerance a horse is said to feel for the bit. The girls slept like travelers who have reached haven after a narrow escape.

On the other side of the wall, Wyn lay wide awake, debating the same theme inside her head. She told herself that Mac would never have sunk so low if she had married him; of course he had those queer tastes, most Winchester boys did, but Wyn knew she could have managed him. Mac was self-indulgent, but he would never have poisoned the air with nagging admonition like the high-minded little bully curled up beside her on the mattress and now peacefully snoring. Tears pricked somewhere behind her eyes, but she forced them back; crying would neutralize the effect of the expensive skin food she had smeared over her face and neck and give her a splitting headache, and she wanted to look her best for the next day, when she was going to *The Second Mrs. Tanqueray* with her favorite man of the moment. She knew she must concentrate on pleasant thoughts, try to convince herself that everything had been for the best. She could easily have married Mac, and she had deliberately chosen to marry Sandy. She had nothing to reproach herself with, and if it had been all to do over again, something told her that she would still have chosen Sandy. The thing now was to get a good night's sleep, and she closed her eyes resolutely.

But the little cushioned hammock braced firmly under her chin irked her. She picked at the buckle, and when it stuck she tore the whole caboodle down over her face and flung it from her.

Pru Girl

WYN WAS HELD UP on her way to bed by the sound of low sobbing coming from her daughter's bedroom. Pushing open the door she found Eileen sitting up in bed with her knees drawn up and her forehead resting on them. Crying her heart out. When her mother came into the room she lifted her head and stopped to moan, "I don't *want* to be a Pru girl," and went on crying her heart out.

Wyn sat on the side of the bed and smoothed the hair away from her daughter's forehead. "You shan't be!" she exclaimed warmly, and put her arms round Eileen's heaving shoulders. But when she saw Eileen cheer up and dry her eyes on the hem of the sheet, Wyn added coldly, "At any rate you can't be for at least another year and a half. It's ridiculous to get worked up so far ahead. Go to sleep." She pushed Eileen's head on to the pillow, kissed her damp cheek, and started for the door. "Go to sleep. It's past twelve. You'll be late for school again." Eileen was now quite sure she would be a Pru girl when she left school. She lay quietly on her back, crying again, but the tears ran into her ears and she had to turn on one side.

The point about getting Eileen into the Prudential when she left school was that one of her uncles had a friend on the Board of Directors. A still greater point, to Wyn's way of thinking, was that the Pru only took girls from nice families. There was practically no entrance exam—you only had to be able to read and write and count—but you had to get a recommendation from a nice person to show that you were nice yourself before you could even fill in an application form, and that was what Wyn, who dreaded Eileen's being forced to let the family down by earning her living, liked about it. Her facile imagination quickly conjured up streams of girls from nice homes who would not spoil Eileen's manners or accent; some might even have presentable brothers.

It so happened that in eighteen months' time the General Post Office planned to take on fewer men and more girls than ever before as soon as its new Hammersmith branch, only a quarter of an hour's walk away, was ready; Eileen could have come home to lunch. The entrance examination was not expected to be stiff, and the pay was better than in the Prudential and carried a pension; moreover, the offices stood in their own grounds with tennis courts and a closed swimming pool, and there were all sorts of language and other courses for self-improvement. But Wyn didn't like the sound of "My daughter works in the Post Office"; people would say "How nice!" and imagine Eileen pounding rubber stamps on forms and envelopes, and selling postage stamps behind a grille. Sandy said Old Wilson's daughter was doing very well in the Post Office, but Wyn considered that only bore her out— they'd take anybody! (Old Wilson was a messenger in the Museum). He reminded her diffidently that she had said herself that Old Wilson looked like a duke, but Wyn said fretfully that real dukes didn't.

Sandy could have got Eileen work copying Latin and Old

English manuscripts for research workers; but, for one thing, though well paid, it was uncertain and you never dared refuse a job, however busy you were, for fear of losing connections.

Sandy, a most conscientious stepfather, would have liked Eileen to go through college, but "Oh the rows and rows of old-maid teachers on his side of the family, and on Eileen's father's!" wailed Eileen's mother. What if the Pru did pay badly? A striking girl like Eileen would be sure to get married before many years passed. Wyn would round up some nice men for evenings, and see that Eileen was thrown with nice men on her holidays. At P.O. tennis courts and holiday camps she would meet nothing but pimply clerks.

Eileen was even unhappier at the Pru than she had anticipated. The girl clerks were utterly uninteresting to her, and as for niceness they were mostly the daughters of small tradesmen and bank clerks. They thought Eileen a mass of affectation with her unmanicured hands and her poetry books and high-brow novels. They themselves scarcely noticed the names of authors and eagerly followed the serial in the daily paper their fathers took in; they even discussed the heroines in Sweetheart Novelettes and other orange-covered booklets that until now Eileen had never seen anywhere but in the drawer of the kitchen dresser. For six months the only work entrusted to her was the copying of names, addresses, and policy numbers out of dirty ledgers into clean ones, omitting heavily erased canceled policies. If she made the slightest slip, the supervisor tore the whole page out of the ledger without a word. Later she was given letters to type, teaching herself as she worked from the company book of instructions. For one week a month everyone had to take a turn at the loathed addressograph.

As a new girl Eileen had no choice of date for her holiday and was allotted two weeks in March. Wyn was in despair. Nobody,

certainly no nice *man*, had holidays in March; she would have
to take Eileen somewhere herself. The only thing Wyn could
think of was a visit to her Aunt Temsy, who was now living in
furnished rooms at Ramsgate. Wyn had had the poor old thing
on her mind for ages. It would be killing two birds with one
stone. *Three*, for the fresh sea breezes—Ugh! shuddered Wyn,
who was as luxurious as a cat—would do her good, after so many
late nights in London.

Temsy lived in her furnished rooms like a gigantic tortoise
sunning itself in the zoo in front of the dark recess into which
it would crawl at night. The bay window of the front room was
dimmed by a crowding aspidistra in an iron-bound tub, with
rings intended for lifting it firmly rusted to its sides. Wire baskets
of ferns swung from the ceiling in front of each windowpane;
there were plush curtains with fringed lambrequins, and the roller
blinds were drawn halfway down to keep out the glare of sea and
sky—but not intrusive glances, for Temsy's lodgings were on the
second floor, so no passerby could see in. There were no houses
on the opposite side of the street, only gently sloping dunes on
which harsh tussocks of grass struggled for a foothold, a narrow
strip of beach beside the road, and then ocean as far as the
horizon; on clear days you could make out a tenuous section of
the coast of France. It was no mere trick of advertising to call
the street Ocean Terrace, and Temsy's lodginghouse had a full
right to the name of Sea View. Temsy, daughter of a British
officer, had followed the nomadic life of a peacetime army, till
her father got his final promotion for gallantry at the siege of
Sevastopol, and finished up his career in what might now be called
the Army of Occupation in India.

Temsy was always moving, and she took with her to furnished
lodgings in Bayswater, Cheltenham, and one seaside resort after
another, the remains of her household gods, adding a Benares

tray, a copper gong with the stick missing, or a Hindu praying
rug to the fern stands and hand-painted vases in each new room.
A new landlady's enlarged wedding photographs were ruthlessly
taken down and replaced over the mantelpiece by enlarged photographs of those gallant officers Uncle Fred and Uncle Dick, whose
bones lay buried in the officers' cemetery at Sevastopol, and a
good wide corner always had to be cleared for the greatest
treasure of all, a portrait tinted on porcelain of Temsy's father,
the field marshal. The dead-white slab was supported on an easel
and draped with a gold-embroidered Cashmere shawl, while his
plumed, three-cornered hat stood, really *stood*, on a small table
in front of him. These, and his bushy mustache and fiercely
hooked nose, were practically all that was left of the field marshal
on the slab. To her mother's grief Eileen took no interest in her
military forebears, could never get the ranks of Uncles Fred and
Dick straight, and scarcely knew where the Crimea was, or what
all the fuss about Constantinople meant.

Temsy's face poked out of a cope of shawls and fichus; her
eyes had the unseeing brightness of a tortoise's, but there was
scarcely a wrinkle in her olive-colored face and forehead, and
her finely cut, sensitive nostrils and the bittersweet lines of her
full lips suggested no batrachian temperament. In fact Temsy was
a bit of a terror, as her maid Eva could have told you any day of
the week. Could have, but never did. Eva was *devoted* to Temsy,
delighted to have Wyn and Eileen come, *astonished* to see how
Eileen had grown—though as she had not seen her for about
eight years, this was not, after all, so very astonishing.

Eva had baked them a special cake in the landlady's kitchen,
and brought them down some raspberry jam from Temsy's stores.
But she had poisoned the strong tea, the country poached eggs on
toast, the cake, and the raspberry jam by standing hand on one
hip at the corner of the table and talking all through the meal:

"Miss Birch this, your Aunt Emily that," the point of every story being that Temsy was always assuring Eva how she loved her, how she prized her, how she could not possibly live without her. For the first time Eileen realized that Temsy was not Temsy's real name. And now her mother told her, tenderly reminiscent, that it had been her little brother, Eileen's Uncle Georgie, whom Eileen had never seen (for he had died at sea), who had christened Temsey. "Auntie Emmie lives on the Thamsie."

The moment Eva picked up the tea tray and went out of the room, Wyn lit a cigarette (she had cultivated the daring habit, chiefly practiced by fast women), gathered up matches and the Guinness-is-good-for-you ash tray of glazed earthenware which the landlady had stolen from the local pub for the use of gentlemen lodgers, and rose briskly from her seat at the table. "Let's go into the bedroom before that creeping Jesus sees me smoking," she said.

Eileen was sincerely shocked; she still believed that people who were *devoted* to your relatives and *delighted* to see you when you visited their employer must be nice. How often had she heard her mother and Auntie Florrie and Auntie Gracie say, "What *would* Temsy do without Eva?"

"But Eva *is* kind, isn't she?" she asked timidly like one in search of Truth, as indeed she was. "Sawney dissenter," Wyn said. "She'd be only too delighted to catch me smoking and tell Temsy. And then out comes the will again and you and I may kiss the little globed crystal watch and the Sèvres tea service good by."

Fascinated, Eileen pictured a bewigged lawyer from a Cruikshank illustration creeping up to Temsy's bedside with inkhorn and quill. She now discovered that she had always disliked an unpleasant gleam in Eva's fishy eye, a nasty polish to her low domed forehead; it was a relief, almost a reprieve, to be at liberty to dislike her. But it was wounding, too; now, when people praised somebody, she would never be quite sure they meant it. But youth is adaptable. "Eva *is* rather like Uriah Heep, isn't she?" Eileen now asked, the searcher after Truth lost in the accomplice.

Wyn hugged her warmly, delighted by her daughter's responsiveness, and how many girls nowadays read Dickens? It was their first night in Ocean Terrace and they were ready to go to bed when Wyn's cigarette was finished and buried in the big pot that held the glossy aspidistra blocking the lower pane of the bay window. "I suppose I really ought to take you for a breath of sea air before turning in," Wyn said reluctantly. "Don't let's," Eileen said reassuringly. "Who wants sea air in March?" Wyn was only too glad to be persuaded.

They had never slept in the same bed before, and Eileen dragged the swathed bolster from under the pillows and laid it perpendicularly down the middle of the bed. "Like the sword on the bridal night," Wyn said gaily, secretly hurt. The bolster took up so much slack that the top sheet and blanket could not be tucked well under the mattress; Wyn woke up in the night shivering, for Eileen had gradually drawn all the covers to her own side. Wyn knew when she was beaten; she got up to get her flannel dressing gown and the heavy quilt which she and Eileen had folded away before getting into bed. With these over her and a sofa cushion for her bare feet to push into, she was soon fast asleep again.

It was a freakishly warm March, and Wyn and Eileen were able to take out books and recline for an hour or so on the sands in the lee of the dunes. Eileen had brought *On the Eve* with her from the drawing-room shelves at home, and Wyn had plucked *The Garden of Allah* from Temsy's single row of books. Eileen

lay on her side with one elbow thrust into the sand and her book
propped against a straggling root; Wyn arranged herself in a
sitting position and pulled her skirt round her ankles. Young men
passing in ones and twos started at the unexpected sight of two
women sitting on the beach so early in the year. Each pair of
eyes rested on Eileen's recumbent figure for a moment. "Darling,"
said Wyn nervously, "I don't think it's quite nice to lie with your
hip humped up like that, and all your legs showing. Those men
look at you in a not-quite-nice way. That last one with the
mustache stepped over your feet on purpose, I'm sure." Eileen
turned onto her back with her arms stretched upwards. "Is that
better?" "Now your tummy sticks out." Eileen brought down her
hands and sat up, her arms clasped round her knees. "I read in a
book," she said thoughtfully, "that a man should never believe
in a woman's figure unless she will keep her arms at her sides
when she lies on her back." "And what kind of a book was that,
I should like to know?" "Oh, *La Vie Parisienne* or something."
Wyn was really shocked now. "Never call a magazine a book,
promise me you never will again." (It might have been the sin
against the Holy Ghost, judging by the horror in her voice.)
"Only servants do that—'a book come for you by the post,
Ma'am'—and it turns out to be only the *Fortnightly*." "Pru girls
do, too." Eileen said it to spite her mother for having insisted on
her going into the Pru. But Wyn was thinking about something
else: "It meant to show that she didn't have a droopy bust," she
said. Eileen picked up *On the Eve*. "I want to go to Russia," she
said. "I assure you there's some girl lying in the steppe reading
Vanity Fair," Wyn said crisply, "and longing to go to England."
"Pity we can't change." Wyn gave a snort of appreciation: "Good
for you!"

Sometimes Eileen roamed the cliff tops for hours while Wyn
sat reading in front of the sitting-room fire, paid a duty visit to

Temsy, and took a short beauty sleep before dinner. Although the
season was months ahead, there were plenty of men, young and
old, sauntering or hastening along the sea front. Without having
given it much thought Eileen had vaguely supposed that the only
inhabitants of seaside towns were lodging-house keepers and that
these probably hibernated all the winter. But now she was always
coming across town-clad youths carrying brief cases and girls who
looked like typists (she thought); for such as these the grocers,
bakers, and stationery shops opened every day, and there were
drapers and milliners who eagerly advertised "marked-down"
cloth and ribbon, hats, gloves and handkerchiefs. Some of the
young men looked as if they wouldn't have minded making
friends, but none molested an untidy, *farouche* girl striding over
the paving blocks with her hands in her pockets. Eileen had
never in her life been "picked up" by a stranger, and the cloth
caps of the Ramsgate young men (or perhaps only the angle at
which they wore them), and the tiny silver-and-copper football
badges on their lapels, put her off. Class consciousness was a
mighty guardian of virtue, and she told herself there would be
nothing for her to talk about with these youths.

After trying the town in vain for some interesting or fortunate
encounter, she began to turn her steps toward the open country
beyond it. The utmost frontier was a curving tramline, after which
the cliff top was unpaved and the wheat in the fields just tall
enough for the wind to sway. A low mass of convent buildings
had been built out to sea on a spur of the cliffs. From the front
it looked low and wide, with a stone path up to the door of a
tiny chapel, but the part where the nuns lived was narrower and
taller. Occasionally Eileen met or passed a pair of nuns speeding
like clockwork mice along the top of the cliff. She liked it best of
all when two, hastening in opposite directions, passed one another
without a word or sign of recognition, like little black trams.

Eileen knew how to take holy water on her thumb from the stone shell in the porch of the chapel. Her mother had gone very High Church since her friendship with the Reverend Herbert Kingsford, and more or less swept the whole family along with her. Kingie was a lantern-jawed curate who wore cassock and beret out of doors. Eileen could spend nearly an hour alone in the chill spicy air inside the chapel. She loved the gray walls and the domed roof, the dim Stations of the Cross on stone pillars round the apse, the flickering candles, the twinkling ruby of light hanging in front of the altar. The atmosphere of devotion absorbed the garishness of statues to the Virgin Mary and the Sacred Heart. Here, somehow included in a sweet marriage of the exotic and the familiar, she rested from the everyday bitterness of life. She lit a candle, dropped a threepenny bit in the tin box below, and tried to imagine she was in France.

After a few visits Eileen made friends with a middle-aged lady who felt an instantaneous fondness for the absorbed schoolgirlish figure which seemed to be at home in every nook of the chapel, though never kneeling in front of a confessional or at Mass. Miss Rogers had taken a room in the convent and spent half her day in the chapel where she was making a private retreat under the guidance of the priest. It seemed to her that the lonely girl could not have been thrown in her way without a purpose; she invited Eileen into her white-walled room and plied her with the innumerable booklets circulated in England by the Propaganda. Miss Rogers could not see why Eileen didn't become a true Catholic, but Eileen thought she was. Kingie had convinced her that the Anglican Church was simply a branch of Rome and somehow it was all Henry VIII's fault that there had ever been a split, so Eileen was perfectly all right where she was and there she stayed, and sweet-faced Miss Rogers failed to pluck this charming brand from the burning, though she redoubled her prayers and votive offerings. She would always pray for Eileen, she said, and Eileen asked: "And may I not pray for you?" "You don't have to pray for my conversion," Miss Rogers reminded her. "I will pray for your happiness," said Eileen, and all these delightful encounters in the white-walled conventual bedroom came to an end in a long, warm kiss, after which Eileen somehow never went near the convent again.

Eileen came home at dinnertime to find the ground-floor rooms she and her mother inhabited empty, but ten minutes later Wyn tapped at the windowpane and Eileen let her in, rosy from her walk. "I was so appallingly bored," she told her daughter, "that I actually thought I'd go for a walk for once and see if I couldn't meet an interesting man." "Would you have spoken to a stranger?" asked Eileen, wide-eyed. "Of course nothing so crude as that, but when two people want to get to know one another they always find a way. But anyhow there *wasn't* anybody. There were lots of men strolling up and down the promenade, but they almost all had those beastly little football badges on their watch chains, and I knew they wouldn't do." "Oh, yes, I know! Isn't it awful?"

"You know what, Ducky?" Wyn said after dinner. "Let's get on a tram and go to the very end of the line. Perhaps it'll take us somewhere interesting."

Fresh from their recent burst of sympathy, they discoursed harmoniously, but Wyn soon spoiled it all by returning obsessively to her favorite theme: Who would Eileen marry? Eileen was only nineteen, but at least, thought Wyn, her endless childhood was over, and it was time to think about the future. Wyn never realized that her whole life was spent in trying to dismiss the tiresome present and "thinking" about the future. Suppose Sandy were to die—not that she wanted him to, poor darling—and she were to marry a distinguished, well-off man. She knew several and though it was true they all happened to be married, you never could tell; supposing she could take Eileen to the Riviera and find a presentable young man of good family and great expectations—no, *she* would go alone to the Riviera and attach the presentable young man to herself, then bring him to the house for Eileen to marry when she had done with him herself. Supposing . . . "It's not that I'm mercenary," she explained for the thousandth time, "but I never understand why—other things being equal, of course—a girl shouldn't fall in love with a *nice* man with a *little* money. Surely it would be just as easy as falling in love with some poverty-stricken clerk!"

It was the leitmotif of the century, the theme of every Victorian novel.

"Well, but supposing one *did* fall in love with a clerk," suggested Eileen, at once putting her finger on the weak point of her mother's argument.

"Ah, but that's just *it*, that's what I *say*," replied Wyn earnestly. "Avoid them—don't give yourself the chance! Keep away from unsuitable people—and at last somebody suitable's sure to come along."

"And supposing they don't?" said Eileen apprehensively.

"Oh, they're bound to."

"And what about you and Dadda?" asked Eileen.

Wyn clasped her hands nervously.

"Ah, that was the Real Thing, there was no resisting it," she admitted mournfully. "I don't suppose a love like ours happens once in a blue moon."

"I should like it to happen to me," said Eileen.

"And *I* want it to," said Wyn, moved by the girl's sincerity. "But I don't see why the Real Thing shouldn't be found among nice men, too. Your father was a schoolteacher, and a Jew, but I

would have loved him no less if he had been—oh, more like the
people I came from."

"But he wasn't, and you *did*," said Eileen obstinately.

The tram did not take them anywhere at all interesting. The
tramlines stopped a short distance from rows of red-brick villas
with slate roofs and gleaming doorsteps, all of which ended
abruptly in a field of nettles and thistles; the sea was out of sight
and but for the clean salty air it might have been any unfinished
suburb on the outskirts of any town in England, clustered round
a church, two pubs, and a few small shops. Wyn and Eileen
partook of a glass of lemonade and a slice of seedcake at a corner
bakery, after which there was nothing to do but go back to the
depot and get on the same tram that had brought them there and
that was waiting for enough passengers to make it worthwhile
to go back; in the course of twenty minutes five women and a
clergyman boarded, and they were off. Wyn and Eileen were
alone on the top, but Wyn couldn't get another word out of
Eileen about the kind of man she would like to marry.

The next day Wyn had one of her headaches and Eileen must
go to the chemist's for the capsule that was the only thing that
ever did her the slightest good. Nobody knew what it contained,
but Sandy, construing with difficulty the doctor's dog Latin, had
whistled and said there seemed to be enough calomel in it to kill
a horse. The chemist's was in the middle of High Street and had
a nice old-fashioned look, with a crimson jar and a blue jar like
the one Rosamund had coveted in the windows. There was only
one customer when Eileen entered, an unpleasant-looking man
like an illustration to a Phil May joke; he wore a light-colored
waistcoat and a bowler hat on one side, and the ends of his
mustache were waxed to thin points. Eileen hated him and turned
her face away from his rude stare. The chemist's assistant, a mere

lad, carried Wyn's prescription, and the one Eva had asked her to take for Temsy, into the room behind the shop, and was back in a few moments to slap three rubber-banded cardboard boxes the size of biggish matchboxes on the counter. The man with the waxed mustache picked up the one of them with no label or inscription on it, handed a silver coin over the counter, winked in Eileen's direction, and tried to exchange leers with the assistant. He, however, only said, "Thank you, sir," without even looking up, and watched Eileen gather up her two boxes and slip them into the pockets of her jacket. Then he said, "Thank you, Missy," and smiled at her very modestly. She smiled back radiantly, and all the way home thought how nice it had been of him not to have smiled in response to the horrid man's leer.

Eva opened the front door to her ring and padded upstairs again the moment Eileen, glancing at the boxes, put Temsy's into her hand. She then went straight into the sitting room and Wyn, hand outstretched languidly, moaned, "A glass of water!" But by the time Eileen was back with one, her mother was sitting up straight, gazing indignantly at a jumble of pink pellets in the open box. "You've brought me Temsy's beastly rhubarb pills. Go and get my capsule from Eva this minute." Before Eileen could turn there was Eva in the room sudden, standing at the edge of the hearthrug with an open box in her hand. "Look at this, ma'am. Miss Birch wants to know the meaning of it." Wyn and Eileen both craned their necks to look at the jumble of soft, floppy objects sticking out of the box. Eileen wondered why her mother gave something like a shriek and why Eva looked really so—so evil. Wyn showed Eva the label on the box: "Miss Birch, rhubarb pills," and then the one on the other box: "Mrs. Hart, painkiller." "The doctor never prescribed them articles for Miss Birch," snarled Eva. "Did you show them to her?" There was awe in Wyn's voice. "She took and opened the box herself." "And what did she say?" "Say? She laughed herself nearly sick. She said: 'Take them away, Eva, I have no use for them.'" "Well, tell her I haven't either."

Wyn held a handkerchief to her mouth to choke back her own irrepressible laughter, and as soon as Eva had gone with Temsy's pills she let it have its way till Eileen's lips involuntarily twitched and she too began to laugh, though why she didn't know. "Oh dear, oh dear, it did me good in a way," Wyn said at last, wiping a tear from the corner of each eye, "but now my poor head's worse than ever." She leaned back and closed her eyes. "I shan't sleep a wink all night," she moaned. "I'm afraid you'll have to take the beastly things back, Ducky, and get my capsule. You don't have to say anything, the rightful owner has probably claimed his property by now." She tapped meaningfully on the lid of the box before slipping the rubber band back in position. "Was there anyone else in the shop?" Eileen told her about the horrid man and Wyn nodded. "They were his." "Why should he need so many?" asked Eileen, plunging her mother into further painful laugh spasms. But Wyn pulled herself together, dabbing at her eyes again. "But darling," she said, "d'you know what they're for?" "I thought—for putting on your finger if you had a scratch." "His fingers'd have to be pretty thick." Eileen's cheeks glowed fiercely; her mother's jape had for some reason brought a memory of early childhood to the surface, and suddenly she knew what "they" were for; she remembered standing beside the pram while a grocer's boy pulled something halfway out of his pocket, which was on a level with her inquisitive eyes, to show to her nurse; and afterward, when Eliza told Annie what a cheek he had, Annie had only said, "It's his way of saying you'd be all right with him." Wyn's speech was usually so excessively refined that her occasional ribaldries shocked more than other people's, and Eileen, deeply offended, stumbled out of the house.

There were three or four people at the counter, and the salesman was standing on a stepladder with his back to them, reaching for a bottle on a high shelf. He just turned his head as Eileen came up and watched her put the box she had brought on the counter. "That's yours," he said, nodding to a little wrapped and sealed parcel, "and I'm very sorry, miss." He began climbing slowly down the steps with a bottle in one hand, but before she fled the premises Eileen saw that his ears were as red as she knew her cheeks must be, and felt gratefully that he was sorry for her humiliation.

"Did the man in the chemist's seem amused?" Wyn asked, after gulping down the huge capsule and handing the glass of water back to her daughter. "Oh, Mother, he was such a gentleman!" exclaimed Eileen. "Both times." "Now don't go falling in love with young men behind counters," admonished Wyn, allowing her head to sink onto the pillow. If Eileen could only tell her mother that nothing would ever induce her to go to that chemist's shop again! "Not to save your life," she ejaculated silently. For that matter she would never turn into High Street again as long as she was in Ramsgate. Not for anything in the world would she risk meeting that darling wonderful chemist's young man again.

Wyn woke up very languid the next morning, but without any more headache. She peered over the bolster at Eileen, who, as if feeling her mother's eyes on her face, opened her own; then she turned toward the wall and Wyn heard her give a long, trembling sigh. "Oh, darling, what is it?" Eileen rolled over on her back, stretched her arms overhead till she could clasp the bedrail, stiffened her whole body right down to her toes, relaxed, and sighed again. "It seems to me that life is rather hideous." "Oh, Ducky, don't say that! You know I would never have sent you back with those things if my head hadn't been absolutely splitting!" "I don't only mean that, but just I don't think I like life much." "*Animal* life," Wyn said trenchantly. "But you can rise above it and then it becomes sacred." "Is it sacred when Kingie comes to tea?"

"Kingie and I are great friends and friendship is always sacred. Exciting too; sometimes I think it's more exciting than the actual *thing*. Of course you sometimes get the two together, but that comes once in a lifetime. Let's get up. I think I can hear Eva on the stairs with the tray."

Wyn always had breakfast in a dressing gown, but Eileen had no dressing gown and when she heard the click of the tray being set on the table in the room across the passage, she hastily pulled her old gym tunic over her nightgown. They washed their hands and faces, combed their hair, and went into the sitting room. There were two letters beside Wyn's plate, and both Wyn and Eileen knew the handwriting on each. Wyn slit open the one addressed in very black crabbed letters, half pulled the sheet out of the envelope, read "Darling Wife," pushed it back with a smile, and opened the other. "Oh!" she cried. "How thrilling! Not specially exciting for you, Ducky, but what a coincidence! Fancy! Old Mr. Arbuthnot from St. Dunstan's Canterbury wants Kingie to exchange duties with him next Sunday, and Canterbury's only three stations away. We'll run in and hear Kingie preach and then—and then—

"And then," continued Wyn firmly, "you can go and see the cathedral and the other sights, and get yourself a nice lunch at a pastry cook's, and I'll be back in the evening."

They parted at the door of St. Dunstan's, Eileen refusing firmly to go in. "I'll go to the cathedral," she insisted, and though Wyn tried to dissuade her, she was really glad. Eileen arrived at

the cathedral only five minutes before the clergyman climbed up
the pulpit steps to give out the text for his sermon. He was an
imposing middle-aged gentleman with a powerful nose, abundant
silvery hair, and fresh coloring; Eileen, a connoisseur, set him
down as moderately High Church, too tolerant-looking for Low
Church, a weeny bit too healthy-looking for a proper Anglo-
Catholic. She didn't like sermons much, but had trained herself
to listen attentively. The text antagonized her: "Be not deceived,
God is not mocked," and when the preacher repeated it, stressing
the word "not" significantly, Eileen contracted her shoulders
irritably. The preacher, in accents as silvery as his hair, began by
saying that people tended to gloss over the Supreme Awareness
of God the Father, who never missed a sinful deed committed
by any of His children. It might be His will to leave it un-
punished at the time; people repented of an unexposed bad
action in the sure knowledge that God the Son would forgive
them, but they forget at their peril that God is Not mocked,
that Truth Will Out, that to God Belongeth Vengeance and
Recompense and their Foot shall Slide in Due Time. Who could
have felt more secure than Haman plotting the downfall of
Mordecai? And yet the King Ahasuerus, sleepless one night (and
we may be sure his insomnia was from God) sent for the book
of records and read therein how Mordecai had saved his life by
informing on two assassins. And too late Haman discovered that
God is *not* mocked. And there was poor infatuated Jonah who
thought to flee from the presence of the Lord by taking ship for
Tarshish and landed in the belly of a whale. Once again God was
not mocked. And let us not forget Lot's wife who believed she
could disobey the Lord's commandment and was turned into a
pillar of salt.

Eileen left the cathedral by a side door, unsolaced by the sermon. It seemed to her that one cruel old man had been telling

her about another cruel old man; for all her piety she had to admit that she disliked God the Father. True, He had (however indirectly) made her, but that was long, long ago and nothing to be specially grateful for as far as Eileen could see. Jesus was different; she was always trying to love Jesus, and there were so many lovely hymns—"Jesus, the Very Thought of Thee," and "Jesus, Lover of My Soul," and "When I Survey the Wondrous Cross"—that presented her with melting moments all through the day. And the Holy Ghost—she loved the Holy Ghost without the slightest effort: It was a dear dove with a soft mauve and silver breast, It was a breath of sweet air, and one day she would go and lie down all alone in high grass and open her mouth and be filled with It. Sometimes she thought of trying this beside the sea waves, but the beach was not a suitable place, much too grubby and gritty, all coal dust and sharp pebbles. There was nothing to prevent her going and lying down in a field of grass and dog daisies just outside the narrow streets of the cathedral, but she felt at the half crown in her pocket and went to look for a nice confectioner's. It was a Sunday and all the shops were shut; the best she could do for herself was to sit at a table in an empty hotel dining room and munch at an éclair and a slice of lemon sponge washed down by a cup of chocolate and whipped cream—and the chocolate wasn't nearly as hot as she liked it to be.

She was back at Ocean View before dark, but she lit the sputtering oil lamp immediately, so Eva would see they were in and bolt and bar the front door. There was a pile of far back numbers of the *Illustrated London News* on the table, borrowed in despair of finding anything better from Temsy (who carried them to every new lodging). The faded pictures of ladies in bustles, chignons, and feathered tilt-bonnets, and gentlemen in Dundrearies and top hats, bored her intensely; she did not even find them quaint, and thought the engravings of Crimean battlefields and groups of royalties positively revolting. Nine o'clock and Wyn not yet back. She dared not go to bed for fear of not hearing her mother's tap on the windowpane; Wyn's parting injunction had been, "Now mind you don't fall asleep!" Overhead Eileen could hear Eva moving about putting Temsy away for the night; lonely as she was, she didn't want to see Eva, however. She turned from the *Illustrated London News* to the novel on her mother's night table—*The Garden of Allah* by Robert Hichens. How could her mother read such trash, she wondered; her mother had good taste, really, but she could read any novel, however feeble, so long as it was fairly new. A letter fell out of the book—the one from Sandy beginning "Darling Wife." It was a nice letter, really. ". . . and I hope you will both come back with rosy cheeks . . . Eileen will be able to start to work with a will . . . I am lonely without you both . . ." Sandy could sound very nice in a letter, perhaps anyone could. Eileen remembered that he had been against her going into the Pru, that he had wanted her to have a college education. Her heart softened to him; perhaps she had not appreciated him.

She opened the novel in the middle, planting her elbows on the table and supporting her cheeks on the palms of her hands until, becoming mildly involved in the story, she sat properly in her chair and turned back to the first pages. After all it could be read, but every ten minutes or so she raised her head and looked toward the window. No Mother! Ten o'clock struck. The lamp gave a final splutter and went out with a gasping plop. Eileen got up and seated herself on a chair at the window. Every ten minutes the policeman on his beat passed along the short stretch of pavement under the window, disappeared, came back, disappeared again. The waves slapped the shore, retreated, slap, hiss, swish, slap, hiss, swish, hushaby baby on the treetop, till the

policeman came back just in time to make Eileen's eyes open
again. She was afraid the policeman would see her sitting all
alone at the window—she hoped desperately he would. Dear
policeman, how lovely his approach, how devastating his departure! But supposing he happened to be passing when Wyn
came back! Wouldn't it be a disgrace, a lady coming back all
alone in the small hours? Eileen prayed her mother would come
up to the house while the policeman was at the end of the street.
But she did not come at all. One o'clock sounded. . . .

Eileen lifted her head from her arms, still folded on the narrow
window ledge, and opened her eyes straight onto her mother's
face, tense and smiling on the other side of the windowpane. She
started up and stumbled to the door, too sleepy to remember to be
quiet; Wyn was in the hall the moment after the key turned in
the lock—in the hall with a finger at her rounded lips; she turned
it again and slid the heavy bolts with greater speed and less noise
than it had taken Eileen to open up, and in a few seconds they
were crossing the threshold of their own room as quietly as cats.
"Quick, quick, to bed with us both!" Wyn whispered, and sat
down on the mattress edge to unlace her high-heeled shoes. "I
know I've been a brute, you poor faithful little pet! But don't
stand there staring. Undress and get into bed."

Another moment and they were lying with their heads on
their pillows, each on her side of the bolster, which even now
Eileen did not forget to lay the length of the mattress. But before
they could sleep Wyn simply had to tell Eileen what had made
her so late. She had been all the way to London and back. By the
next train, truly she had.

The holiday, which had at first seemed as if it would never
pass, suddenly began to rush to a close. It was invigorating to
go shopping for souvenirs—miniature jugs and cups with local

crests on them for Eileen's schoolgirl collection and for presents—and positively stimulating to pull the cabin trunk (relic of better days) out from under the bed and start dropping things in it. Back at the Pru, Eileen could see that people had only just begun to notice she was not there before she was back among them. "Did you have a nice holiday?" Miss Earl said, slapping a bundle of policies in front of Eileen, and passed on to the next girl before she heard "Very nice, thank you."

Call It Love

THE ROOM WAS as still as a floor display in a furniture shop, with a mannequin from Gents' Clothing seated beside a gas stove borrowed from Lighting and Heating Fixtures to give an effect of intimacy. The folds of the window drapes were as rigid as organ pipes, and each crystal drop on the chandelier hung motionless on its wire; not a leaf of the plants on the bamboo stand stirred; the eye of the mouse in the wainscoting, the fan of flame in the gas bracket, were as still as if they were figures on a blueprint. The only moving objects in the room were the eyes of the stout gentleman reading his newspaper beside the fireplace, but he never once upset the equilibrium of the bentwood rocker. An abortive tinkle from the clapper over the door scarcely disturbed the stillness; only the prudent mouse withdrew its eyes and the reader, tightening his grip on the sides of the newspaper, halted his traveling glance. Then came a grinding clamor that sent the mouse scuttling into the wall and brought the reader to his feet. The chandelier jingled to his tread and the fronds of the plants brushed against one another; when his foot came down violently on a loose plank, the fan of flame in the gas bracket contracted and shot upward with a frantic screech.

The stout gentleman opened the door and a tall young woman with short, unevenly cut black hair stood in the doorway. "Eileen Shelly," she said. "Miss Page says you want a typist."

The gentleman closed the door, ducked his head, and felt in a waistcoat pocket from which he produced a solid white square and held it out to the visitor. "Belkin," he said, and ducked his head again. She took the card uncertainly, holding it loosely between her finger and thumb. Mr. Belkin pulled a chair away from the round table in the middle of the room and murmured, "Take a sit please," but she stood while he rolled back the heavy plush tablecloth and set a portable typewriter and a letter file on the cleared space.

She then stepped to the table, sat down, and slipped Mr. Belkin's card furtively under the file. "What a funny typewriter!" she said.

Mr. Belkin glanced anxiously at the dark head and jutting profile bent over his beloved Oliver. "It is very convenient machine," he pleaded. "Very subteel. One may write in four languages." He leaned cautiously over her shoulder and tapped out, "Dear Sir, in reff. to yours of fifth ult." "See?" he said. "English!" He hooked the drum out with one finger and took another from a box on the table. "Now we may write French!"

"No, no! Russian!"

Obediently, he returned the French drum to the box and fixed the Russian one in the machine, then seated himself to bang out a line of mysterious hieroglyphics.

"More, more!" she cried. "I've never seen Russian letters!" He tapped another two lines. Then she wanted to see if she could change the drum herself, and after some fumbling managed to extract the Russian drum and replace the English one. "Now you can begin," she said.

Mr. Belkin drew a letter from the file, held it close to his eyes, cleared his throat, and began dictating. "Dear Sirs, In reply to yours of the 17th inst."

Instead of typing, Eileen Shelly sat with her wrists against the edge of the table, fingertips poised lightly on the keys of the typewriter, and asked, "Where did you learn business English?" He took a volume from a row of books on the top of the upright piano and handed it to her triumphantly. She held it with the spine toward her and read out the title—" 'How to Conduct Business Correspondence' "—ruffled the pages fastidiously, stopping here and there to read, and handed it back to him. "Of course you know there's no such thing as business English."

"Perhaps you are right. But is more convenient to make like others."

"I thought you were a revolutionary!"

He gave her a startled look but only remarked, as if to close the subject, "I did not think a little business English is so dangerous."

"I thought after the revolution there wouldn't be any more of all this sort of thing." Her denigrating glance traveled from the plush tablecloth to the Nottingham-lace curtains, the useless chandelier. "And now you say there'll always be business English."

"There are perhaps more important things to change," he said mildly. "Shall we continue?" He cleared his throat again nervously. "Excuse, please. It must be business English. I can no other."

Mr. Belkin seemed to take delight in watching the rhythmic dance of the typist's fingers. "The touching system," he said. "I see you are a very professional." But no, Eileen told him, she was self-taught and not very quick. But she never made spelling mistakes.

When the letters—there were only six, all addressed to agricultural-machinery firms in the provinces—were in their envelopes, and while Eileen Shelly was closing the typewriter with unaccustomed movements, Mr. Belkin sat silent, his hands on his knees, gazing at the floor. All of a sudden he raised his head and stared at her over gold-rimmed pince-nez. "Who tell you I am revolutionary?"

"Beatrice Page. Miss Page, you know, who recommended me to you. She says you're a political émigré."

"And what do you know about political émigrés?"

"I've read Prince Kropotkin's *Memoirs of a Revolutionary*, and I have a socialist uncle and aunt."

"And are you socialist?"

"Sort of. That's why I left home really. I couldn't stand the atmosphere."

"Too reactionary?" he suggested.

"That's it! Reactionary!" she echoed radiantly. "My mother's quite broad-minded—she believes all politicians mean well, and it doesn't matter much whether they're liberals or conservatives. But my stepfather's awfully reactionary. He made me learn the names of all the books of the Bible by heart when I was sixteen, and I felt so humiliated I resolved to leave home the moment I got hold of the money my father left me. It just about covered the move and six months' rent in advance. And I bought myself a typewriter. I still have ninety-seven pounds four shillings and sixpence in the bank."

Mr. Belkin smiled. "A capitalist!"

Before she left, he asked her for her card, reminding her with a twinkle behind his glasses which might have been quizzical, that he had given her his.

Eileen snatched his card from the table and nudged it into the webbing at the top of her skirt. "I have no card," she said.

"You ought," he said. "'Miss Eileen Shelly. Very Good Type-writer.'"

She wrote her name and address for him at the top of a sheet of typewriting paper, and added "Fairly Good Typist."

Mr. Belkin took the sheet and held it close to his eyes. "Golden Square? I think you live in Hampstead."

"I do, just round the corner."

"But Golden Square is in the center. It is little little street out of Ridgent Street."

Eileen thought it astonishing that a foreigner should know London so well, and said so. "My Golden Square is just a cobbled yard off the Grove. You know the Grove."

Mr. Belkin knew the Grove—he passed through it on the way to the Heath.

"Then you must have passed my house," said Eileen. "It has an empty garage in front of it, on the corner of the Grove and Golden Square. And an enormous tree."

Mr. Belkin made a hesitant offer to see her home, but Eileen's sharp "No, no!" intimidated him, and he did not persist. Sorry as soon as the words had escaped her, Eileen stepped alone onto the pavement, enlivening with agreeable visions the steep pull up High Street to Golden Square: appreciative Russians only waited to pay her generously for a few hours' typing and pleasant chat, with an occasional remunerative English lesson thrown in. Mr. Belkin would teach her Russian, and as soon as the war was over she would go to St. Petersburg, marry a count or a Cossack, and write her life.

When a week passed without any summons from Mr. Belkin, Eileen began to think she had frightened him off by her fierce refusal of his offer to see her home. So she was very glad when a knock came at the door one morning, and even though it turned out to be only Beatrice Page, she was still glad.

"I come charged with a message from the Slav," Beatrice said. "The poor man isn't sure if it would be correct to call and let you know he has some more letters to dictate. I explained the postal facilities of London as best I could, but he seemed doubtful. Shall I tell him he can call? I've never been in your digs before, you know. Rather divine!"

"Of course he can come."

"I'll tell him then. Is that another room?"

"Just a prophet's chamber."

Beatrice lifted the latch of the narrow plank door and popped her head inside, noting a chair piled high with clothing, and a bowl of unwashed dishes on the floor. "More like a chamber of horrors," she said. "You have a magnificent view of the privies back of Heath Street, though." She drew back her head, letting the latch fall into place. "The low ceiling is sort of cozy, but it must be a bit stuffy sometimes. I should find it much too poky, of course. I couldn't expect Todd to live in such a hole."

"Who's Todd?"

"My maid, didn't you know?"

"I thought everybody's maid had been taken for war work."

"If looking after me isn't war work, I don't know what is," Beatrice roared. "Doesn't your mother keep a maid?"

"Oh Annie's about a hundred, and she's spavined." Beatrice laughed heartily; a kind of derisive sympathy seemed to have been established.

Beatrice's roving glance now fell on Mr. Belkin's card, which was propped against a brass candlestick on the mantelpiece. "Looks like a coal merchant's card. Only needs 'All orders punctually executed' across the corner, and a list of illustrious patrons on the back. The man doesn't even know that visiting cards have to be engraved, not printed."

"Does it matter?" Eileen said.

"Not a bit, of course, only it looks utterly putrid. I wonder what the S stands for—Shadrach or Solomon?"

"It's a D. His name is David."

"Sorry. I was misled by the flourishes. I don't suppose Belkin's his real name, anyway. They're all wanted by the police."

"I don't believe it!" Eileen said indignantly.

"I see you've taken quite a shine to him."

"I think he's awfully nice."

"Pidgin English and corporation and all? And have you seen his room? It's one of those matching rooms—two of everything but the piano."

"The usual furnished lodgings," Eileen said indifferently.

"What d'you bet he considers it the Ideal Home?" All this time Beatrice had been standing in the middle of the room, pointedly ignoring the chair Eileen pushed toward her. She now dropped abruptly on the seat of an armchair on the hearth, but got up quickly to sit on an unpainted deal stool against the wall. "Stuffed furniture has to be so awfully luxurious to be comfortable. I have nothing but an old wooden settee and armchairs molded and polished by the backsides of three generations. My mother was a Talbot, you know, or perhaps you don't. I must be off. I hope you get on with the Slav. He's rather a problem for me, always luring Samson to his room and stuffing him with liver sausage and stinking cheese. Samson is a scientifically fed cat and I will not have his figure spoiled by any damned political refugee!"

Eileen put a pained solicitude into her voice that she did not feel. "You should ask him not to."

"I've *told* him not to."

"And does he go on just the same?"

"He brings Samson to my door every now and then and says, 'Receive your cat.' But I don't know what goes on when I'm out. The other day Samson was a good half-hour trying to wash specks of red caviar out of his whiskers."

"I always thought caviar was black."

"They buy a red sort in Soho—bright orange. The man must be an utter cad, of course. On the other hand, I suspect he may be rather a pet. You must try and find out which preponderates."

"I'm sure he isn't a cad," said Eileen.

Day after day came and went, with no sign of Mr. Belkin, till one evening, chancing to look out of her window, Eileen saw a burly figure standing irresolutely at the wicket gate. She watched behind her curtain for him to lift the latch and walk up the irregular flagged path to the open street door, but instead of doing this he turned and stepped rapidly away in the direction of the tube. Having spoken and thought so much about Mr. Belkin, Eileen did not like to see him slip through her fingers, and muttering, "There goes ten shillings!" she plunged down the stairs into the yard and ran after the compact, rapidly disappearing figure. "Why did you go away?" she panted, when she caught him up.

He turned, showing a countenance blurry with embarrassment: "I think I make mistake."

"The street door was open. Perhaps you couldn't see the number?"

"No, I see. But I see also policeman coming out."

"It was only Mr. Lambert going on point duty. He's my landlord."

"Foolish of me. Excuse please."

"Do you want me to come and take some letters?"

"If it is convenient."

They crossed Heath Street into High Street. "Is it because you're a revolutionary that you don't like policemen?" Eileen asked.

"We are perhaps too ready to see everywhere surveillance. Our life make us suspectful."

Eileen opened her eyes wide. "Did you think I was a spy?"

"No, no, never could I think that."

"Then why did you run away?"

"First—I see policeman coming out of house. I don't like. Then I see such simple house, with door open and narrow wood stairs like in slums, and I think I make mistake."

"Don't you like my corner? All my friends envy me. They say, 'Hasn't Eileen placed herself well?'"

"No, I like," said Mr. Belkin politely, but he obviously could hardly believe that a young lady of good family lived in a workman's cottage from choice.

"This is very nice, too," Eileen said, as they turned off High Street into Perrin's Court. "I love that peep into the old cobbled square. And that old tree in the middle. So peaceful."

Mr. Belkin looked doubtful. "*My* friends think I found me very poor place to live."

"Where do they live themselves?"

"West Hampstead. Parliament Hill—"

"Parliament Hill! Horrors!"

"They have every convenience. Do *you*?"

"I have a gas ring, and there's a tap in the garage."

Mr. Belkin pointed to the screened window of the veterinary dispensary at one side of the entrance to his house. "What is so nice about living over an animal doctor?"

"It's very convenient for Miss Page when you make her cat sick."

"Ah, Samsòn! You know Samsòn?"

"I know you lure him with foreign foods."

They were by now on the first-floor landing, at the door of Mr. Belkin's room. He fitted a clumsy key into the lock and admitted Eileen, with a smile that she found enigmatic, therefore attractive.

There were not many letters, but Mr. Belkin said they were urgent. When they were typed, folded, and enveloped, Mr. Belkin produced from one of the twin mahogany whatnots either side of the fireplace a tea caddy and a metal coffeepot with a mistletoe pattern stenciled on the lid and down the curved handle, and a medallion with a smiling woman's head on each side. Eileen was surprised to see him fill it with water from a carafe and place it carefully on a gas ring in the fender. "Haven't you got a kettle?" she asked, and blushed at her own tactlessness.

Mr. Belkin explained that the coffeepot had been more expensive than a kettle. "My principle is—buy the best. Coffeepot three-and-six, kettle half crown. I buy coffeepot."

"You can't always go by that," Eileen said.

He looked hurt. "Is it—'horrors'?"

"A kettle might be more convenient for making tea."

From the same whatnot Mr. Belkin took a chubby britannia-ware teapot. "I hope you like teapot."

Eileen was just beginning to say that teapot was a very fine teapot when a loud knock startled them both. Before Mr. Belkin could get to the door, it was pushed from the other side and Beatrice Page's head appeared in the opening. "Sorry if I'm *de trop!*" she sang out, flashing quick glances round the room. "I'm looking for Samson. I thought you might have been seducing him again."

"I do not seduce her," Mr. Belkin said with dignity. "She seduce me."

"*He!*"

"In my country is cat 'she.' "

"The vet downstairs could tell you Samson's been an 'it' for years, but we still say 'he,' not to hurt his feelings."

Mr. Belkin obviously had no idea what she meant, but invited her to take a sit and have a glass tea. Beatrice thanked him curtly, withdrew her head, and slammed the door.

"Does she always burst in like that without even ringing?" Eileen asked.

"Bell does not ring. It never ring again after you come."

"D'you mean to say I broke it?"

"It never ring again after you come," he repeated, smiling.

When, after drinking two glasses of tea and lemon and eating two Garibaldi biscuits, Eileen got up to say good-by, she was surprised to feel the light brush of a cat's body against her legs. "Samson was here all the time! And you never said a word!"

"I am not informer," said Mr. Belkin.

Mr. Belkin began to feel a need for Eileen's professional services several times a week, and a habit of fixing the next appointment each time was soon established. She broke his typewriter when trying to change the drum from Russian to English, Mr. Belkin made matters worse by trying to mend it, and they were soon on the best and easiest of terms. Each session ended in tea and conversation. Mr. Belkin always had a great many questions to put, and Eileen would have been glad to answer a great many more. He was amazed to learn that not only had she never been to college, she had not even stayed in school after the sixth form. "My mother doesn't believe in school," Eileen explained, "and my father died when I was only six. His side of the family are quite different. They were always egging my mother on to send me to college."

"Your socialist aunt," he murmured.

"Do you go to the Russian Club in Charlotte Street?" Eileen asked abruptly. "My uncle, Dr. Moss, has lots of patients there. Perhaps you know him."

Mr. Belkin's face brightened. "I hear about Dr. Moss, certainly. He save my comrade when all other doctors would operate for tumor on the brains. Dr. Moss say he recover without operation and he recover."

"Uncle Saul's a dab at diagnosis," Eileen said, gratified.

"And he cure another friend of mine from syphilis. He was first doctor in London to use Salvarsan."

Eileen had never before heard anyone acknowledge a friend with venereal disease. She had taken it for granted that only people one never met had syphilis. "My uncle used to be an anarchist when he was young," she said. "Now he's only a socialist. I wish I knew the difference."

"Shall I explain it to you?"

"Not now!" she said quickly. "Let's have tea!"

Smiling, Mr. Belkin began turning macaroons from a paper bag onto a metal dish. "My sister's favorite biscuits," Eileen said, watching his hands.

"And what are your favorite biscuits?"

"I like those squashed-fly ones you gave me the first time—Garibaldi biscuits, you know."

"I take them for name, but now you say squashed flies I shall never eat them again."

"Oh, how sensitive! Do you know ginger nuts? They're my real favorites."

Out came Mr. Belkin's little notebook and silver pencil. "Spell it, please!"

"G-i-n-g-e-r . . ." Looking over his shoulder, she saw he had written in a narrow, slanting hand, "Jinjer nutts."

Loud steps were heard on the stairs. "I bet that's Beatrice," Eileen said. "Don't you ever lock your door?"

"I lock when I am alone, but when a young lady visit me . . ." He placed a hand, plump, warm, and firm, on her shoulder, smiling very kindly.

A streak of lightning leaped from somewhere inside her to meet the pressure.

"What?" he said huskily, though Eileen had not said a word.

A peremptory rat-tat on the door gave Mr. Belkin just time to remove his hand. Beatrice didn't enter a room; she invaded it. "Are you aware that it is strictly forbidden to keep people awake with clattering typewriters all hours of the night?" she barked.

Eileen was awed by the dark ferocity of her face, but Mr. Belkin was imperturbable. "She cannot clatter with lid on, I think," he said, glancing at the covered machine.

"Typewriter is *it*," Beatrice rapped out. "Inanimate objects are neuter in English." But she sat down when Mr. Belkin pulled out a chair for her.

"Always I forget. But why is sheep 'she'?"

"Sheep aren't inanimate—they eat grass and have lambs," Eileen explained.

"I meant sheep on the sea, not ship which eat grass and have lambs."

"Bottom marked top to avoid confusion," said Beatrice.

Mr. Belkin reddened, but laughed with the girls.

Glass after glass of tea was drunk and the macaroons consumed to the last crumb, but conversation limped. Yawning noisily, Beatrice took off her glasses and rubbed them with a folded handkerchief. "Sorry!" she groaned hollowly through another great yawn. "Let's go, Eileen; I'll see you to the corner."

Mr. Belkin accompanied the girls to the front door, but Beatrice discouraged him from going any farther by the simple expedient of slamming the door in his face.

"Why are you so rude to him?" Eileen asked.

"It amuses me. I'm always hoping to make him rude to me one day."

"I don't think you'll succeed."

"Are you in love with him?"

"Madly," Eileen said. "I mean I think he's awfully nice. Are *you?*"

"I easily could be," said Beatrice.

It was not Eileen's day for dinner at her former home, but she could not wait to tell her mother about her new gentleman friend. Before she had time to ring the bell, the door opened and her sister Doris, in a pink cloak trimmed with swansdown and a candy-striped fascinator over her dark head, stepped out. "Is Mother in?" Eileen asked eagerly, and Doris waved a flannel shoe bag toward the dining-room door at the end of the hall, and made to pass down the steps onto the pavement. Eileen checked her. "You're wearing my fascinator!" Doris began tugging with a great show of energy at the scarf, but did not, Eileen observed, make any real effort to get it unwound. "Take the beastly thing!" she said, still fumbling, but hastily tucked the ends inside her cloak when Eileen, with an impatient gesture, went into the house.

Her mother was in an armchair in a black tea gown and velvet slippers, reading a Mudie novel. Eileen noted jealously that the table was laid for three. Wyn looked up, smiled, read on for a few lines, but placed the book open face downward on her knees when Eileen stooped to kiss her. Both stayed very still at the sound of the front door being opened with a key and then gently closed. After a short pause, uneven steps were heard

in the hall and another door was opened and closed with the
same deliberate gentleness.

"I'd forgotten how he *limps*," Eileen said. "Regular dot-and-
carry one."

"It's the daily stampede to the tube, always holding that heavy
brief case in the same hand," Wyn said unfeelingly.

Eileen glanced again at the table. "Who are you expecting?"

"It's Grace's day," Wyn said, raising her voice as a bell rang
in the hall. "I was beginning to hope she wasn't coming. Sandy
makes such a fuss about having more than one person to
dinner."

"I'll go!" Eileen cried.

"Go?" echoed her Aunt Grace, entering the room. "Just when
I've come?"

"You can't go now," Mrs. Hart said nervously. "Sandy'll have
noticed your things in the hall."

"There aren't any things. I came just as I am."

Aunt Grace was shocked. "I should feel like a housemaid sneak-
ing up the area steps if I went out without a coat."

"I'm always telling her," Eileen's mother said fretfully. "Of
course you must stay, Eileen, now you're here. It's only that Sandy
likes to know beforehand when people are coming to dinner.
Meat coupons, you know."

"You said I wasn't to make a fetish of coming on Wednesdays."

"I'm always glad to see you, darling. You know that."

The door opened, and a small man in a gray suit lurched into
the room. "Ah!" he cried uncheerily. "Grace! Eileen! Quite a
meeting of the clans!" He thrust a scoured mauve cheek obliquely
for Eileen's kiss and leaned forward with rounded elbow to offer
Grace a dry, tight-skinned hand. He then delivered a peck on
his wife's cheekbone, and all took their places at the table. Eileen
turned in her chair and rummaged in the middle drawer of the

Sheraton sideboard till her fingers found a knife and fork and a napkin thrust into a bone ring. The flabby damask seemed to be the only thing at home to welcome her. Aunt Grace examined her own napkin doubtfully before slipping it out of the orange celluloid ring. Wyn took hers quickly out of its threaded tortoise-shell bracelet, and Sandy, with solemn ceremony, drew his out of a heavily embossed silver ring, held up the limp square by two corners before spreading it across his knees. An elderly maid came in with a dish supporting five rissoles on a bed of mashed potatoes, which she placed before the master of the house. Sandy divided the odd rissole into four minute portions before beginning to serve with precise movements.

The silence was broken by Aunt Grace. "Is your house anywhere near Frognal, Eileen?"

"Quite near. The top of Frognal kind of debauches on the Grove."

"Surely not, darling," said Mrs. Hart.

Aunt Grace rambled on amiably. "The Dudley-Clarkes had an enormous place in Frognal. They used to give the most superb garden parties, but cabbies said their horses foundered on the way up, so they sold it and took a villa on the Riviera."

"If you know Frognal, you can easily find the way to me," Eileen urged, as if there were nothing she so much desired as a visit from her tiresome Aunt Grace. "You go straight up from the tube till you come to a cottage with a garage sticking out in front. You can't miss it, there's an enormous tree at the corner, it's said to be at least a hundred years old."

"An oak?" Aunt Grace asked reverently.

Eileen was sure it wasn't an oak. Its leaves were too light and twinkly.

Sandy put down his knife and fork, propping them against the rim of his plate. All waited while he chewed the morsel in his mouth and swallowed it. Even then he had to wipe his lips and take a sip of water before speaking. "It is probably affiliated to the poplar family—*Populus tremula, Populus nigra,* or *Populus alba.*"

"It isn't a poplar, I'm sure," Eileen said carelessly. "Poplars are tall and narrow, and it's ever so branchy."

"Only the *Populus fastigiata*—vulgarly known as the Lombardy poplar, owing to its incidence in the south of France—is tall and narrow."

Mrs. Hart put in her word. "'The blast that turns the leaves of poplar white,'" she said. "I suppose Tennyson meant the *Populus alba.*"

But the word "alba," it appeared, referred to the whitish color of the bark, in distinction to the darker trunk of other species, notably *Populus fastigiata.* And since Eileen had mentioned the incessant twinkling of the leaves, her tree was probably the *albus tremula,* so frequently met with in the streets of cities.

"Don't you feel lonely all by yourself, dear?" Aunt Grace asked hastily.

"I have friends quite near," Eileen said. "Beatrice Page lives only ten minutes away."

"One of Eileen's school friends," Mrs. Hart explained. "Her mother was a Talbot, you know."

Aunt Grace beamed.

"Whether that is so or not," put in Sandy, who had been listening intently, "it seems to me that Eileen's friend incurred a grave responsibility in encouraging her to relinquish a secure livelihood on the strength of chimerical private employment."

"I've kept myself ever since I left the Prudential, haven't I?" Eileen said rudely. "I haven't asked you for help yet, have I?"

Mrs. Hart looked across the table at her daughter imploringly.

Aunt Grace could not resist joining in. "All your relations think it was rash to leave the Pru, Eileen."

"Not all," Eileen said meaningly. "The Shellys never thought Dadda's daughters would have to go out as clerks. They were sure Doris and I would go to college."

"Had there been the slightest cooperation on the part of either of you, mine would not have been lacking," Sandy said gravely.

"The Shellys would like Eileen and Doris to be teachers," Mrs. Hart broke in. "Share digs with women friends, meet nothing but schoolmarms, and spend their holidays in Y.W.C.A. hostels."

"At least they earn the money they spend," Sandy said.

Eileen made what she could of her work for Mr. Belkin. Her stepfather looked impenetrably grave, and Mrs. Hart said she hoped neither of her daughters would marry a foreigner. But Aunt Grace, who would rather see a daughter of hers dead and in her grave than married to a Corsican, admitted to having met some fascinating Russians at a hotel in Berne.

"This one isn't particularly fascinating," Eileen told them. "But he's awfully nice."

"And what profession does this alien in our midst pursue, if I may ask?" said Sandy, between prolonged bouts of chewing.

"The letters I write for him are mostly to English firms trying to sell farm equipment to Russia. But there were two people who wanted Russian lessons."

"Probably a cloak for more netarious activities," Mrs. Hart said easily. "Well, so long as he doesn't teach you to throw bombs at the King."

"In any case, a precarious means of subsistence," Sandy said. Even the high-minded Sandy seemed to regard every new male acquaintance as a potential husband for Eileen.

Doris, who suddenly appeared in the doorway, having broken

the heel of her shoe, came in for the end of the discussion. Hers was the last word. "How old is Mr. Belkin?"

"Forty," Eileen said quickly, and Doris quickly disappeared again.

Again days passed with no word from Mr. Belkin, and Eileen began to be afraid he had identified her with the insolence of Beatrice. But a week later a postcard with a Nottingham post-mark came addressed in that sloping foreign handwriting she was already familiar with. Mr. Belkin wrote that he had been called away on business but would be back in a day or two and would venture to call on Miss Shelly when he got back. And two days later Mr. Belkin appeared at her door, holding his portable type-writer and brief case, explaining that he would rather prefer to work in her room if she had no objection. "I think perhaps it will be less interruption."

He stood uncertainly in the middle of the floor, where the ceiling drooped within inches of his head. "It won't fall on you," Eileen said in reply to his nervous upward glance. She took the typewriter from him and set it on the floor against the wall. "I have my own. And do sit down."

He dropped into the armchair on the hearth. "Is like room of Russian student," he said, looking around the sparsely furnished whitewashed chamber, uncurtained and uncarpeted. He drew the familiar letter file from his brief case. "Where can we work?" he asked.

"Here," said Eileen, and lifted the flap of a gate-leg table pushed against the wall. He was astonished to see her turn in the chair she had fitted herself into at the table, raise the latch of the little door behind her and thrust her arm through the opening, still more astonished when her hand came back holding a type-writer.

Mr. Belkin held a typewritten letter up to his glasses and cleared his throat, but instead of beginning to dictate he said, not looking up from the letter, "I have something to ask you."

Eileen blushed thickly.

"Will you give me perhaps English lessons?"

He looked up sharply and Eileen was sure he had observed her crimson cheeks. "I've never given a lesson in my life," she faltered.

Mr. Belkin leaned back in his chair, even crossed his knees. "If you could explain me the use of the present perfect?"

"Which would that be?"

Mr. Belkin sighed. "We could read," he said, and sighed again, and asked permission to smoke.

After taking out a cigarette, he laid the pack on the table, and Eileen shook a couple onto the letter file. "There's hardly any tobacco in them!" she said.

"Russian cigarettes. Together with mouthpiece. Very hygienical."

"Can you get them in London?"

"I bring them with. They wished to take them away at Dover —too many, they told—but I say, 'I thought England would let me to smoke cigarettes of my native land.' And custom man smile and put crosses on every box. I hear him say to man next him, 'Chap homesick.'"

Eileen took the lid off her typewriter, but at that very moment a high clear voice was heard from the bottom of the stairs, asking the landlady if Miss Shelly was in. Eileen darted to the door and turned the key in the lock. The unseen caller mounted the stairs and knocked again and again, trying the handle between knocks, before giving up and clattering slowly down the stairs. Even after they heard the click of heels on the flags outside, the two in the room only ventured to speak in undertones. It was beginning to get dark in the room, and Eileen lit the gas before sitting down

to nudge a sheet of paper into the typewriter. She typed Mr.
Belkin's address and the date at the top right-hand corner of the
paper and swung the carriage back to write "Dear Sirs" lower
down. But there was to be no more typing that day. She got up
and perched on the arm of Mr. Belkin's chair. Immediately his
arm came round her waist and drew her against his hard, firm
thigh. She felt urgent kisses in the very middle of her cheek, but
when she turned to receive them on her lips Mr. Belkin moved
his away. "Not hygienical," he said. Eileen pulled herself back
and sat bolt upright on the arm of the chair. He passed a plump,
white hand over his flushed face and smoothed the hair off his
forehead. "In my country," he said, "girls do not kiss unless they
are ready for all."

Eileen could not honestly tell herself that she was ready for All
at the moment—a few more preliminaries, she thought, would
have been in order—but she could not refuse something that
sounded like a challenge to her integrity and slipped back into
his arms. All, she discovered, was not much, but something prevented her from showing her disappointment. He still could not
be persuaded to kiss her "properly." Even the most proper novels
ended with the words "Their lips met," and Eileen asked in all
innocence if he didn't like this.

"No, I like," he assured her, "but is not hygienical," and added
with devastating realism, "Besides, I cannot breathe through the
nose only. I think perhaps I have an obstruction."

"You should have it out," Eileen said.

And yet she would not mock at him as she had mocked at
many a young man with far less provocation. There was a warmth
and solidity in him that she had need of.

When her lover had gone, Eileen went down the wooden staircase to lock the cottage door, but was tempted out into the yard
by the sweetness of the night. Houses and pavements were white

under a huge moon, and the branches of *Populus alba tremula* hovered over their own inky pool of shadow on the cobblestones. A light breeze came hushing through the leaves and lifted the short hairs on Eileen's temples. She stepped into the garage to wash at the faucet with icy water before going up the stairs to bed. She felt no elation, but a great calm seemed to have descended on her, and she got into bed and slept for nine hours.

The first thing Eileen saw when she opened her eyes was Mr. Belkin's portable. "He'll have to come back for his typewriter," she told herself, unconsciously betraying her fear that perhaps he would never come back. Had not her mother taught her it was practically fatal for a girl to give all before marriage? She spent a good part of the day at her window, and by eight o'clock began planning how to return Mr. Belkin's typewriter. She was just wondering whether to take off the cover and stick a dignified note in the carriage, or get Mr. Lambert to take it back to his lodging and deliver it to him without a word, when she heard a light step on the stair, a discreet knock on the door.

Mr. Belkin greeted her with his usual grave courtesy, and kissed her hand, which she thought nice; nobody had ever kissed her hand before. His first words, after hanging up his coat and hat and seating himself at the hearth were, "My footsteps were dogged all the way home last night."

Eileen was startled. "By Beatrice?"

"Oh, no, no!"

"Not by the police, surely!"

He beamed at her. "By a dog! A little white doggy! She followed me all the way to your house, and when I went out she was waiting for me at the corner of the Grove. I think—she is like me, she has no home."

Eileen went up to him and laid her head against his shoulder, happy now to receive his warm hygienic kisses on her cheek.

"You are brave girl," he murmured. "You trust a stranger, foreigner. I like. You shall not regret. Much money, lives of many comrades have been trusted in me, and none was lost. And you will be safe."

"You make me feel ever so safe," said Eileen. "I don't know why."

"You will always be safe with me," he repeated, "but when the drum of Revolution sound I shall follow it wherever I am, even if I must leave you."

"I'll go with you. So nobody will have to leave anybody."

"You will be revolutionary?" He smiled.

"You must tell me how," said Eileen.

It is a truth not so universally acknowledged as it deserves that as soon as people are happy in one kind of relationship they are eager to change it for another. The hardened revolutionary and the rebellious daughter were soon spending an inordinate amount of their freedom discussing legal marriage. These discussions, always exciting, were sometimes alienating. They brought the world into their intimacy, and a certain fragrance of secrecy was gone forever from their relations. David considered that a revolutionary ought not to form family ties, but had to admit that most of them did. He was easily brought to admit that he would like to live alone with Eileen, to be spared the pain of constant partings. And this, of course, entailed marriage, because David as an alien would be forced to register any change of address with the police and a landlady would be quick to discover from his papers that they were living in sin. Having got David to this point, Eileen invariably withdrew in alarm. "Supposing we were to change our minds afterward and wish we hadn't?"

"I do not change the mind."

"Don't you ever have any doubts?"

"When the mind is made, doubts are waste time."

"So you do have them? What are they?"

David cleared his throat, put a cigarette between his lips, took it out again, crossed his legs and began, "First, it is against my principles to marry, and I make vow never to marry bourgeois girl. And then you are so untidy. I live so long alone and am accustomed that all things have their place."

Alarmed now, in the opposite direction, Eileen said, "You shall have a room to yourself. None of us ever go into my stepfather's study and it's the only tidy room in the house."

David protested that he did not want a study his wife could not go in and out of freely. He was sure Eileen could learn to be tidy if she really wanted to. All that was required was to put everything back in its place as soon as one had done with it.

Eileen did not consult her mother about getting married, but she bombarded her socialist aunt with the tale of her doubts and desires. Aunt Enid listened with patient amiability, believing that people seldom ask advice until they have made up their minds what to do. Once, tired of Eileen's endless arguments for and against marriage, she exclaimed, "Well, then, *don't* get married! Why not just go on as you are?"

"We want to live together," Eileen faltered.

"Do you have to be married for that?"

"Well, you know—landladies, registering as an alien, and all that. David said he might be called up any day, or have to go back to Russia."

Eileen's Uncle Saul looked up from the *Clarion.* "Of course they have to get married," the old anarchist said. "How long can people stand the emotional tension of love for love's sake?"

"Then go ahead and *get* married!" said Aunt Enid.

That same evening, Eileen told David that Dr. Moss thought

they ought to get married as soon as possible. Others thought so, too. Mrs. Lambert kept asking her when they were going to church; she said the neighbors were talking about her.

"And do you care what the neighbors say?"

"We-ell," said Eileen.

"I know someone else who is greatly interested in our getting married," said David, his eyes twinkling behind his glasses. "I met your friend Miss Page on the stairs yesterday. She ask me when may she congratulate me. And if I see your parents yet. I say no, but looking forward to make their acquaintance, and she say, 'I suppose you know they're filthy Jews.'"

Eileen was appalled. "I had no idea people could be like that!"

"You think it isn't any anti-Semitism in England?"

"Perhaps you'll call my mother anti-Semitic. My father was a Jew, but she sent me and Doris to school half an hour away because most of the girls in the nearest school came from Orthodox Jewish families, and she said why should we brand ourselves?"

"What will she say about me?"

"I haven't told her you're a Jew. She thinks you're just a Russian, the way we think we're just English—with Jewish blood, you know. And my father died so long ago. She loves Jews herself, but she's afraid other people won't."

Eileen had not expected David to allow himself to be so easily led to the home of her parents; she had yet to learn that no one is so conformable to the lesser social conventions as your professional revolutionary. Once having decided that he and Eileen were to be legally married, it seemed to him the most natural thing in the world that he should be shown to her parents, and he followed Eileen with imperturbable gravity into the crepuscular gloom of a small passage in which the spicy fumes from a joss stick struggled with the smell of fog and cooking. A stained-glass lantern swinging from the ceiling threw shafts of red, blue, and orange over the surface of a tall mirror, picking out a shifting network of stars on the wall. David could see nowhere to hang his coat, but Eileen stepped briskly through the stars, which immediately revealed themselves as nothing but beads in a rattling cascade of bamboo stems. Eileen held them apart for David to hang their outdoor things on an empty hook and dropped them, causing another light rattle and starry panic.

Wyn was waiting for them upstairs in a corner of her drawing room, her head and shoulders bathed in the amber glow shed by a standard lamp. A Moorish table at her side held on its octagonal top a tarnished silver cigarette box, a bronze ash tray in the form of a lily pad encircled by the arms of a drowned-looking naiad, and a Mudie novel held lightly open by a crumpled lacy handkerchief. The wide sleeves of her pleated tea gown fell away from a lean forearm as, without rising, she gave her hand to David. When she leaned forward to greet him, the light, no longer filtered by the kindly lamp shade, fell full on a drawn face, where rouge stood out on haggard cheeks and thin smiling lips.

David might pass for an easygoing, simple fellow, but he had knocked about the capitals of Europe and knew a professional siren when he saw one. He took in the dense black curls ranged over the high narrow forehead, the strings of beads rising and falling in the deep V of the lace collar, the slender, carefully exposed ankle, the arched foot crushed into a high-heeled satin slipper. He surrendered his hand to a warm knuckly grasp, there was a grinding of rings in his own well-cushioned palm, a light, quick release, and his hand, slightly smarting, was his own again.

"So this is David," Wyn said tenderly. "Sit down beside me and let's get to know one another."

David ducked, emitted a resonant, respectful how-do-you-do,

and sank cautiously into the arm chair indicated by his hostess's gracious gesture. Below him, a wire twanged musically as the cushioned seat touched the floor.

Sandy hastened in, crablike. "Don't get up! Don't get up!" But David had already struggled to his feet to meet the pumping action of his host's handshake and was looking around surreptitiously for a less engulfing seat. "What about a little light on the subject, Mem?" Sandy said, and touched a switch. Everyone flinched at the harsh glare from the ceiling, and Wyn moaned and put a ringed hand to her eyes.

The room instantly lost all resemblance to a corner in a seraglio and became a comfortable London drawing room, complete with thick rugs, Oriental vases, and a Broadwood piano. All this seemed imposing enough to David, whose myopic glance did not at once take in the dingy colors of the upholstery, the missing rings on the window curtains, the dusty Cape gooseberries in the vase of gap-toothed mosaic. Mellow sounds—a Chinese gong struck in the hall—summoned them down carpeted stairs to the dining room, where the table looked pretty in the light of a hanging lamp with rose-colored fringed shade. Here, too, David was impressed by the atmosphere of comfort and did not notice the drop handle missing from a door in the sideboard, or that the clock of black marble, like the gilt-and-ivory timepiece in the middle of the drawing-room mantelpiece, had no crystal over its paralyzed hands.

The dinner was bad, but David disliked English cooking anyhow, and after all it was wartime. Wyn tried to draw him out with sympathetic questions, fixing a melting brown gaze on his face. Sandy was an assiduous host, a conventional English gentleman—a type David recognized and respected. Aunt Grace, invited to meet Eileen's fiancé, was bright-eyed and vivacious. Doris was there, too. She was off to a dance; nothing but curiosity to see her sister's young man could have kept her at home to dinner, and after a quick gobble she pushed back her chair and rushed past the diners, whispering in Eileen's ear, "I love him!"

In devout conformity with upper-class tradition, Mrs. Hart, followed by Aunt Grace and Eileen, swept out of the room after the melancholy blancmange with stewed prunes had been coped with, leaving the men to sit over the decanter of whiskey and the soda-water syphon. Aunt Grace would not climb the stairs; she had a long way to go—living, as she had taken pains to inform David at dinner, "only ten minutes from the House of *Lords*." Eileen had often heard her aunt say this to new acquaintances, but the absurdity of it came home to her for the first time when she caught the malicious twinkle behind David's glasses.

Her mother lit a cigarette and nestled into a corner of the sofa, watching the blue spiral of smoke on a level with her eyes. "I like your David," she said, a shade too heartily. "He's so human. When are we to dance at your wedding?"

"There ain't going to be no wedding."

"At least you'll go to a registry office?"

"David will if I want him to, but he says it won't bind him. He says nothing can bind him but his own feelings."

"Oh, yes it can," said her mother sagely. "The law will bind him."

"I'd rather trust to David's feelings."

"Even so," her mother said, leaning forward and pausing a moment, then continuing in low rapid tones, as if a revelation had been vouchsafed her. "Even so, if you stick to conventions you have everyone on your side, but if you ignore them you have to be content with a narrow circle of cranks and eccentrics."

"But Mother, the people you call cranks and eccentrics are the only ones who interest me."

"Of course they are—me, too. But you can have them as well. Why alienate the majority—the ordinary people one has to live with? You can keep the artistic bohemian sort for amusement."

"David isn't a bit artistic, and his friends aren't half so bohemian as you are. It's simply that they've worked out principles of their own."

"Isn't that rather a waste of energy? Conformity would save them a lot of time and trouble if they only knew it." She lit another cigarette. "What ages Sandy's keeping him! Boring him stiff, you may be sure."

"Oh, I don't suppose so. David's awfully conventional in some ways. Much more than you are."

"I hope your David likes me. Has it ever struck you that you and Doris are rather lucky not to have some frump for a mother? Men can see *you* won't be so bad either when you're older."

The thick, mustard-colored blanket of fog, burning throats and searing the insides of eyelids, had rolled away, leaving behind it a strange blackness that dimmed the arc lights and shrouded houses to the chimney pots but no longer tasted of sulphur. The church in the middle of the square was still only a formless bulk, but its spire floated above the layer of blackness, and when their eyes got used to the murk they could even make out stars twinkling palely here and there above the rooftops. By the time they reached the long emptiness of Earl's Court Road, they could see the curb and the stone coping under the railings of front gardens.

"Could you believe my mother was going on for fifty?" Eileen asked eagerly.

"Easily I could," was the ungallant reply.

"Don't you think she's . . . beautiful?"

"She has beautiful eyes. Your eyes, only not so—"

"So what?"

David did not quite know how to put it. "Too sweet a little bit, I would say. She seems to be begging you to like her."

An empty bus trundled by, with clickings of ghostly hoofs and harness. Its lamps were mere smudges of light, and the driver passed them, heedless of their cries. So they plodded on through the gloom to Kensington High Street. There was not a wheeled vehicle of any sort in sight—even the cab rank was deserted— and David steered Eileen across the road to the steep flagged walk running between the grounds of Holland House and the garden walls of Campden Hill. An occasional gas lamp illuminated the ground for a few steps, and when they reached the top of the walk they halted under an ancient plane tree, unwilling to emerge from the leafy tunnel into the gaslit spaces of Notting Hill. The last of the fog had gone. "It stayed in West Kensington," Eileen said, leaning against the pied trunk of the plane tree, her face and neck spotlighted by the slanting rays of a street lamp through the branches.

"Did anyone ever tell you you are beautiful?" David asked.

"Artists have wanted to paint me."

Placing a hand under her elbow, he hurried her out into the street as if he had said too much. "I meant ordinary people," he said.

"Somebody once told my mother that I had moments of spiritual beauty," Eileen said, but added apologetically, "He wasn't an ordinary person, he was a poet."

"Ah!"

"What's the matter?" asked Eileen, alarmed.

"A sort of agony," he said and stopped to pull her toward him and hold her close against him, till the footsteps of an approaching policeman seemed to wake him from a deep trance.

By the time they got to the Notting Hill Gate tube, houses and shops stood out as clear as day under the street lamps, and more stars showed in the upper reaches of the sky. David was not sure if they were in time to make the connection for the Hampstead line, and Eileen said she hated changing in the tube anyhow. David knew a short cut to the Hampstead Road by way of the Harrow Road and Baker Street. If Eileen was not too tired? Nothing tired Eileen so long as she was allowed to talk, and they set off along the Bayswater road, closely linked, meeting nobody but occasional policemen on point duty, each of whom looked at them sharply before wishing them a civil good night. One added, "And bless you!"

They crossed Edgware Road into Marylebone, coming out half-way down Tottenham Court Road. Eileen thought again how well David knew London—she would have gone miles out of her way if she had been alone. Now the Hampstead Road was almost in sight, and at the end of it was only a short stretch to the Hampstead tube, the Grove, Golden Square, and bed. Eileen's feet were beginning to hurt, but she hardly noticed them in the pleasure of having David where he almost had to listen to her. If they had been in a room, he would long ago have picked up a newspaper, being unaccustomed to giving or receiving confidences. She had discovered that all conversation except on political subjects or points of practical interest wearied him. But walking beside her on the resounding pavements beneath the light from the street lamps and the pallid sky, he had nothing to do but listen. Eileen's tale of a harassed suburban childhood, bullying nursemaids, a perpetually nagging stepfather, a mother who alternately dealt out ruthless punishment and exaggerated caresses, of the sudden return from boarding school to become her mother's confidante and plaything at the age of fifteen—was so far beyond anything he had ever known as to be all but incomprehensible to him. When she told him of constant anxiety about money, he was simply puzzled. "You had two servants, a house and a garden for only your family, you went every year to the seaside, you had dancing lessons, music lessons. How could you do all this if you were poor?"

"I don't know. That's the way it was. Sandy was always saying we had our backs to the wall and must cut down on expenditure, and my mother could never see anything we could do without. Mother and Sandy quarreled incessantly; Doris and I were in agonies all the time. Our one thought was to reconcile them, and we were often on Sandy's side—he sounded so rational and he was the man, after all."

This reminded David of his own long-forgotten childhood— the fierce quarrels of his parents, which always ended in threats of divorce. "My blood freeze," he said. "I think what will become of me! It is the end of the world for me if they separate."

Once the news of their engagement was out, the lovers were in such a hurry to get married that many people were sure Eileen must be well on the way, though this was not the case at all. No, it was a sudden longing to live together—more powerful than any sexual drive—that made them use every spare moment of the day in searching the heights of Hampstead and Highgate for lodgings, and spend the evenings looking through the local newssheet and underlining advertisements of rooms to let. Either would have agreed that there had not been anything inevitable in their early relations. David might have left England as suddenly as he had arrived there; Eileen might have been sent far away on war work; each might have found someone else and never met again. But now nothing, nothing must prevent their living together as man and wife in the face of the world. Every time a landlady—put off perhaps by David's thick English and

Eileen's shaggy appearance—changed her mind and refused to
rent them rooms half promised the day before, he was visited by
wild surmises of conspiracy or anti-Semitism, and the law's
delays, though only amounting to a week or two for the establishment of residence, drove him to frenzy. Would not this
interval be filled with potential danger for their union? He even
contemplated fleeing London and hiding in some obscure pro-
vincial town where "they" would not be able to find him, to
come back under cover of night on the eve of the day fixed for
their marriage. Eileen kept looking at her pale face and in-
somnious eyes in shopwindows—was she going into a decline?

But nothing untoward happened. They found rooms on the
top floor of a five-story house, with a view over the ponds and
copses of Hampstead Heath, and were made man and wife at
the Hampstead Town Hall on a day in February, 1917, when
there had been no news from the Russian front for over a week.
Before a month was over, the drum of Revolution sounded, and
it was just as they had both said: he followed its summons and
she went with him.

Apartheid

THE SOROKINS RENTED a different dacha every year; Oleg said there would be something wrong in each, so they might as well have stuck to the first one, but Lili always hoped to find the perfect dacha. The one they chanced on this summer was practically an ideal spot—not too far from Moscow for Oleg to commute, and quite countrified when you got away from the shops beside the station.

They—the Sorokins, that is—rented a room and a glazed porch in the front half of a dacha standing on a spacious plot, the owner retreating to the back of the house with Milochka, her four-year-old granddaughter. The proximity rather worried Lili (you never know with other people's children) till she discovered that the gate in the fence between the front garden and back yard was a gate in name alone; it was shrouded in poultry wire, its rust-devoured hinges would never again turn in the sockets, and the latch was ground permanently in its groove. The fence itself was reinforced by dense thickets of unpruned raspberry canes; the potentially undesirable Milochka could not break through and fraternize, and visitors to her grandmother who

93

came to the front entrance of the dacha had to be waved away
and instructed to walk to the end of the block and turn the
corner. Isolation couldn't have been more complete.

It was isolation, chiefly for the children's sake, that Lili desired.
Most of her friends sent their children to State crèches and
kindergartens, but Lili didn't intend to surrender her power till
her children were old enough to go to school, when she knew
she would have to. But she knew, also, that it was the first five
years of life that count and was determined to use these formative
years (stretched to seven) to instill good manners and the elements of French in Valya and Fedya, never doubting her ade-
quacy for the task. She took them to the boulevard every day
in the winter, herself sitting patiently on a bench among grand-
mothers and nursegirls, whose charges were never out of sight
for a moment. At the dacha Lili could relax, knowing that Valya
and Fedya, though not particularly obedient children, would
never go into the street by themselves. But it isn't so easy to
isolate children who can see and hear one another—even if only
through a locked gate covered from corner to corner by wire
netting. Valya and Fedya soon found a gap where the wire had
worked loose on one side, through which small objects—a toy
wristwatch, a safety pin with colored beads threaded on its shaft,
a varnished pawn—all the surrealistic litter that accumulates in
playboxes (and workboxes)—could be pushed. Valya and Fedya
had great quantities of playthings in various stages of disrepair,
but Milochka's toys were stored away in a shoe box and carried
into the house every evening; as a rule, she only brought two to
the trysting place—a one-legged celluloid duck and some odd
playing cards. Duck was a very inconvenient toy—he couldn't
stand and he was too lumpy to lie either on his back or his side—
but Milochka, abetted by Valya and Fedya, tied bows round his
neck and his one ankle, and bound colored rags over his slippery

head; the connivance of Valya and Fedya consisted in thrusting ribbons and Lili's best pocket handkerchiefs through the gap for Duck's adornment. Both sides were fully involved when the playing cards came one by one out of the box. Lili was fascinated to hear Milochka's long monologues as she held a single card against the netting, interrupted every now and then by a question from Valya (three-year-old Fedya never said a word, only looking into his sister's face whenever she spoke). Lili longed to know what it was all about, but all she could gather from Valya was that the court cards were portraits of Milochka's relatives.

Lili began to wish Milochka could play in the garden with her own children. She asked her landlady if she didn't think Milochka needed the society of other children.

Paulina Efimovna said Milochka could play with her own toys. "Your children have one another," she said. "They don't need Milochka. People have different ideas of bringing up children."

Lili reddened. "I only meant Milochka's alone all day," she said. "Didn't you ever think of sending her to a kindergarten?"

"I sent her to a crèche and she got measles," Paulina Efimovna said. "Then I sent her to a kindergarten and she got whooping cough."

This, of course, made Milochka a still more desirable playmate, and Lili had difficulty in concealing her delight and forcing her features into lines of decent commiseration.

"I wonder why Paulina Efimovna doesn't want Milochka to play with our children," Lili said to her husband.

"It was you who didn't want it," Oleg reminded her. "You let her see that from the very first day."

"How could I know Milochka would be such a darling? She might be a very *good* influence on our Valya."

"Perhaps Paulina Efimovna is afraid our Valya might not be a very good influence on Milochka."

Going about the dachas, picking up a kilo of strawberries at one, a liter of milk at another, Lili also picked up a hint or two about her landlady's past. All that was known for certain was that Paulina Efimovna had left the village thirty years before, and had come back to Stepanovka with a baby grandchild in time to gladden the last two years of her own aged mother's life. Manfully, unaided, Paulina Efimovna had patched and propped the tottering dacha till the front room was fit to let. With the rent money, she was able to pay for fundamental repairs. In another five years, she would be out of the woods.

Lili had to go to the market several times a week. It was a change from the exacting society of young children and she rather enjoyed wandering from stall to stall, pricing fruit and vegetables. On Saturdays Oleg went with her to carry back potatoes and vegetables. Lili never took Valya and Fedya with her to shops or the market—it was another of her strict rules—and now she could leave them behind without anxiety; Milochka was as good as a nurse.

One Saturday Lili's roving gaze was arrested by a doll dangling from a hook on the post of a haberdashery booth. She needed hairpins and stopped Oleg, but what she really wanted was to get a better look at the doll. It was an exceptional doll, with an expression of grave kindness on its rosy face, and it had dense black eyelashes and chestnut curls; its clothes were fastened by exquisite small buttons, so that it could be dressed and undressed like a real child, and its shoes and socks were not just painted on the feet but were made of real goods. The saleswoman, who had been tatting flimsy edging at the back of the booth, now came up to them. "*Eemportnaya,*" she said and showed them its name

—Greta—on the price ticket. Then, sure of her customers, she went back to her tatting.

The doll packed in its box and paid for, Lili was eager to leave the market. But the sight of an old man selling baskets and reed besoms at the entrance stopped her again. A new besom has an insidious charm, and Lili tried to check her husband's urgent stride with a hand on his wrist. But he went straight on, and she would have followed if she hadn't caught sight of a miniature besom displayed all by itself on a flat stone, a mere whisk finished off with a crimson tassel, with three rows of crimson silk dividing the rococo bulges of the handle. Oleg looked back and Lili held it out in silence for him to see. What was it for, he wanted to know. The old man lifted his head to enlighten them: it was for dusting wall carpets or carpet tablecloths. Saying they had none, Oleg steered his wife out of the market with a hand under her elbow. When he saw the bus wasn't even in sight, he put down the bag of potatoes and went back to buy the little besom; he was ashamed of his surliness, knowing very well that he might have bought it himself if he had been alone, or even if he had happened to catch sight of it before his wife had. On the way home in the bus, Lili carefully removed the price tag from the doll's skirt. She had decided to call it Héloïse so as not to confuse the children, who thought the only language in the world but Russian was French. Not for a moment must they be allowed to have a doll with a German name.

Valya scarcely gave herself time to take in the beauties of Héloïse before she was off to the fence, holding her up for Milochka to kiss. Lili knew Héloïse would never look new again, but the sight of those remote, passionate kisses and Valya's earnest attention overcame for a moment her possessive instincts and she said not a word of reproof. "If only that stiff-necked

female would let me buy Milochka a doll!" she moaned. That had
been tried. Oleg had thrown a little ball over the fence to Milochka
the day he brought Valya and Fedya a big one, and though
Paulina Efimovna had not actually wrenched it from Milochka's
grasp she effectively inhibited further charitable impulses:
"Milochka doesn't need presents."

Lili had at first been too busy to do more than take perishables
out of her market bag, but in the evening, when the children
were in bed, she bethought herself of the whisk. She knew
better than to ask Paulina Efimovna if she had seen it, but was
thoughtless enough to call to her husband across the porch, "Oleg,
I can't find the whisk. Did you take it out of the bag?" An
abrupt sound from the back of the house reminded her that
Paulina Efimovna could hear every word said on the porch. "I
wish I hadn't spoken so loud," she said to Oleg.

"You should think before you speak."

"You know I can't."

"You can. You never have an accident with the kettle because
you've trained your hands to be careful. You can train your
tongue, too."

Lili approached the table with the kettle in her hand. "Are
you quite sure you're not being rather a prig?" she asked, neatly
controlling the flow of the boiling water into the tiny opening on
top of the Japanese teapot.

Oleg didn't answer, only smiled as he slipped a wafer of lemon
into his tea. They drank in silence, helping themselves to a tea-
spoon of jam between swallows of tea. When Lili got up to pour
second glasses, she heard a sound from their side of the door that
made her put the kettle down. She turned and beckoned to
Oleg, so urgently that he joined her. "What?" he began, but she
held up a finger, and he fell in with her listening pose. What
they heard was a woman sobbing.

Lili stooped to the keyhole. "Paulina Efimovna, what's the matter?"

The sobbing stopped for a moment, but began again, loud, uncontrollable.

"Paulina Efimovna, open the door! Let me come to you!"

The sobbing went on as if it couldn't stop.

Lili handed Oleg a knife, and after a questioning look he inserted the tip under the latch on the other side. Pushing the door open gently, they both stepped into the room. What they saw made them first step back, then go farther in. Paulina Efimovna, still sobbing, was leaning over the cot in the corner. Milochka was fast asleep, one hand resting on what Lili at first took to be a doll tucked snugly in beside her but quickly recognized to be the missing whisk, a square of flowered silk knotted under the top bulge of the handle, like a kerchief tied under a chin.

Oleg moved closer and jerked Paulina Efimovna away just in time to stop her pulling the whisk from under Milochka's hand. "Give me a hatchet!" he whispered. "I'm going to knock a hole in that blasted fence." Strangely submissive, Paulina Efimovna moved toward a low closet, but Lili begged Oleg to wait till morning; it might take longer than he expected to break down the fence.

"We found a use for the whisk," Oleg said when they were back on the porch.

"Didn't you think Milochka's cheeks were a bit bricky?" Lili asked. (Till now they had never seen Milochka's features except through the poultry netting, and reality was a little harsher than imagination had suggested. Women were fools to have allowed veils to go out of fashion, Lili reflected.)

Oleg, flushed with the rare pleasure of having indulged a chivalrous impulse, wasn't going to have his Andromeda denigrated. "Milochka's a country child," he said, "and none the worse for that."

Breakfast was eaten in a rustic arbor at the end of the garden, and Lili had the children dressed and in their places before nine the next morning. She would not rouse Oleg—he had a right to get up as late as he liked on a Sunday—but she longed to have the ceremony of breaking down the fence over as soon as possible. Since it had been announced, and tacitly consented to by Paulina Efimovna, decency (taste, anyhow) required that it be done quickly. "Go and tell Papa breakfast's ready," she said to Valya.

Valya slipped obediently from her seat and tiptoed up the steps to the porch. She was back again in a moment. "Papa says he's asleep."

It was a hallowed family joke, but Lili only frowned and bit her lip. "Who gave Milochka the whisk?" she said.

"I just held it up to her and she looked at it so . . ."

Lili understood that Milochka's glance had been compelling. The children ran off to the gate, and still Oleg didn't appear. Lili told herself she wanted to wash the dishes and be free, but in reality it was the thought of hatchet and fence, the memory of Paulina Efimovna's dark glare, that was gnawing at her peace of mind. Paulina Efimovna would think Oleg had been dissuaded from a generous act by his wife, she might take back her unspoken consent. Impatiently, Lili began washing the dishes. The minute she had, unthinking, run off all the water in the samovar, Oleg was upon her, demanding hot water for a shave. As if he couldn't shave afterward! As if he didn't stay unshaved all Sunday as a rule! Lili suggested that he'd enjoy his breakfast more if he could have it at leisure. Oleg assured her that he fully intended to enjoy his breakfast at his leisure. He would do it his own way, Lili knew, and she began tidying the children's room and the porch, only going out to the arbor when she felt sure her husband must have shaved and finished breakfast. Oleg was peacefully reading Saturday's paper, a half-smoked cigarette propped against his saucer. He looked up when she came to the table. "Let's hear the news. Bring the box, will you?" In silent fury, Lili went for the transistor and set it on the table next to his elbow.

When the news was over, Oleg pushed back the antenna, ostentatiously gulped down the cold tea in the bottom of the cup, let the newspaper fall on the grass, and made one last attempt to get a rise out of his wife. "I ought really to go to the station and get a *Pravda*," he said, but she would not be drawn, and he sauntered over to the fence.

First he had a look at the rust-bound gate. Nothing doing there —it would be easier to hack an opening through the fence. More watchful than their parents knew, the children on either side crept nearer; Lili could almost feel Paulina Efimovna peering from her doorstep. All expected—Oleg, too, perhaps—a gallant climax. A few strokes of the hatchet would bring down a section of fence and there would be a gap anyone could step through. But a glance showed Oleg that this would not be so simple. Before he could get near enough to strike a blow at the rotting palings, the bushes would have to be cleared. His thoughts darted to a spade standing against the wall, but Paulina Efimovna, who had come out of her house to see the fun, shook her head and went back for a two-handed saw. From that moment till a way had been hacked, sawed, and sheared through the bushes, she only left Oleg's side to fetch a wheelbarrow, which she heaped with spiny branches and trundled away somewhere behind the house. Seven times she took it away full, seven times brought it back for reloading. The audience dwindled away—Lili to see to the dinner, the children to carry on their endless con-

verse through the gate. But when there was nothing but roots
between the hatchet and the fence, all assembled for the final
collapse. The atmosphere of anticlimax that had hung over the
proceedings prevailed to the end, the palings, too soft to be
chopped, having to be plucked out of the earth one by one, with
ignominious effort. As soon as they lay flat on the ground, the
children moved up to the ugly gap and stood staring at one another across it. Paulina Efimovna puffed out the loops of the
white nylon bow atop Milochka's round skull, and gave her a
tiny, involuntary push; Lili half restrained Valya and Fedya with
a no less involuntary pull at their clothing. Then the children
freed themselves and rushed with hoarse strangled cries toward
one another.

A new life began at the dacha. Milochka came every day. A
silent, staring presence, she haunted the place, whether Lili was
giving her children their meals, feeding them vitamins, or striv-
ing to teach them French fairy tales and nursery rhymes.
Milochka resolutely refused all offers of food and could not be
persuaded to listen to or learn *contes* and *chansons*. Her blue stare
antagonized Lili, who didn't get any fonder of Milochka as the
summer wore on; if anything, she disliked the child, resenting
her ascendancy over Valya. She read derision into Milochka's
innocent Russification of French words. Thus *Mon fils* became
"Mawfisochka," *Ma fille*, "Mayfiyochka," names that completely
replaced Fedya and Valya, so that soon even their parents never
called the children by any other. Héloïse inevitably became
Elochka, and the little whisk was always known as Venichka, a
tender adaptation of *venik*, the Russian word for a besom.
  Milochka did not seem impressed by the belongings of her
grandmother's lodgers. Lili expected her friends to ignore a

cracked mirror, a gap-toothed comb, a regiment of worn, shape-less footwear—anything would do for just one more summer at the dacha—but Milochka's appraising glance exposed them in all their squalor. Lili once caught her pinching the felty blanket on Valya's bed, for all the world like an old woman pricing goods at a flea market. Valya came to the supper table that night looking sulky and discontented. "Milochka says they had silk eiderdowns in Magadan," she muttered when her mother told her to drink up her milk.

"In Magadan," echoed Fedya. The parents exchanged startled glances over their children's heads.

When they were sure the children were fast asleep, Lili waited for Oleg to say something, but had to begin on the subject herself. "Magadan! Could that mean Paulina Efimovna was in the labor camp there?

"Magadan's a big town," Oleg said, not lowering his news-paper. "There must be a permanent population, you know."

"You know very well I'm not talking about the town. But what on earth can Paulina Efimovna have done? Perhaps her daughter was in the camp and she went out to fetch Milochka."

"Perhaps," Oleg said.

"But Milochka must have been a little baby, and what does she mean about silk eiderdowns and the gilt furniture she's always chattering about?"

"Tales of a grandmother," Oleg said and went on reading.

Valya's playthings were gradually exchanged for Milochka's miserable possessions. The smaller ball replaced the bigger one. "Milochka says it's easier to catch," Valya explained. This was true, but where had the bigger one disappeared to? Two of Valya's best picture books vanished from the playbox, in which Lili was disgusted to find an artificial poppy, an imitation leather belt minus the buckle, the benevolent severed head of a Teddy bear.

"And what is this?" Lili cried, holding up a strip of sapphire-colored plush embroidered in gilt beads.

"Milochka said it would make a nice skirt for Elochka," Valya said defiantly.

And one day even Elochka vanished, and in her cradle, solicitously wrapped in the sapphire-colored strip, lay Venichka. Lili had to admit that the black buttons sewn on Venichka's chubby face were very expressive. She understood how it was that Valya found her so sympathetic. "But Elochka has very nice eyes, too," she expostulated.

"Yes, but they're always the same. When I'm sad, Venichka looks sad, and when I smile at her she smiles back."

"Oh, Mafiyochka, and isn't Mama sorry when you're sad?"

"You don't always notice. Venichka never doesn't."

The taboo against leaving their own territory without permission still held, and for some time Valya and Fedya did not invade the back yard. But when Polkan, the yard dog, stopped snarling at them and wagged his tail instead, the taboo weakened and Lili had the mortification of seeing her children prefer the back yard to the lawned and bedded garden. One morning she couldn't bear it, especially as she saw almost the last of their toys being carried away under the arms of Valya and Fedya; she called to them to come back this minute, and then, bethinking herself of Paulina Efimovna's sensitive pride, added in coaxing tones, "You'll be in Babushka's way."

The nights were beginning to get chilly, and Lili set up a portable cot in the children's room, leaving Oleg to sleep alone on the porch. But tonight, tortured by the remembrance of her tactlessness, she crept into his bed and told him what she had done. Confession, even the sharp scolding it brought upon her (perhaps because of it), lightened the burden, and they were falling asleep in perfect amity when a curious intermittent squeaking rent the silence of the night. A faint light showed from the back of the house and Oleg, sitting up to look out of the window, could see a figure moving away in the darkness; a few seconds later, movement and sound grew more distinct. "Babushka shoving the wheelbarrow backwards and forwards," Oleg said. "Now she's gone in and put out the light. Sleep, darling."

Daylight showed what the squealing in the night had meant. The gap in the fence was loosely filled in by an amorphous mass of branches, lifeless but still thorny. The children, as if not noticing anything out of the ordinary, made straight for the gate, and all morning Lili could hear Milochka's monologue: "In Magadan we had chicken every day . . . in Magadan we had cream with our kasha . . ."

Babushka

THE ENGINE CHECKED the headlong plunges of its piston
rod and drew up at the wayside halt with loud, impatient blasts,
while one passenger, a woman with a rucksack strapped to her
shoulders and a bulging brief case at her side, stepped out of the
train. Before she was fairly off, the engine gave her a friendly
jolt: *Have you forgotten anything?* Not a hope!

The woman, young really but worn-looking, stood on the not-
platform to watch the train disappear screaming round the curve
with an insolent flick of its last coach. The tracks at her feet
stretched from nowhere to nowhere, and Irina seemed to have
become part of the stillness, like the telegraph poles and the
signal box, or perhaps more like the cart wheel leaning against
the iron strut of the signal box. The wheel had been there so long
that a seedling yew had thrust its crown between the spokes, but
it was not a permanent part of the landscape; at any moment
somebody might come and trundle it away. Irina, not being made
of wood or steel, had to move under her own power, so she
shifted the leather straps of her rucksack and crossed the line by
a sleeper.

The countryside waited with furled flags for the approach of spring; tufts of grass, limp and bleached as prisoners of war, straggled through melting snow. Only the black-and-white stems of the birch trees wore a festive air; all through the winter they had believed spring would soon be back, and now here it almost was.

Irina's thoughts turned around the train she had just left. Cares will grow on any soil, and the journey had nourished hers. The passengers, a few old men and women, had started talking the moment the train left Moscow, and Irina had taken every word they said to heart, for their theme was the ingratitude of children. They mangled it, strophe and antistrophe, the whole way. In summer, when town people travel back and forth to the country, there is little or no general conversation, but the few passengers on suburban trains in winter, simple folk in rough clothes, huddle together instinctively and talk more to strangers they will never see again than they ever do to their families and neighbors. When the complaints began, Irina had expected to hear the usual accusations of drunkenness and dissipation, but the talk was all of the indifference to their parents of student sons and daughters.

"You feed them and clothe them, and nurse them when they're sick," the old women chanted, "and they go to their colleges and get married, and forget all about you till they need you to dandle their babies." "All they think of is their pleasure," chanted the old men. "They forget how we had to work early and late so they could study." A middle-aged man in a quilted jacket glanced censoriously from above round spectacles at Irina, bent over her book in a corner. Voices were timidly lifted in defense of learning: "What about the Metro? It took learning to think up that one, didn't it?" "My daughter is a radio announcer, and a better daughter you couldn't wish for."

But it was the wails of the malcontents that pursued Irina as

she trudged over melting snow and slippery clay through a
tangle of bushes. Some birds maintained an intermittent shouting
and Irina thought they, too, were reproaching her, though of
course birds are never expected to do a thing for their parents.
And yet, she kept reminding herself, *she* had not been the one
to suggest that her mother-in-law stay behind. Had she not
repeatedly urged her to go back to town with them at the end of
the summer? It had been Nikolai who said his mother knew
what she wanted. It wasn't as if they were leaving her with
strangers; they had been summering with Praskovya Egorovna
seven years now. And nobody had worked harder than Irina to
see that Babushka had everything she needed. She had taught
Praskovya Egorovna how to give subcutaneous injections, and
Babushka declared that she did it quite as well as the district
nurse; she had left Praskovya Egorovna the telephone numbers
of the local hospital and the flat in town; she had seen to it that
there was a supply of digitalis drops on the top of the chest of
drawers; and she had fully intended to visit Babushka every week.
But what with one thing and another—Vova and Mashenka
down with the measles, Nikolai's lecture tour, the almost intolerable burden imposed on a wife and mother who is at the
same time a wage earner—she had only managed three visits the
whole winter.

   Clutching her burden of guilt to her, Irina was at the bank of
the river before she saw it. Never before had she seen it so full
and swift. The last time she was here it was frozen hard, with
snow piled on its surface, a mere undulation in the blanketed
landscape. In the summer, as Irina knew it best, the water scarcely
covered its stony bed and children played in its coves, paddling
out to reefs and islets. Piles had been sunk for a bridge long ago,
but today the only way to cross was by primitive ferryboat. The
watchful ferryman had already spied her from his hut a few

yards away, and Irina reflected that the bridge would put him out of work, only he might be dead by the time it was ready. Nor could she repress the reflection that Babushka would certainly never see the bridge. And the three thoughts, coming one after the other, were like the planning of three crimes, linked each to each. The old man now came shambling into sight, closely followed by a duck. His name was Vasili Ivanich, and the name of the duck was Vaska. Vaska was locally regarded as assistant ferryman. When Vasili Ivanich died, Vaska would be out of a job, and that was something else to worry about.

Vaska stopped just short of the ferry and launched his curved breast on the water; he then dived briefly, and emerged almost at Irina's feet. Vasili Ivanich waited courteously for Irina to seat herself before he began to haul with the deceptive languor of the expert at the waist-high cable slung across the river. The slow, imperious movements of his hands summoned a hidden landscape into view: a tracery of paths up the slope of the opposite bank, wooden houses rising and subsiding like the cogs of a mill wheel, a leafless coppice expanding and contracting with the gentle undulations of the ferry, and suddenly—just when Irina expected to see Praskovya Egorovna's house—the whitewashed wall of the school. Irina had to reinstate this wall in her memory every time, and the lapse always vexed her (after all, she was supposed to be a topographer). When the gnarled hands released the cable, ferryboat, trees, and buildings came to a stand with a soft bump.

Some children playing on the bank tossed obviously inedible husks toward Vaska, who stood uncertainly at the water's edge but turned away after a single beak-thrust in their direction. Touched by what seemed to her a look of disappointment in the round, high-placed eye, Irina groped in her brief case and threw a fragment of sweet cracker. It fell on the ribby orange webbing of one splayed foot; Vaska recognized this as the real thing without having to look, and scooped it up in his flat beak before slipping onto the water and propelling himself frantically after the departing ferry. The children left their play to stand and eye Irina in silence, scarcely answering her cheerful greeting. They were three little girls and a swathed baby strapped onto a sled.

Irina pulled another cracker out of her brief case. She tried to find the baby's hand among its shawls, but, changing her mind, gave the whole packet to one of the watching children, who deftly fitted a cracker into the baby's mittened grasp. All breathed *"Spasibo!"* in chorus. One even smiled. Only the baby, who was the soul of honor, munched on the cracker in complete independence of spirit. *"Dosvidanya!"* Irina said, and braced herself for the climb. And they all removed the crackers from their lips, to echo *"Dosvidanya!"* All but the baby, who munched on in silence.

Irina was prepared to see the bench farther up the slope— just a plank nailed to sawed-off logs—but for a moment she did not recognize it in the fairy banqueting table spread at her feet. It was covered for about a third of its length by a strip of coarse linen on which were neatly laid rounds of cardboard, each holding a tiny mud pie centered in a ring of scarlet berries, each with an acorn cup propped beside it; at the ends stood medicine bottles half filled with pink and blue liquids, and the centerpiece was a candle end on a scrap of tinfoil. Fascinated by the unexpected radiance and the spirit of loving care hovering over all, Irina stood gazing. Then once more she adjusted the straps of her rucksack on aching shoulders and took the hill with resolute steps. At the crest of the slope, she looked back. The sled had been pulled up to the bench, and two of the children were now squatting in front of the banqueting table; the third had taken off her shawl and stood holding it like a hammock. A ray from the setting sun touched her flaxen head to gold. The others

plunged their hands into the shawl, bringing them back with
small dark objects (twigs?), which they tossed contemptuously
aside. Suddenly one of them punched the shawl from below, and
the twigs (if twigs they were) flew up and scattered on the
ground. A quarrel, Irina thought uneasily, and was relieved when
shrill laughter sprayed and sank. The owner of the shawl shook
it vigorously and bound it over her head and shoulders. Their
movements became private and purposeful, as if they were weav-
ing a nest, and Irina stepped out, pursued by the sound of their
amicable twitterings.

Almost before Irina was in the room, her mother-in-law was
asking her if she had brought Volume III. Olga Dmitrievna was
sitting up in bed chopping dark crinkly leaves of parsley on a
board. On the night table, a large book that Irina recognized as
The Home Cook's Best Friend lay open, and a corner of one of
the blue volumes of Tolstoy's collected works showed under a
pillow—Volume II, which Babushka had nearly finished.

Olga Dmitrievna had an insatiable appetite for information.
She wanted to know about Vova's exams, and whether Mashenka
had grown; she must hear all about the new branch of the Metro.
She took delight in the thought of trains into which she would
never step, asked how Irina had crossed the river, and was vexed
to hear that the bridge was not ready yet.

Praskovya Egorovna brought two plates of soup and slices of
dark bread on a wooden platter. Olga Dmitrievna sprinkled the
chopped parsley over the soup and sat up without touching the
pillows. Praskovya Egorovna came in again with potatoes for
them to eat with the fragments of meat lurking in the depths of
the soup. While they were eating, Irina told her mother-in-law
about the children she had seen playing on the bank of the river.
Olga Dmitrievna brought the palms of her withered hands to-

gether with a hollow thud. "Wait! After she takes away the things, I'll show you something!"

Irina produced a lemon from her brief case and went to the kitchen to make tea. When she came back with a steaming glass on a saucer in each hand, she found her mother-in-law on her feet beside the bed, looking vaguely round the room. "What are you looking for, Mama?" she asked reproachfully. "Do let me get it!" But purpose came back into the old eyes. Olga Dmitrievna stooped with alarming abruptness and dragged a suitcase from under the bed. After some fumbling, she brought out a flat cardboard box, and sank heavily onto the side of the mattress. Irina pushed her gently against the pillow and pulled up the sheet. "You're awful, Mama."

Olga Dmitrievna silently handed her the box, stroking the lid with her fingertips to indicate that Irina was to open it. She did so, and a rich feast was spread before her enchanted gaze—a lobster intensely scarlet on its oval dish, a bunch of grapes on a compotier, a trussed chicken, a scaly trout, an embossed golden jelly, and a three-inch highly varnished French roll.

Olga Dmitrievna held open the lid of the box, enjoying her daughter-in-law's ecstatic admiration. "I played with them myself when I was a little girl," she said. "Our Miss Pollock brought them from Leeds. Look!" She closed the lid and held the box upside down for Irina to read the inscription on the other side: *For my sweet little pupil from her fond 'Miss Allie.'* "Kolya played with them. He was very careful; not one is missing. When the lobster came off, he pretended to let it nibble from the other plates, but in the evening he glued it back on its dish. You can give them to those children you saw playing house. I meant them for Mashenka's birthday, but she'd only lose them. Besides, she has everything."

"And if I don't see them?" Irina asked jealously. The exquisite morsels were too precious to be allowed to go out of the family. And Nikolai had played with them.

"You can keep them till the next time you come," Olga Dmitrievna said placidly.

A taste of imperfectly digested antagonisms curdled on Irina's tongue; she could remember days when that tone of calm authority had brought tears of rage into her eyes. Even now Olga Dmitrievna's Olympian complacency, her firm assurance that she would be obeyed, had the power to irritate her daughter-in-law.

The old voice droned on. "Perhaps the new bridge will be ready by then, and the truck won't have to go all that way round." She closed her eyes and Irina wondered if she had fallen asleep, but she opened them suddenly to say sharply, "Not that I mean you to go to the trouble of a Moscow funeral. I intend to be buried in the village. Praskovya Egorovna knows what to do. Tell Kolya."

She turned her head on the pillow, and this time Irina saw that she really had fallen asleep. She looked about the room to see if there was anything to do for her mother-in-law before leaving. A candle and a box of matches stood on the chest of drawers, and she removed them to the night table, unconsciously digging her teeth into her underlip. More guilt. Kolya had spent hours fixing the overhead lamp and nailing a cord to the wainscoting so that Babushka could turn the switch without effort, only to discover that the flat prongs of the new fixture would not go into the round holes of the outlet; he had bought a new plug, but it still lay in its wrappings in the drawer of Irina's desk, and if Babushka was burned to death one day it would be Irina's fault. She tiptoed to the door, but was brought back by a sound from the bed.

Olga Dmitrievna had opened her eyes and was looking at her daughter-in-law from the pillow. "Put those library books on the night table," she said a little thickly. "I promised to get them labeled by tomorrow." Irina took a few calico-bound volumes from the chest of drawers and set them on the table. "And my fountain pen," came the insistent old voice, "and the labels. They're in the top drawer at the very back. Have you left me matches?"

"Everything, Mama." Irina bent to kiss the loose silky skin on the old cheek. "Good night, Mama. Sleep well. I'll be back ever so soon. Next week."

There was a glitter between the almost-closed lids, but Babushka neither answered nor moved to show that she had felt the routine caress, heard the routine promise.

Irina opened the kitchen door to say good-by to Praskovya Egorovna. "I didn't like to take away the matches," she said in a low voice. Praskovya Egorovna assured her she'd take them away herself before going to bed. Babushka could knock on the wall if she wanted anything in the night. "You won't forget?" Irina said anxiously. Praskovya Egorovna asked her if she thought she wanted her house set on fire, and this was final reassurance.

In the darkening village street Irina stopped a little girl—she thought it was the fair-haired one who had taken off her shawl. "Were you and two other little girls playing house on the river-bank when I passed?" she asked.

Pale eyes danced under pale brows. "We were playing wed-dings." (*A wedding feast! Oh, how right!*)

Irina took the flat parcel out of her brief case and handed it to the child. "Babushka—Vova's and Mashenka's *babushka*—sends you this for your dinner table."

The little girl accepted the parcel listlessly, murmured "*Spasibo*" from the folds of her shawl, and went on her way without a look at Irina.

Irina could not help thinking of the vociferous delight with which her own children received presents, forgetting how quickly their interest failed and how soon the new toy was lost or broken. A high-pitched cry made her turn. The little girl had broken into a trot, the parcel held high over her head, and was calling to shawled figures starting from adjacent wicket gates. "Dusya! Nadya! Come and see what I got!"

Sheafed buds were on the lilac bushes in the squares, tulips were being sold at the curb, and still Irina had not found time to get to the country again. She knew from Praskovya Egorovna's faithful weekly postcard that Babushka was all right, and any day now the whole family would be going to the dacha for the summer. Last year's bathing trunks and cotton vests had been hunted out, new sandals bought for Vova and Mashenka, the lid of the basket in which the cat Murka traveled found and tied on with string. It only remained to order the truck for them all to go down to the dacha with the tables and chairs, the pots and pans, and the new refrigerator. The hiring of a truck was Nikolai's business, but every evening when he came home from work he brought news of postponement. One day he had not had a moment to get to the telephone; another time there had been so much to do at the office it had gone completely out of his mind; the telephone had been engaged all day; or nobody answered from the garage. Nikolai said this dacha business was an antiquated survival, more trouble than it was worth. Next summer the children should go to Pioneer Camp and he and Irina would go to a Crimean rest house.

Rather to Irina's dismay, the children capered with delight. "And Babushka?" she asked.

"We'll take Babushka with us."

One question sobered the children: What would they do with Murka?

This summer, at any rate, they were committed to the dacha, and there came an evening when Nikolai told them the truck would be at the door at nine o'clock the next morning. The children were called in from their play in the yard and sent to wash their hands for supper. "Hurry up! We're going to the dacha tomorrow!"

When they were all seated round the table, Irina noticed that Mashenka was holding Murka on her knees under the table. "Put Murka down this instant!" Irina said.

Mashenka obeyed almost at once, after giving Murka a kiss on her stripy peaked head. "Murka smells of feet," she said dreamily, and was sent to wash her hands again.

"It's not Murka's fault she has to sleep in the boot cupboard," Vova said.

"Never mind, Murka'll be smelling of buttercups soon," said Nikolai, who was fond of Murka.

The talk at supper was all of the move. Vova boasted he would go swimming with the older boys this summer; Mashenka thought of the new kid that was to be Dusya's reward for feeding the goats all winter. They wondered if Dusya and Nadya still had Babushka's dinner set. Irina had told them about the wedding feast on the riverbank, and now she could not resist improving the occasion. "Of course they have. Village children appreciate their toys." She turned suddenly to her husband. "Don't you think we ought to send Praskovya Egorovna a telegram to say we're coming, Kolya?"

Before Nikolai could answer, Vova said, "Praskovya Egorovna called up."

"Oh, Vova, and you never told us! What did she want?"

"She wants certificates."

"What for?"

Vova began counting on his fingers. "One, a certificate from the doctor. Two, a certificate from the pensions office. Three, a certificate from the housing office—"

"Vova! Did she say anything about Babushka?"

"She said she needed the certificates for Babushka."

Irina and Nikolai exchanged glances over the children's heads. Nikolai half started up in his seat.

"Wait!" Irina said wildly. "What else did she say?"

"She said she must have the certificates at once. She needs them for the funeral."

Nikolai sprang to his feet and pounded out of the room.

"Where are you going?" Irina cried. "It's too late to do anything tonight."

But Nikolai was out of the house almost before she finished speaking. They heard the front door slam. It was as if he had rushed away at a call from Babushka.

But Babushka was dead—even Mashenka understood that. "Only," she said when her mother came to kiss her good night, "I'm not quite sure if I know what dead means."

"It means there is no more Babushka. She has gone away from us."

"But she hasn't really, has she?" Mashenka corrected gently. "Papa's gone to see her, hasn't he?"

Vova put in his word from his bed on the other side of the room. "She can't move. That's what being dead means—you can't move."

Nikolai called Irina up from his office and told her to keep the truck till the coffin came from the undertaker's; it could go with the other things. Irina did her best not to give away by her answers what they were talking about; she could see that Vova was bursting with curiosity. Morbid curiosity, she thought severely, and was glad to get both children off to her sister's, not wanting them to see the coffin being unloaded at the dacha with the refrigerator. The funeral was fixed for the next day. Nikolai would go down on the truck to show the driver the way over the bridge, finished at last, and Irina would have to get in touch with the textile plant where Babushka had worked for thirty years, and go in the train with any relatives or old friends who might wish to attend.

At the graveside Irina heard her mother-in-law praised for qualities that never yet won love—punctuality, conscientiousness, diligence—qualities she must have shared with hundreds of her comrades in the plant, where she was still remembered by a few aging people. An old man with a leonine head and baby-blue eyes said simply, "The deceased gave us a lot of trouble on the works committee. She would have her way." This too was praise, everyone knew; it was not for herself Olga Dmitrievna had wanted anything.

Back at the house the mourners downed their short drinks of vodka and munched flaky *piroshki* with murmurs of approbation. "She was a good woman in every sense of the word," one said. "After all, seventy-six is a good age nowadays," said another. There seemed a danger of the funeral orations beginning all over again. But it soon became obvious that most of the mourners, especially those from Moscow, were really only wondering how soon they could escape with decency, and pious sentiments were checked by thoughts of the timetable.

Praskovya Egorovna wanted Irina to stay and look through Olga Dmitrievna's possessions, and Irina herself was glad of an excuse to avoid the journey back to town in company, with the necessity of talking against the rattle of the train, but she could see that Nikolai was longing to get away. "Go," she said. "The children will be alone. I'll come as soon as I can."

"You didn't bring Vova and Mashenka," said Praskovya Egorovna.

"We thought they were too little for funerals," Irina said apologetically.

"She was a good grandmother to them," said Praskovya Egorovna. "She was always thinking of them. The last thing she did was mend the doll Mashenka left in the closet. We found one of its legs on the dust heap, and stuck it on. It was Olga Dmitrievna's last request, and we fulfilled it."

She brought out a bundle of odds and ends. As Irina loosened the knot, *The Home Cook's Best Friend* fell out. She picked it up and handed it to Praskovya Egorovna. "Keep this in memory of her."

Praskovya Egorovna blew her nose respectfully and fingered a pair of horn-rimmed spectacles wrapped in a clean handkerchief. "Could I keep these?" Noticing a shade of hesitation on Irina's face, she added quickly, "Perhaps you or Nikolai Stepanovich need them. Or you may want them for when the children grow up."

Irina hastened to assure her that neither she nor her husband could have any possible use for the glasses and that they had no intention of making an heirloom of them. Praskovya Egorovna might not have believed the reason for her moment's hesitation—that nobody ought to use another person's glasses without consulting an oculist.

Other relics were disposed of, and a small parcel of books—the volume of Tolstoy Olga Dmitrievna had been reading in up to the day of her death, a book of Ukrainian fairy tales, some odd numbers of *Novy Mir*—was wrapped in paper and tied up with string for Irina to take back to town. A polite argument over Olga Dmitrievna's flowered flannelette dressing gown, which Irina tried to press on Praskovya Egorovna and Praskovya Egorovna said might come in useful for Irina, was settled by Irina's taking it out of her rucksack at the last moment and laying it on the bed while Praskovya Egorovna was out of the room. Some neatly folded nylon hair ribbons came out with the dressing gown, and Irina tucked them into the pockets. They would not be needed anymore. Irina intended to cut Mashenka's hair—a thing she had been longing to do for years.

The sweet May evening was beginning to take possession of the landscape, absorbing the green from grass and trees, but it was not yet dark when Irina picked her way cautiously down the slope to the new bridge, avoiding the twin strips of churned mud and smashed grass made earlier in the day by the truck that had brought Babushka's coffin to the dacha. On the patch of bare earth round the bench halfway up the bank, a tire had left a neat imprint, like a signature, before going on to crash into the bench. A muddy rag underneath showed that the wedding banquet had been spread that day, and spots of scarlet and white, purple and blue gleamed like flowerets springing up in the wake of the juggernaut. Irina knew these were the crushed remains of Babushka's dinner set. A few paces farther on she caught sight of a bigger spot of color in the mud. It was the lobster, wrenched from its dish all in one piece. Irina meant to stoop and pick it up, but before she could stop herself she had brought her heel down on it, grinding the fragments firmly into the soft earth.

She ran to the bridge with an impetus that landed her on the very middle of it; when she stopped to take breath, she became aware that Vaska was keeping up with her on the river. Irina stopped and put down her rucksack for a moment. Vaska stopped, too. Hopefully? There was nothing eatable in the bag but a few of Praskovya Egorovna's *piroshki*, wrapped in a lace-embroidered doily—one of those so patiently worked at by Babushka in her spare moments. Irina took out a couple, meaning to throw them to Vaska and put by the rest in the doily for the children. But somehow she did exactly the opposite, putting the two she had taken out for Vaska back into the rucksack and throwing the others, in Babushka's beautifully worked doily, over the railing into the water. Vaska had a little trouble retrieving one pie before all the rest sank to the bottom, and the white square of linen floated serenely downstream.

Irina scraped the two pies out of the rucksack, tossed them into her mouth, and clapped her hands smartly to free them from the rich crumbs. Then she tripped briskly to the end of the bridge, reaching the halt just in time to jump into the last coach before the train started.

Bright Shores

I. PORTRAIT OF A LADY

Everyone in Svetli Bereg could see at once that John Brough was a foreigner. It wasn't just the spirited styling of his tailor's bench trousers and natural-shoulder crease-resistant jacket, or even his antique-brown casuals—he looked just as foreign in the striped pajamas and leatherette slippers issued to patients in the sanatorium, still more so in an embroidered "peasant" blouse he bought at an Intourist shop in Tbilisi. It could have been his straight mat of hair, which looked gray in some lights, merely drab in others, but always looked, among the close-cropped heads and shaven skulls of other patients, as if it needed trimming. Or it could have been John's purposeful stride, when most people dawdled or sauntered in holiday relaxation, or his expression of grave friendliness, when other people looked either amicable or aloof, seldom both at the same time. Whatever it was, something marked him out for an Englishman.

If Svetli Bereg found John Brough exotic, John Brough did not find Svetli Bereg even picturesque. The local bus had dumped him in front of the post office in the middle of Lenin Prospekt. The folded map in his pocket had shown him that he was stand-

ing between the Caucasian Alps and the Black Sea, but the mountains at his back were obliterated by the post-office building, and
the stores and offices on the opposite sidewalk effectively screened
the sea and its beaches from view. John knew it must be there;
he had only to cross the road to find it. A passing truck held him
up, and he stood for a while at the curb to watch the people
lining up at the bus stop or diving into cafeterias. Women and
girls in light flowery dresses and youths with transistors slung
across their elaborately patterned pullovers; a few old women with
Byzantine features and shawls banded over their brows, some old
men with gaunt tanned faces and fierce mustaches, in belted
blouses and knee-high boots, who stood apart like shadows that
had come unstuck. A swift glance at his watch showed John that
he had time to walk along the coast to the sanatorium without
arriving late for supper, if he could only find his way to the cliff
top. The crowd was thinning rapidly, and by the time he was on
the opposite sidewalk it was almost empty. He was disappointed
to find nothing but blind alleys closed by dense thickets between
each block, but a cold twinkle here and there through the network
of swaying branches showed that the sea was not far off, and
stores and sidewalk soon gave way to a railed-off square. John
pushed into it through a turnstile and made his way past mounded
flower beds and plaster statues of Young Pioneers beating taps
on plaster drums, to the granite war memorial in the middle. A
booming in his ears was getting louder every minute. Across the
square and through another turnstile he came out on a broad
unpaved walk; and a few steps brought him to a gap in the trees
and bushes where a side lane entered. Here was evidently a
passage to the sea at last, and John turned confidently into this
gap, but he was almost beaten back by the unexpected onset of
returners from the beach, all hurrying toward the bus stop in
family groups and in twos and threes. Alarmed by an inter-

mittent rain of grape seeds from rouged lips, a rhythmic flapping of wet swimsuits and violent blasts of pop music from transistors, he turned again; it would be easier to be borne along by the crowd than to make his way against it. He would cross the road and go back by bus.

A few weeks later, the tourist season was almost over in Svetli Bereg. The sun's warmth was still benign, figs and grapes were plentiful, roses and dahlias bloomed in their stony plots, but the schools and universities had opened all over the country, and beaches and park benches were empty. John Brough thought it was high time for him to go home, too, but the doctor refused to grant him his discharge. John was given to understand that he was accident-prone; there were things it would be dangerous for him to do for some time. He had been seen boarding a bus; that was wrong—he might be tempted to run for it, to get on after it had started; there must be no bathing, no mountaineering. "Supposing you got a dizzy spell, with nobody near to help you?" John objected that he had had no dizzy spells so far. But Dr. Zlotov said wait till he hadn't had one for three months after the operation. He could smoke, eat anything he liked, drink in moderation—Georgian wine never did anybody any harm. Seeing that his patient still looked glum, the doctor told him of the scientist who had won a Nobel Prize after a trepanning, of the pugilist who had fathered twins. John's face did not clear. The delights of reading *Pravda* with a dictionary and exchanging stilted remarks at the table d'hôte had lost novelty; he was even tired of exploring the countryside on foot. He longed for his work, for idiomatic conversation, for his wife and his two children.

The passage to the beach that had been crowded a few weeks earlier was deserted now, and one day John paused at the corner. The simple words "Steep Lane" were written by hand in purple

ink on a board nailed to the trunk of a eucalyptus tree, but it was
not steep at all, and more like a woodland glade than a lane. It
was too short to give any illusion of perspective, but where the
cypresses on either side came to an end, arching bushes framed a
blue shimmering screen that John at first took for the sky. It was
like standing a few yards from the horizon, till John's mind overtook his imagination, and he realized that this blueness must be
sea and not sky. There were railings behind the trees; as John
passed them on his way down the lane, he counted four intricately
wrought iron gates at well-spaced intervals on either side, each
with its number and sagging mailbox. All ended at the edge of
a cliff, from where John could see the true horizon and a steamer
silhouetted against a sky several shades paler than the sea. He
knelt to get a sight of the beach, and then it was that he saw the
mermaid. She was asleep at the edge of the waves, her head a
sunburst, something blazing furiously in the palm of one out-
flung hand. If this was a dizzy spell, John thought he rather
liked it.

He closed his eyes for a moment. When he opened them again,
the mermaid was still there, sitting bolt upright, but the green
tail had been switched aside, uncovering two perfectly good legs.
After stowing the blazing sphere into the mouth of a beach bag,
she began fastening her hair, which now appeared to be sandy
rather than golden, in a loose bun at the back of her head. This
enchanting pose was held for less than a minute, after which a
striped dress was pulled ruthlessly out of the bag and as ruthlessly put on and buttoned all the way down the front. Now an
ordinary young woman sprang to her feet and nuzzled her toes
into brown sandals that had been lying out of John's sight till
she stood.

Instead of picking up bag and robe, as John expected, and
starting toward the base of the cliff, she turned her back to him

and stood with hands loosely supported on narrow hips, as if looking out to sea. "Breathe in, breathe out," John murmured, and moved behind the trunk of a many-pillared yew when she turned and began toiling up the cliff. At the top she passed near enough for him to discover that she was not so young as she had seemed at a distance, and that she had blunt northern features and one of those pulpy infantile mouths that the years set in a firmer mold but never really change. In the streets and cafés of Tbilisi, John had seen women with antique perfection of form and color, but it was revealed to him in a flash of self-knowledge that a mild blue eye and a naïve mouth were more in his line than sultry glances and chiseled lips. The word "sandy" as applied to a woman's hair had simply dropped out of his lexicon.

One of the reasons, perhaps the only reason, for Vera Ivanovna's leaving her family on a two-months' vacation every year was her growing need for solitude. A child of the revolution, she had never had a room to herself, and after the birth of her first baby she had never been alone in a room for a single hour. When her son brought a wife into the cramped flat, and in due time a baby was born, Vera Ivanovna knew she never would be. She went to Svetli Bereg on the Black Sea coast because it was still "undeveloped" (no sewage plant, no running water) and, though long popular as a holiday resort, not yet built over; she went there out of season because she hated crowds, and because rooms were easy to get, and because the sun no longer blazed overhead but slanted benign warmth from nine till six; and she went to Steep Lane because it was only a three minutes' walk to the edge of the cliff and she could walk to the beach in a bathrobe. Most circumspect of ladies, Vera Ivanovna allowed herself a five-minute sun bath every day; people who live in Svetli Bereg all the year round do not go in for bathing, and Vera Ivanovna was certain she would hear approaching steps in plenty of time to pull her terry-cloth gown over her.

Vera Ivanovna bathed in solitude as well as in sea and air, but she wrote long letters home and always went to the corner of Steep Lane to meet the postwoman, and one day she was forced to admit to herself that a little congenial company wouldn't come amiss. That was the day her landlady brought her a *Morning Star*. Vera Ivanovna wondered what demand there was for the *Morning Star* now the students had all gone back to school and college, but Klavdia Mikhailovna told her that Tamara, the girl at the newsstand, had a regular customer—a teacher of English who lived a short way up the mountainside. She had not been for her copy, and Tamara had offered it to Klavdia Mikhailovna for her *Anglichanka*. It appeared that Tamara's *Anglichanka* was an old friend of Klavdia Mikhailovna's *Anglichanka*, and meant to come and see her one day. So the next time Vera Ivanovna went to the post office she stopped at the newsstand and left her address to be passed on to Tamara's *Anglichanka* when she came in. If Tamara had known her address, Vera Ivanovna would certainly have taken a bus up the hillside and looked up this old acquaintance.

The day after the discovery of the mermaid, John Brough's legs took him to the beach at the end of Steep Lane as soon as he was through with his medical shower and massage. There she was—the lady, not the mermaid—clothed and spectacled, reading a book in the lee of an upturned fishing boat. To his horror, loose pebbles sprayed from under his shoes, one actually hitting the book and ricocheting into the reader's lap. His apology burst from him in English, but the lady understood him, and after a moment's pause, during which she smiled and took off her spectacles, bowed her head graciously, and said, "Nothing!" He was delighted to find that she knew English, even though, as she hastened to explain, she spoke not very good.

An enchanted period began. John was now always first in the breakfast room at the sanatorium, first in the queue outside the massage room, and off to Steep Lane before any friendly soul could engage him in conversation or involve him in a hygienic stroll round the park. Very soon he was cutting the shower and leaving immediately after massage, and a little later he abandoned this, too, bolting from the room the moment breakfast was over.

And Vera Ivanovna always waked with a smile now.

There was plenty to talk about from the very first. John listened in charmed amusement while Vera Ivanovna, astonished to find a *kulturni Anglichanin* so ignorant of his country's literature, discoursed of Gollswordzy, of Somerset Moham and of Cronnin. The discussion of the best translations of local names never palled on either of them. Would Svetli Bereg be "Bright Shore" in English? "Shores" would be better, John thought, but could not explain why he thought so. And were all Englishmen called John? Quite a lot, but what about Vera—there were two Vera Ivanovnas in the sanatorium, the matron and the dietician, and the doctor in the Moscow hospital had been Vera Ivanovna. That was nothing: there had been three Vera Ivanovnas in the library where Vera Ivanovna had worked as a girl; to distinguish them from one another, one was called Vera Ivanovna, the second Verochka, and Vera Ivanovna herself was called Malishka—the Little One.

But it was in quiet moments that intimacy flowered. When a leaf wrenched itself from the branch of a fig tree, with a fuss and bustle like the whirring of an old clock before striking the hour, they waited in silence for the heavy thud of its fall; even the tinny chime of a real clock, striking twelve from a distant interior, could strike them dumb; and when the breeze carried a pungent whiff to them from the eucalyptus tree at the corner, they moved instinctively nearer one another on the outspread robe.

John was always teasing Vera Ivanovna to find some more private place for their meetings. Ignoring the urgency in his voice, she tried to put him off with brisk evasions. John didn't have to be told that the woods were still less private than the beach—in fact, there were no woods, only the bare hillside and parks full of benches and playgrounds. But Vera Ivanovna had a room to herself, hadn't she—why should she care what her landlady thought? "I care," Vera Ivanovna said gravely. She had been staying with Klavdia Mikhailovna every fall for the last five years; how could she suddenly bring a strange man, a foreigner, into the yard and lead him up the outside stairway to her room? John had seen a hotel near the station—couldn't they take a room there? She challenged him to ask the director of the sanatorium for his passport and explain what he wanted it for. Well, then, wouldn't she consider leaving Svetli Bereg when he did and taking him to her room in Moscow? She had to tell him that there was nowhere to put him up in the two-room flat, where her son and his family occupied one room and she and her husband—

"Your *what*?" John said, so violently that Vera Ivanovna started. "You told me your husband was dead!"

"How could I?" She looked at him palely. "He is *living*. Like your wife is living!"

"You told me you lived in Moscow ten years with your second husband!"

Vera Iranovna moaned. "I had to say, 'I *am* living ten years.' No, no, the present perfect! The present perfect *continuous*. I had to say—I—have been—living—ten years. Then you understand me."

Then he understood her. But after all, did it make so much difference? Not to be put off by a discussion of English syntax,

John returned to his point as pertinaciously as a cat that jumps
on the table as often as it is shoved off. Couldn't Vera Ivanovna
ask some friend to lend them a room for a few hours?

"My friends should be greatly surprised," Vera Ivanovna said.

John felt quite desperate. "What do Russians do when they
want to—to be alone together?"

"We divorce ourselves," Vera Ivanovna said.

"Isn't that rather drastic?"

Out came Vera Ivanovna's scribble pad, the "Bloc-Not" she
always kept handy for jotting down a new English word. Her
pencil hovered, she looked at John sideways, bright as a bird
that has just espied a worm: "Drastic"?

John had trouble finding a synonym. The word "extreme"
came to mind, but it was not rich enough in content.

Vera Ivanovna wrote it down anyway. " 'Severe,' perhaps?" she
suggested, her pencil still poised over the paper, and seeing him
doubtful added the word "severe." She had him neatly side-
tracked, but she couldn't help asking herself what sort of a conversation this was. How had she been led into the discussion of
ways and means for committing adultery? She, who always
evaded the explicit in her relations with people!

The last day but one came. Tomorrow evening John would be
leaving the Soviet Union and they would probably never meet
again. Surely Vera Ivanovna would allow him to take her out to
dinner! They had fresh trout in the restaurant.

"Warmed-over trout," Vera Ivanovna said scornfully. "Come
to lunch in my yard tomorrow, I will give you really fresh trout."

"What about your landlady?"

Vera Ivanovna told him, blushing, that her landlady would
be in Sukhum for the day. John's eyes blazed fiercely and she
hastened to add that after lunch they could take a bus to Silver
Bay, where there was a famous view: "The mountains come right

down to the sea. Stalin was living there sometimes, but now his dacha is a sanatorium."

Everything should be just as she wanted it, John assured her, and he would bring a bottle of wine to the beach the next morning to go with the trout. But Vera Ivanovna told him she would not be at the beach the next morning; there would be too much for her to do. He must bring it straight to the house at one o'clock.

"I don't even know where you live."

She looked at him mischievously. "I will show you. Come!"

John knew she lived quite near, but he was not prepared to be halted only a few steps from the top of the cliff, at a gate he had passed daily for nearly a month. "I don't believe there's another woman in the world who could have kept that from me so long!" he exclaimed in honest astonishment.

"Are Englishwomen so quick?" Vera Ivanovna asked.

As soon as Klavdia Mikhailovna left for Sukhum the next morning, Vera Ivanovna went up the stairs to fetch the heavy market bag she hoped she had hidden from her landlady's inquisitive eyes. At the door she turned and gave a backward look at the room. It was immaculate, and she glanced complacently at *The Quiet American* on the chair beside her narrow bed (there were two in the room; there are no single bedrooms in Svetli Bereg), and the oyster-colored rose displaying every frill it had in a glass jar on the window sill, between starched yellowing lace curtains. Then she put down the bag for a moment and went back to straighten the flimsy square of matting in the middle of the parquet flooring (once the house had been a proud mansion in the middle of a huge estate) and push her worn carpet slippers out of sight under the bed.

An uneasy sense of being untrue to herself for the first time in

her life prevented her from singing over the elaborate preparations for what she intended to be a choice though simple meal,
but her eyes sparkled and each detail of her work seemed of
enormous importance. A rattling sound from the gate made her
look at her watch with amused vexation. Only twelve, and she
had told him to come at one, by which time the table would have
been laid under a tree and her dress changed. It never for a
moment entered her mind that it could be anyone but John at
the gate, and the sight of a woman's figure between the metal
flourishes was a threat from the outer world. But hostile emis-
saries must be treated with respect, and Vera Ivanovna said
politely, "Klavdia Mikhailovna's gone to Sukhum. She won't be
back till the evening."

The woman outside said in a loud, plangent voice, "Malishka!"

Vera Ivanovna felt as if she had been shot; it was wonderful
to her that she could lift her hand and pull back the iron bolt.
She looked at the back of her hand as if she didn't know what
it was, before pulling the heavy gate toward her to admit a
stranger who was no stranger but a once-familiar being she had
never thought to see again. She heard herself say sharply, keen-
ingly, "Verochka!" and wondered again to find that she could
move, could make sounds.

The woman on the other side stepped in, and an old, an almost
ancient familiarity drew the two bodies together close. Vera
Ivanovna came out of the embrace strengthened. The other, too,
seemed to have shaken off something hesitant, anxious. "Malishka, Malishka! There wasn't a single day out there when I
didn't ask myself, 'Is Malishka all right? I wonder where Malishka is.' And you've been all right all the time. You haven't
changed a bit, I'd have known you anywhere."

Vera Ivanovna recognized an undercurrent of reproach in the
words, and felt she deserved it. She felt almost guilty—to have

been all right all these years while her friend had been wearing her life out in a prison camp! She pushed the bolt back in its socket before putting her arm through the older woman's and turning her in the direction of the house. "Sit here a moment," she said. "I was just getting dinner. And do take off your coat, did you really need it?"

"You can't trust the weather here for a moment, it's always changing," Verochka said peevishly, and Vera Ivanovna remembered how tiresome this old friend had often been, how little but the intimacy that springs up between people working side by side every day had bound them, and how that little had fallen away altogether when this bond was broken. But she remembered, too, that Verochka had once sat up with her all night before auditing day, tracing an error that had crept into her accounts and might have cost Vera Ivanovna her chance of promotion. And how she had encouraged her to read English and guided her taste, till modern English literature became what it was now—the abiding interest of her life.

It didn't seem worthwhile to drag everything out into the yard, and Vera Ivanovna laid plates and forks on the scrubbed kitchen table. She returned the wineglasses to the cupboard and thrust the choice hors d'oeuvres (chopped chicken livers and chopped nuts and a biting Caucasian sauce) back into the refrigerator. This she did in no grudging spirit but rather from an instinct of tact, not wishing to overwhelm her friend by indications of luxurious living that were, actually, fictitious, since Vera Ivanovna's meals were generally as Spartan as meals in Georgia can be, which is not very in that favored land. Fresh trout baked with garden herbs and fried potatoes was a sumptuous feast for two lonely women, and the splendor of a piled dish of persimmons is never ostentatious when it is practically a duty to pick them before the birds get at them. Verochka opened her eyes wide at the sight of the golden crinkly skin of the trout—she had thought it was illegal to sell trout.

"My landlady knows a fisherman," Vera Ivanovna said simply. "It's just a bit of luck you happened to come today." The words cost her another brief pang, but from that moment her old peace of mind returned to her—for keeps, she was sure.

Vera Ivanovna knew that the greatest kindness you can do a returned prisoner is to listen to his tale of woe. She did not know, hardly anybody does, that this is a tale that cannot be told. The hearer is not really with you, wants only facts. But facts must be selected even by the unskilled narrator, and the bald consecutive chronicle that might contain interesting details but would take all day to unfold is rejected for a handful of striking anecdotes that somehow miss impact. Still, Vera Ivanovna listened as attentively and sympathetically as she could, while one thought and one only really occupied her mind—what was she going to say to John? She went to fill the pail at the tap in the yard and stood thinking till her shoes got wet; another time, she went to the gate and looked through the railings into the lane; then, remembering that she had not locked up after Verochka came in, she hesitated a moment, and turned the key in the padlock. She suffered no agonies of doubt, not for a moment did she consider admitting John—but what was she going to say to him? What? She could think of nothing he would understand. Her friend could have been told she had a prior engagement. She could have come another day, couldn't she? No, John would never understand.

When the rattle at the gate came, Vera Ivanovna pretended not to have noticed it.

"It's a man," said Verochka, peering over her shoulder through the open doorway of the kitchen.

Vera Ivanovna jumped up from her seat at the table. "It might

be somebody about a room," she said. "I promised my landlady
. . ." She was right at the gate, near enough to have touched
his smiling face with the tip of her finger through an iron
curlicue, and still she hadn't made up her mind what to say.

John helped her out without knowing it. Seeing a dim, bowed
figure standing in the doorway under the raised porch and peering inquisitively toward the gate, he cried impulsively, "Didn't
she go?"

Vera Ivanovna looked at him strangely, slowly shaking her
head. She said nothing, but her eyes seemed to have turned a
darker blue and John read in them love and refusal.

Cursing the useless love, almost loving the stony refusal, he
shook the handle of the gate in peevish wrath. "You never meant
it!" Seeing her look nervously over her shoulder, he sank his
voice to an angry growl. "You and your English literature!" Suddenly his other hand came up and he struck the ironwork with
something that flashed for a moment in the sunshine; there was
a glassy tinkle outside the gate, and water gushed over the front
of Vera Ivanovna's blouse and trickled inside the opening, but it
was not water; it dried practically at once and it smelled of men
drinking.

Vera Ivanovna put her hand over the stain on her blouse and
ran back to the house. Her friend was seething with curiosity.
"Oh, just a man looking for a room. I told him to come tomorrow,
and he was annoyed."

"Annoyed! He must have been drunk! I saw him throw a
bottle at you."

"Not at me, at the gate. I'll just run up and get out some clean
sheets. I'm sure you'd like a nice rest after coming all this way.
Wait till I call you."

Up in her room, she pulled the blouse over her head and put
it away in a drawer out of sight, but not all crumpled up. No, she

smoothed it out carefully before shutting the drawer. She hardly had time to take off her skirt and get into a flowered print gown before Verochka appeared in the doorway.

"You rest, too, Malishka," Verochka said, seeing that there were two beds in the small room.

"I will," said Vera Ivanovna. She lay down and closed her eyes resolutely.

Half an hour later there was a noise at the gate. Verochka, dozing over *Catcher in the Rye,* was aroused immediately. "Malishka!" she said softly. Vera Ivanovna lay with her face to the wall, and by her breathing her friend supposed she must be asleep. Verochka got out of bed and tiptoed to the window. She could see across the yard into the road, where a man just outside the gate seemed to be picking up stones, every now and then straightening himself to peer through the iron scrolls and curlicues. Verochka wondered, with the quick fear of violence that would now never leave her, if he was going to throw stones at the windows. But the house stood too far back for that, and soon he turned away and walked up the lane toward the road. "Malishka, it's that man!" Verochka cried. But Malishka's head on the pillow never stirred. Verochka reflected how easy it was for people whose nerves had not been shattered to sleep whenever they felt like it. She closed her eyes and was soon snoring rhythmically.

On the other side of the room, Vera Ivanovna lifted her head and quietly, quietly turned her pillow on its other side.

II. FLIGHT FROM BRIGHT SHORES

Svetli Bereg
6th Oct.

Dear Vera:

*Here I am firmly established in your old room at Steep Lane,
only it isn't called Steep Lane now, it's Medicinal Beach.*

*When I came out of the airport the square was a maelstrom,
enormous motor coaches swooping in from all directions with
obvious intent to kill. There wasn't a porter in sight, like you said
there wouldn't be, and people ran from one stopping place to
another, dragging heavy bags; they didn't have any Vera Ivanovna
to tell them what to do, poor ducks. Holding tight to your list
of instructions, I left my suitcase in the cloakroom and passed
through the square like a breeze (or would have if those glorious
new shoes I stood in line for so long hadn't hurt like hell) and
across the footbridge and round the wall of the market till I got
to Lenin Prospekt, and there was the dear little local bus waiting
outside the post office just as you said it would be. I got off in
the most knowing manner at the third stop and crossed the road
to the eucalyptus tree at the corner of Steep Lane (I will not
call it Medicinal Beach!). From your description I had pictured
a leafy tunnel ending in a landscaped "O" for Ocean, instead of
which the fig trees and magnolias have been ruthlessly felled,*

137

*and your woodland glade is now a strip of asphalt running bang
into a fence with "Welcome to Medicinal Beach—entrance ten
kopecks" painted in sham Slavonic lettering on a kind of wooden
rainbow over the top.*

*Klavdia Mikhailovna received me with landlady's smiles; she
is even more disagreeable than you said, but the house and the
situation are lovely and I well believe she's clean and honest, and
you can't have everything, as no one knows better than you
and I. I have your old room at the far end of the porch, where
the vine is thickest. The radio just outside is, I am happy to say,
still out of order. The room is all right, if it weren't for the second
bed, which I don't like; it takes up space and tempts one to dump
things on it. Klavdia Mikhailovna told me she rented three beds
in this room in the season and actually tried to make me pay for
the second bed, but I reminded her firmly that the season was
over, and she agreed to charge me for a single room. She has
sent a boy to the airport for my suitcase and as I can't do anything
till it comes I thought I'd write to you, only of course there's
really nothing to say. I wonder if I shall come across an English
gentleman. I think I could sit on the cliff top and talk about
English literature just as well as you.*

Putting down her pen, Darya Lvovna flexed and unflexed her
toes inside her stockings. The new shoes stood side by side under
the table like silent inquisitors. The door of the room opened on
the porch and the window was a generous slit framing crowns
of fruit trees, most of them heavily festooned by grapevines. The
persimmons hung like Christmas-tree decorations from leafless
boughs. The fig trees' leaves were beginning to fall, one at a time,
but there was still enough foliage at the top to shelter a few
shrunken purses. Apples and pears could have been picked by
leaning a little way out of the window, while clusters of grapes—
the light showing right through the green ones, the purple ones
faintly luminous—were too far away to be reached. Darya remembered she had had nothing to eat since leaving Moscow. She

emptied her bulging pocketbook onto the second bed and heterogeneous objects fell on the quilt. A coiled dog leash, a receipted laundry list, a library ticket were evidently there by the workings of simple inertia—Darya had forgotten to clear out her pocketbook before leaving. But tweezers and a pack of miniature playing cards did not belong in a pocketbook; she had abandoned them purposely, thinking to give her chin a rest and to break, if only temporarily, her exhausting addiction to solitaire. The only explanation of their presence could be that son Volodya's eye had fallen on them at the last minute and he had rounded them up and thrust them into the pocketbook, unable to imagine that his mother could do without them for a month.

Darya now chose from the sprawl on the quilt what she needed to take with her to the cafeteria—money, a handkerchief, *The Centaur* (translated into Russian as *"Kentavr"*). Wincing and grimacing, she slipped her feet into the cruel shoes. In the salesgirl's hands they had looked as supple as a pair of gloves, and they now fitted her shrinking feet like gloves indeed, but gloves of iron; the new leather of the uppers had swiftly discovered the strategic points of corns—one incipient, the other dormant—on the little toe of each foot, and there were burning sores on her heels that would be blisters soon. Darya hobbled out onto the porch, not daring to stand and admire the crimson sky behind the gap-toothed mountains, because if she stood still for a moment it would be painful to start walking again. She counted three padlocked doors and three shuttered windows between her own room and the staircase into the yard. A small table was pushed against the wall under one of the windows. Darya was sure it hadn't been there when she came, having particularly noticed there was nothing on the porch except the radiola, but the sight of her landlady stepping buoyantly from the top of the stairs and holding Darya's large suitcase as if it were weightless, prevented

further speculation. "Let me take it!" Darya said, but Klavdia
Mikhailovna held onto the handle and Darya could only walk
back to the room beside her, murmuring apologetically. With a
gesture of emphatic delicacy Klavdia Mikhailovna left her lodger
to open the suitcase unsurveyed, but Darya Lvovna, who had not
missed her swift glance at the table, thrust the open letter into
her pocketbook before going out of the room. She now noticed
what she had not seen before: that the top of the small table was
marked out in squares. She called down to Klavdia Mikhailovna,
who was already on the piazza: "Does your husband play chess?"
but got no answer; Klavdia Mikhailovna had turned into the
open-fronted kitchen under the house—perhaps she hadn't heard.

When Darya Lvovna got off the bus opposite the cafeteria she
noticed a man crossing the road. She noticed him because he
looked different from everyone else, in fact he looked foreign,
perhaps on account of his tan brogues and the cut of his Norfolk
jacket, which was just enough like the Russian *Tolstovka* to
emphasize the difference. His fawn-colored hair was almost the
same shade as the jacket, and badly needed trimming. His face
in profile showed gaunt, almost haggard. Before Darya reached
the sidewalk he had disappeared.

Darya dined off the borscht and meatballs with boiled buck-
wheat that she knew would be her fare for most of her stay at
Svetli Bereg, except for those few and happy occasions when
there would be chicken cut open and roasted flat as only Geor-
gians know how to roast chicken. She propped the *Kentavr*
against the cruet and finished her meal with a glass of thickened
cranberry juice. Before she got up from the table she took the
letter out of her pocketbook and added a sentence to it, smiling.
Out on the sidewalk again she caught herself looking round for
the foreign-looking gentleman.

The high road lay between the mountains and the sea (both invisible) and Darya turned the first corner she came to, knowing that every turning must be a passage to the coastline and thinking to go back to Steep Lane along the cliff top. The side street she had chosen was unpaved and seemed to end in a thick copse, but she struggled through the bushes and there was the sea, though the cliff was too sheer for a view of the beach. She thought she caught sight of a man dodging in and out of the copse before her, but the thought only made her step out more briskly. The path ended abruptly at the foot of a fence and this time she was almost sure she saw a figure lurking in its shadow, but when she got closer there was nobody there. Unable to walk along the line of the cliff any farther, she turned to look for a strip of park land at the side of the high road that Vera Ivanovna had told her of, and followed its paths till she came to the other end and there was the eucalyptus tree at the corner of Medicinal Beach.

The sky was still streaky in the west, but the moon was a polished disc over the horizon and its reflection was a broad shaft of light all the way to the fence at the end. Darya felt an irresistible tug to follow the path down the cliff and to the edge of the waves, but first she must go in and change her shoes. From the top of the staircase she looked eagerly round the porch to see if the chess table was still there. It was, and now a yellowish knight with flaring nostrils was champing impatiently on a white square, faced by two impassive-looking rooks and a sprinkling of yellow and black pawns. A bishop, a queen, and more pawns sprawled from an open wooden box tilted on the table.

In her room she stood on one foot, then the other, to draw her aching toes out of the new shoes and ease them into an old pair of bedroom slippers. Next she extracted from her suitcase a bulky volume of Dostoevsky. Vera Ivanovna had asked her to

take it as a present to Klavdia Mikhailovna. Klavdia Mikhailovna
wasn't what you'd call an educated person, but she was an avid
reader and had trained her taste on books and magazines left
behind by her lodgers. The last time Vera Ivanovna was in
Svetli Bereg there had been a tragedy—Klavdia Mikhailovna
had got into the very heart of *The Brothers Karamazov* when
the owner had written asking for it back. Vera Ivanovna had
found a copy of the book in a secondhand bookshop but she had
never got round to mailing it. Darya Lvovna left her pocketbook on the table, but remembering her landlady's roving glance
she took out the unfinished letter, locked it into her suitcase,
smiling again as she remembered the sentence she had added in
the cafeteria: *"Did your English gentleman play chess?"*

Something new had been added to the chess table—a stool,
salmon-pink and comma-shaped, on three flared black legs. Could
she have overlooked such a vivid object against the shingled
boards? She didn't think so, but brushed the thought aside, tired
of groping in her memory.

Piggy eyes gleamed out of the dusky kitchen below when
Darya approached, the big book in her hand. "I'll put it away
till the winter and read straight through from the beginning
again." In Klavdia Mikhailovna's voice was the memory of endless winter evenings when windows were shuttered both sides
of the street and storms were perpetually putting the electricity
out of kilter; when the neighbors crept into bed and allowed the
roaring of sea and sky to lull them to sleep, and Klavdia
Mikhailovna lay with her back to her snoring husband, reading
Chekhov or Dostoevsky by the light of an oil lamp with a cracked
chimney and chipped porcelain shade. She stood on a chair to
put the heavy volume atop a clothes closet and immediately
became the dour woman Vera Ivanovna had described. "I shall

have to find something to send Vera Ivanovna," she grumbled. "Perhaps you'll take her a jar of persimmon preserve when you leave." Darya secretly vowed she would do nothing of the sort, she had had experience of carrying pots of preserves among the clothes and papers in her suitcase. "Klavdia Mikhailovna," she said, "you don't have to send Vera Ivanovna anything. It gave her the greatest pleasure to find *The Brothers Karamazov* for you."

"She took her time over it," Klavdia Mikhailovna said grimly. She looked at her lodger's slippers. "You going out in house shoes?"

"I thought I'd just go and have a look at the sea," Darya Lvovna said apologetically. It was a solecism for summer guests to go out of the house in bedroom slippers. As soon as she was out in the lane she became aware, from certain sounds, that Klavdia Mikhailovna had followed her across the yard and was now standing outside the gate, probably watching her.

A few steps brought her to the fence at the end which she now recognized as one side of an enclosure like the one that had prevented her from coming home along the cliff top. She knew there must be a door under the wooden rainbow she had described in her letter to Vera Ivanovna, and found with her finger tips a wider crack between two palings, which meant hinges. A door or a gate there was, but barred and bolted on the other side. Darya Lvovna turned impatiently. Yes, she had been right, her landlady was standing outside the gate staring after her. Her Gothic features were shaded into softness by overhanging branches, but her powerful figure stood out in bold contour. There was nothing angular about the supple lines of her rather thick waist, her small high breasts and elongated hips. Darya remembered how lightly she had carried the heavy suitcase upstairs, and how easily she had bent and unbent while taking in laundry from a line. A man might find beauty in the strong womanly figure, she reflected, and forgive the grimness of the visage held erect on the majestic neck. Darya spoke to her as soon as she came within hearing: "Will the gate be open in the morning?" Klavdia Mikhailovna told her the beach was closed for the year, she would have to go by the road till she found a pathway to the sea a little farther on. Forgetting that there had been no fence in Vera Ivanovna's time, Darya Lvovna said, "But Vera Ivanovna used to sun-bathe on the cliff straight from the lane."

"Everybody knows that," Klavdia Mikhailovna said with an ugly sneer. Vera Ivanovna had warned her friend that Klavdia Mikhailovna was a disagreeable person, but Darya had not been prepared for such extreme disagreeableness. She walked quickly to the head of the lane and into the highroad. There she slowed her steps till she came upon a rutty pathway through a field and followed it to the edge of the cliff, down the steep side, all the way to waves dashing against pebbles, retreating more slowly than they had advanced, clinging desperately to small stones they had a moment before flung themselves upon so heedlessly. Here, Darya told herself, she would come early next morning to bathe in the sea, lie in the sun.

The house was in pitch-darkness when she came back, but there was a faint gleam over the door of her own room. Other houses, on both sides, kept a light shining in the yard all night long, but Darya Lvovna was not surprised to find Klavdia Mikhailovna mean about electricity. The chess table was not in its original place on the porch, but it was there, next to her own door, evidently for the sake of the light coming from the one tiny bulb screwed into the wall. And there was a man seated at it with his back to her. He rose at the sound of her footsteps, pushed the table aside and disappeared. The table and stool were back in their original place farther down the porch.

When Darya passed the shuttered windows and padlocked doors on her way to breakfast the next morning there was no chess table, no colored stool on the porch. She drank her coffee and ate the unleavened Armenian bread and keen-tasting cheese of goat's milk, slipped a big persimmon into her beach bag, and went to look for the path across the field she had found in the evening. It was nearer than it had seemed in the moonlight and she followed it over the side of the cliff to the beach. Darya took off her sandals and paddled back to Medicinal Beach through limpid curling wavelets to the side of the fence which marched a few yards into the sea, getting lower all the time till its palings hardly showed above the water and she had no difficulty in rounding the last of them. Now she saw what people got for their ten kopecks. On the cliff top there was a small tarred shed with a pay-desk window in one wall, and a little farther down the cliff an open-sided pavilion stacked to the roof with deck chairs and canvas cots. Darya had an impulse to pull out a cot and treat herself to a free sun bath, if only for the pleasure of cheating, but a strip of grass at the foot of the fence looked so nice and shady that she decided she would rest there after her swim. "I bet that's where they used to sit and talk," she told herself. She stayed a long time floating in the lazy swing of the tide, till a subtle change in its rhythm sent her swimming back to shore. She climbed painfully up the shingle to the cliff top, where she peeled off her swimsuit, spread the bathrobe on the grass, and let herself down in the lee of the fence. A great ship was outlined against the sky, its bows dipping; Darya wondered idly how long it would take to disappear behind the horizon. Her eyes closed of themselves against the golden scintillations from sea and sky.

Something was throbbing like a heart under the wrinkled folds in the hood of the robe; a tiny breeze, the merest zephyr, nuzzled up one wide sleeve like a roving hand; the ground was rising and sinking like the sea. She was not on the grass under the fence, she was lying on shuddering boards, aware of the thrusting of a piston in the engine room, its smooth recoils, insistent returns, in a realm where anything could happen. She felt not the least surprised to see a gaunt face that she somehow knew, suspended over hers. The strokes of the piston grew longer and slower. They stopped. Darya opened her eyes and pulled the robe closer. A bee sailed out of the calyx of a flower. Darya looked out at the shimmering surface of the sea. The ship had disappeared; only a plume of smoke on the horizon showed where it had been. Then her muscles contracted and helped her to a sitting position. She stretched and stood up. "That was nice," Darya Lvovna said.

She staggered to her feet and came down heavily on something horribly soft. Stooping, she saw a red stain spreading over the white gown. The persimmon. She snatched it up, looked at it reflectively for a moment, hastily sucked up the juicy mess, and flung the skin into a bush.

In the yard she stopped at the pump for a few minutes to rinse out the stain and hang robe and swimsuit on the line. As she passed the kitchen on the way to the porch her landlady looked up from her ironing and said, smiling unpleasantly, "Sunbathing?"

In her room Darya unlocked her still-unpacked suitcase and rummaged in it till her fingers found a narrow cardboard box that, emptied of pencils and reels of cotton, would just take the coiled leash, the pack of cards. The tweezers she only glanced at and left where they were on the night table. The unfinished letter she left in the suitcase; the box she would take to the post office, where she would buy a shiny picture postcard to send to Vera Ivanovna. On the way she composed the lines she would write on the empty space next to the address:

Firmly established in Steep Lane only it isn't Steep Lane any more, it's Medicinal Beach but everyone still calls it Steep Lane and I shall too. Klavdia Mikhailovna was delighted to get the Dostoevsky. Had my first bathe. Everything fine. Love Dasha.

Darya Lvovna spent all her mornings on the unenclosed section of the coast, never again swimming at Medicinal Beach or taking a sun bath in the shadow of its fence. Why, she could not have said. Every now and then she took the unfinished letter out of her suitcase, added a few lines of teasing reference to Vera Ivanovna's English gentleman; the letter got quite long and she had to begin another sheet. She knew now she would never send it.

The chess table had disappeared from the porch for good. Nor did an elusive figure in Norfolk jacket and brogues start up at odd corners when she walked into town. But one day she had an encounter that, while it did not touch her near or deep, interested her vitally. She was standing at the counter in the cafeteria, and had just moved away to pick up a worn aluminum soupspoon and a fork from a side table (knives were not supplied), when she noticed that a woman who had been behind her in the line was looking at her earnestly from sad, beady eyes. Darya chose a seat near the huge plate-glass window where she could amuse herself by watching the passers-by as she ate. The woman hesitated for a moment with her tray in her hand and then came straight across the floor—though there were as many empty as occupied tables—and pulled out a chair exactly opposite Darya with an appealing look that was more expressive than her murmured apologetic request to sit down. A lonely soul, reflected Darya unkindly, but then bethought herself that *she* was lonely too, and smiled the consent that she could scarcely have withheld. The stranger opened conversation with the usual gambit: was this the first time her neighbor was in Svetli Bereg? Was she staying near the sea? How did she like it? Darya replied with stiff amiability and the two women began on their dinner in silence. After a few mouthfuls the other put down her fork, and effectually prevented Darya Lvovna from lifting a spoonful of soup to her lips by leaning forward and saying in a low voice, "You don't remember me?" Darya put down the spoon, smiled faintly, and said, "I'm afraid not. Ought I to?"

"We have a common friend—Smirnova. Vera Ivanovna Smirnova. Vera Ivanovna and I worked at the Foreign Library. You used to come for English books. I worked in the accountant's department."

Dim images crowded into Darya Lvovna's mind—Vera Ivanovna emerging from a huddle of bowed figures in the back of the library to greet her at the book counter. A head—was it the one opposite?—raised from the huddle to regard her as if for identification and sinking back over papers again. "Vera Ivanovna told me you were here," she said. "You live somewhere in the mountains, I think. And I think (smiling) your name is Vera Ivanovna, too. But I can't say I remember seeing you at the library."

"Did Vera Ivanovna tell you about me?"

Darya drew a long face. "She told me you had been—away a long time."

Gradually the strain of making conversation relaxed; as soon as the two women got fairly on to the fascinating subject of a mutual friend, they found plenty to say.

"I think you were a great friend of Vera Ivanovna's."

"I am," Darya said. "But your friendship is older than mine."

"She was scarcely more than a child when I first knew her. We called her Malishka because there were three Vera Ivanovnas in the office."

Darya smiled. "I know. She told me how you came to see her at the end of her last visit here."

"Did she?" Vera Ivanovna was visibly moved. "And did she tell you about her Englishman?"

"She told me she met an Englishman staying at the sanatorium," Darya said coldly, but felt such curiosity to know more about the English gentleman that she consented almost eagerly when the new acquaintance suggested that they finish up their talk over a glass of tea. Vera Ivanovna took half a lemon and a short knife with a black handle from a plastic sack in the pocket of her sagging cardigan. Admiring the forethought, Darya watched her slice thin wafers from the lemon. "You'd think the cafeteria would provide knives for customers. Are they afraid we'd take them home?"

"Perhaps they think people would start knifing one another." Both women laughed, surveying the sparse clientele of the cafeteria peacefully gulping cabbage soup or munching scraps of meat too soft and stringy to require cutting up.

"I found Malishka very much changed," began Vera Ivanovna.

"Did you? It seems to me Vera Ivanovna's a person the years have changed less than anyone I ever knew. I still think of her as almost girlish-looking, not a single gray hair and hardly a wrinkle, and her figure so slender and willowy—"

"Oh, not outwardly, it was her behavior I was thinking about."

"Her behavior! I've always regarded Vera Ivanovna as a model —not to say a reproach—to us all. She may seem a little prim at first, but very soon you see it's only shyness. I don't know anyone more kind and tolerant."

"Yes, yes! I love Malishka, but she behaved very strangely the

last time she was here—lying naked on the beach with a man—
a foreigner from the sanatorium—and spending all her time
snuggled up against him on the cliff top."

"For goodness' sake! Where did you get all that from?"

Vera Ivanovna looked a little ashamed. "Tamara told me,"
she said.

"And how does Tamara know anything about Vera, stuck up
in her newsstand all day?"

"She got it from an authoritative source—your landlady told
her."

"Klavdia Mikhailovna! And you'd believe what that foul-
minded hag says against what you know of your friend!"

"Ah, but that's just *it*. I have firsthand knowledge, too."

I oughtn't to listen to her, Darya Lvovna thought, but, far
from dealing the merited snub, she encouraged further revela-
tions. "D'you mean to say and actually *saw* Vera do anything
bad?"

"I saw plenty. I went to her without warning one day and I
could see at once that she was expecting a man. She hadn't
prepared such a chic little lunch just for herself. I saw her hide
the wineglasses. And while I was there a man came to the gate—
twice. She didn't let him in, told me it was someone for the
landlady. I think I spoiled that little rendezvous."

"And you are proud of it?" Darya asked, appalled by the
malice in Vera Ivanovna's voice. "Do you grudge your friend an
hour's happiness?"

"Happiness! Nobody thinks *I* have a right to happiness! Vera
wouldn't have that clear baby complexion if she'd spent ten
years in a camp! Look at you—for all I know you may be older
than me, but nobody would think it. *Your* mouth hasn't fallen
in through losing all your teeth from scurvy! *You* weren't bald

as an egg before you were forty!" Almost frenetically Vera
Ivanovna put her hand to her head and pushed back a coarsely
made wig, exposing an expanse of waxy skull.

"We know it," Darya Lvovna said, "and we respect you for
what you went through. But you are not the only one; my
younger sister is just the same, and *she* wasn't in a camp—she
survived the siege in Leningrad. And Vera Ivanovna, what you
say is true—your friend *was* expecting a man she cared for; she
had prepared a farewell lunch for him, but she couldn't bear to
hurt your feelings. Another woman would have asked you to
come the next day. Don't cry. People are beginning to look at us.
Let's go out and sit in the park."

They sat down on an unoccupied bench in a bushy, blossomy
niche. A tubular ash can crowned with a saucer-like rim was at
their service, but it was inconveniently placed, too high to be
used from a sitting position, so after lighting up each contributed
a spent match to the litter of cigarette butts and candy wrappings
on the gravel at their feet. A cinema hall in front of them was
closed and silent, its columned portico and white walls against
a semicircle of cypresses pleasingly Greek to uninstructed eyes.
Behind them in a raggedy, sanded enclosure, swings and seesaws
stood motionless; the children were in school.

"You despise me, of course," Vera Ivanovna said in a low
voice. "I never really thought any harm. I always loved Malishka
and I always shall. If she were in trouble there's nothing I
wouldn't do for her."

Darya thought, But her happiness was hard for you to bear.
Aloud she said, "I don't despise you. Probably I'd feel just the
same in your place." She reached out and took from Vera
Ivanovna's lap a hand she had already observed to be surprisingly shapely—the one elegant note in the ungainly figure beside

her on the bench. Vera Ivanovna received the warm clasp gratefully and threw the half-smoked cigarette from her with a fine
recklessness. "Do you think Vera is happy?" she asked.

"Who's happy?" Darya said wildly.

There was a letter from home waiting for her on the kitchen
table. She got one a day; her husband sent his letters on the
conveyor system, starting the next as soon as he had posted the
one before.

"*Dear wife*," he wrote, never having discovered how the affec-
tionately facetious words infuriated Darya.

Dear wife,

*I've been roped in lately to give a series of lectures on the scien-
tific characteristic of communist economy. I know you take not
the slightest interest in what has always been my ruling passion,
and I hope I can take a hint as well as the next man, so I won't
bother you with the details, though they say the attendance and
subsequent applause were greater than anyone in the office can
remember for a lecture of this sort. I began by stating that the
establishment of communism is in itself a natural historical
process, each stage of social development arising objectively from
the preceding, while there can be no arbitrary omission of a given
stage. Practically a truism, you will say, though it required to be
stated as a point of departure. But there are people who will
contest any statement whatever, and that ass Kuznetsov has to
send in a note at question time: "Inasmuch as I understand the
speaker to describe communist economy as a purely rational
process, it would seem spontaneous elements are entirely ruled
out. Is this in accordance with the Party Line?" I had to remind
him of the word "natural" in my thesis, allowing for the occur-*

rence of spontaneous phenomena even under socialism. Such are,
e.g., . . .

Darya Lvovna rapidly turned page after page till she came to
her children's names:
Nurochka is seldom home before twelve, and Volodya treats
his home as if it were a doss house. I seldom if ever see my
children.
The letter ended, as all her husband's letters ended:
Come back soon. I miss you. Your loving husband.
The next day Darya Lvovna didn't go to the cafeteria, but
mustered her little store of fruit and cheese and milk to eat at
home. She felt, compunctiously, that Vera Ivanovna would be on
the lookout for her, and, unkindly, that she didn't want to gratify
Vera Ivanovna. Standing a spray of syringa in a milk bottle on
the flowered linen cloth, Darya couldn't help thinking of the
lunch of the two Vera Ivanovnas and checked herself in the act
of setting out plates and cutlery for two. The illusion was so
strong that a rattling at the gate set her heart thumping. She
knew the gate was locked and bolted; Klavdia Mikhailovna,
though no farther away than the poultry yard at the back of the
house, would have seen to that. Darya started to her feet to get
there first, and recognized immediately the shabby squat figure
of yesterday's acquaintance.

"History repeats itself," said Vera Ivanovna, sidling purpose-
fully through the unhospitably narrow opening Darya Lvovna
left in the gate. "You looked just the way Malishka did when
she let me in—as if you were expecting somebody else."

"I wasn't expecting anybody at all," Darya said ungraciously.
"I was just having my lunch."

"And I just had my dinner. Shall we go for a walk? We could

take a bus to Golden Bay. Stalin used to have a villa there—
they say it's a wonderful view."

Darya Lvovna excused herself, but invited her visitor to sit
down and have some grapes. Vera Ivanovna, abashed by the cold
welcome, sat for half an hour at the table, and went away without repeating her invitation to Golden Bay. Of course Darya felt
a beast. Yesterday she had received a lonely stranger's tears,
clasped her hand, all but revealed her own heart, and today she
couldn't stand the woman. But when she remembered the callous
words "I think I spoiled that little rendezvous" she hardened her
heart, or rather she seized on the memory as justification for her
own callousness.

After her guest had left, Darya Lvovna, exhausted by the most
exhausting of indulgences—the indulgence in remorse—stripped
to her shift and flung herself on the bed, pushing aside the padded
crimson quilt; the room was still warm with the rays of the
evening sun, and a sheet was covering enough for the short nap
she intended to allow herself. But depression had got a firm toe-
hold in her mind and sleep would not come. She tried to brace
herself by considering the *real* troubles of other people—of Vera
Ivanovna, lonely, neglected, resentful, her health shattered, pay-
ing out her life trying to teach English to Georgian children; of
her sister in Leningrad, a confirmed hypochondriac, surrounded
by medicine bottles and doctors' prescriptions, practically lost to
society; of the friend with the sixteen-year-old spastic daughter;
of the girl at the office no man had ever dated. What had she to
complain of in comparison with these? She didn't care for her
work in a government office, but neither did her fellow workers;
the light and feeling had long faded from her relations with her
perfectly good husband, but that wasn't so uncommon either; her
children, kind and dutiful, had stepped out of her orbit, and
what could be more right and natural? What was eating her?

She didn't know. It was not given her to uncover the roots of her pain. At last she slept.

She awoke to music; piercing, sweet, forlorn. The bow soared in the hand of a master in a triumphant crescendo, plunged home in consoling diminuendo. Everything is ineffably sweet and no less ineffably, sweetly sad, the bow assured Darya's soul, but a voice joined in and familiar trivial words mocked her. She smiled scornfully, with her lips only.

> *I'll be loving you*
> *Always,*
> *With a love that's true*
> *Always.*

Twenty years ago this foolish song had been her husband's favorite record. He had learned the idiot words by heart, and though Darya laughed at him she had aided and abetted the placing of the phonograph on the night table, where he could switch off the record in bed and, constitutionally nonintuitive, come to her crooning the word "Oalways—s." The tradition had lapsed from inertia like an unwound clock—first the crooning dropped off; then another record was put on the player; and last of all the gramophone was left for weeks at a time on the floor of the clothes closet, from which it did come out occasionally, but never to recapture its place at the bedside. The irony of it was that the fatuous words were true: they had indeed been loving one another for a good slice of "always," upward of twenty years, and their love was now prison diet, indispensable but insipid. Darya told herself again and again she had nothing to complain of—he was her husband, she was sure of his love. Perhaps you couldn't say worse of a man.

Strange sounds like shuffling footsteps, interspersed by irregular thumps too heavy to be dance steps, were added to the voice and the violin. Darya got out of bed and tiptoed to the door, which opened just wide enough to give her a view of the porch. She saw at once where the sounds came from: Klavdia Mikhailovna, wearing a flowered sarafan and a white head kerchief, was hopping and shuffling in time to a record on top of the radiola, her right foot tethered to a thick pad; near her stood a pail with a cloth on its rim and a straw besom propped against its side: the cloth was stained a deep chrome, the besom tapered forlornly to one side—Klavdia Mikhailovna was polishing the boards of the porch.

As Darya watched, a dim figure approached from behind to place a hand on the waist of the floor waxer, to join her rhythmic movements.

Klavdia Mikhailovna's small eyes radiated light from their dark centers and the lips Darya had only seen grimly compressed parted to show strong teeth, exquisitely white.

Now a third figure, bowed, meek, popeyed, stole up. Klavdia Mikhailovna seemed not to notice her, but her partner extended his other arm and drew the newcomer into the dance. Immediately an elderly frump was transformed to drowsy beauty; she dropped her head on the shoulder so conveniently near, and fell into step. The music accelerated furiously, the abandon of the dancers mounted to frenzy, Darya poked her head farther out of the doorway. The women did not heed her, but the male dancer, who had seen her at once, extricated himself effortlessly from his partners and strode up to her. Instantly the record ground to a finish, Klavdia Mikhailovna closed the gramophone, bent to unfasten the pad from her right foot, picked up the pail, and clattered toward the stairs. The other woman had vanished the moment the music stopped. Darya was left face to face with the chess player, the haunter of sidewalk and cliff. She took one step forward, laid her cheek against his shoulder and closed her eyes. The rough-looking wool felt as smooth and cool as a pillow. It was a pillow.

When she opened her eyes again light was streaming into the room, and the quilt lay huddled at her feet, where she had pushed it before getting into bed. How many hours ago was that? She had gone to bed before nine and now the clock said it was seven. Too early to get up. (She didn't like to go into the kitchen till Klavdia Mikhailovna's husband had left for the day.) But she got out of bed and dressed anyhow, buoyed up by the realization that she had slept eleven hours on end. And what is more, she packed her things and went down to breakfast fully determined to go home by the next plane. Every day she had a letter from her husband. The last three had ended: *"When are you coming back?"* There was a letter from him on the kitchen table now, warning her to profit from the prolonged spell of good weather—any day it might break and flying become impracticable. "I will go home," Darya Lvovna said.

The Boy Who Laughed

I.

THE SPECIALISTS CONSULTED by Slava's anxious parents all agreed that Slava was retarded. None would commit themselves further. All had known, or at least heard of, otherwise normal children who did not speak till they were five, six, indeed seven years old. By the time he was eight everyone could see that Slava, while patently a human being, would never be a full member of society; the slack underlip, the straight, spaced fingers, the curious angle at which he habitually carried his head, were more articulate than poor Slava's unmanageable tongue. Many people advised Yuri Vladimirovich and Valentina Matveyevna to send their child to a Home. Yuri Vladimirovich might have agreed, but he never dared propose it to his wife or mother. And many who knew Slava in his home thought it would be a tragedy to send him away. One doctor went so far as to say that to deprive Slava of the only things he understood—his mother's affection and the passionate devotion of his grandmother—would cause a trauma from which Slava would never recover. "And it would kill Babushka," Valentina Matveyevna said. Yuri Vladimirovich knew it was true—his mother lived for Slava, without him her life would have no meaning.

The move from Odessa, where Slava was born, to Moscow—occasioned by Yuri Vladimirovich's astounding success in nuclear physics—had a most unfortunate effect on Slava. In Odessa the family had inhabited the ground floor of a dilapidated two-story house, in a weed-grown yard where Slava spent hours on end picking grass stalks which he afterward placed one by one on the stone path in subtle, never-repeating patterns. Upstairs lived two old ladies who had known Slava all his life and were used to him. In Moscow the family had two rooms in an old-fashioned communal apartment on the ninth floor. The yard was a thoroughfare for motor traffic and Slava had to make his patterns from spent matches on the top of a trunk in the tiny room he shared with Babushka. He soon came down with a severe case of flu. Thanks to Babushka's fanatical conscientiousness in carrying out the doctor's orders, still more perhaps to the purity and intensity of her love, Slava recovered, but he was a different boy in his relations with the outside world forever after.

Before his illness he had taken no notice when the other tenants spoke to him; now he responded to the kindliest greetings with maniacal chuckles. He was quiet with his gentle mother and grandmother, but on Sundays and in the evenings when his father came home, harsh laughter was heard in the other room every time a door was opened. Housewives at work in the communal kitchen set down a rolling pin on a floured board or upended an iron to shut out the horrid sound with a hand at each ear. And one day Yuri Vladimirovich packed up his bag and went away never to return. And no wonder, the other tenants said. It was all the fault of his mother and wife for not sending Slava to a Home; how could one of the most promising young physicists in the Soviet Union be expected to live at close quarters with a hopeless imbecile, even if it *was* his own child? Where was he to write, to receive his friends and colleagues after work hours? There were even people who said Slava should have been "allowed to die" of the flu. They asked: what would become of Slava when his grandmother died or (more delicately) if anything happened to his mother? They said such children live for ever. Valentina Matveyevna and her mother-in-law shrugged their shoulders helplessly. What was meant by "allowing Slava to die"? Were they to withhold succor from a sentient being who gazed trustfully at them from fringed eyes, and accepted their ministrations with the wavering smile only seen on the lips of infants and dying persons? Did Slava need love and security less than other children? Or, he being defective, didn't his needs matter? For the first four years of Slava's life had she not been as proud and happy as any mother? Was his mother to give him up because he was unfortunate?

Two attempts were made to put Slava in a day school for retarded children, once when he was six years old and once after his father left them. Each had ended in catastrophe; the doctor said Slava could only be dealt with in a Home, but held out no hopes of a "cure"—the trauma might be too strong for treatment to be of any use. And gradually, under Babushka's gentle, unrelaxing pressure, Slava became amenable to certain social disciplines: he learned to stand aside to let a neighbor pass him in the hall, to wait till everyone else was in the lift before stepping in himself, to wipe his boots on the mat. He still snarled quietly at play, but the horrid outbreaks of harsh laughter grew less frequent, only occurring under stress of novelty or fear.

Slava loved to draw. He drew by the hour during the day, and in the night Babushka was sometimes awakened by a low continuous growling from the window and knew it was Slava standing behind the window curtains, drawing by the light from the neon lamps in the street. Friends encouraged Valentina Matveyevna to believe Slava had artistic talent (weren't Van Gogh and Utrillo both mad?). But the obsession subsided; the albums and crayons lay untouched in the top drawer of the bureau. And yet the indefatigable Babushka managed to graft certain skills on what the doctors said were the empty cells of Slava's brain. She taught him to read. He would read aloud in a low murmur by the hour from any book put into his hands, without any apparent preferences; Russian folk tales, *Robinson Crusoe*, and *Tales for Tiny Tots* seemed to give him equal pleasure, and once his mother had had trouble in tearing him away from a street guide to Leningrad which had been given to him in mistake for a copy of the *Arabian Nights*. Apparently the only thing Slava couldn't do was to make sense out of his senses.

Babushka's supreme achievement was teaching Slava to play the piano. Her method was crude to the point of subtlety: she placed his great paws over the backs of her own delicately arched hands and played a few bars of music over and over again, then slipped her hands from beneath Slava's hollowed palms, leaving the tips of his fingers poised on the keys; Slava's excellent ear and sense of rhythm did the rest, and soon he had a repertoire of six songs, ranging from the "Song of the Volga Boatmen" to "Silent Night," all of which he played "with the left hand too," as Babushka never failed to point out, by which she meant she had somehow taught him to shift from the tonic to the dominant and back again. Hopes of musical talent were now indulged in. As a little girl Valentina Matveyevna had been taken to hear Pachmann play Chopin at the Petersburg Conservatory. All she could remember of it was that Pachmann's antics on the piano stool had made the audience laugh. Poor Pachmann was mad. But that had not prevented him from being a great pianist, had it? A teacher said to have had much experience with "maladjusted" children was found. Slava played his six pieces for her and waited for the outburst of admiration to which he was accustomed. When the teacher said nothing but took up his forearm to demonstrate the proper position of the hand before striking the note, Slava tossed her hand away with a powerful gesture and once again went through his repertoire, wagging his heavy head and laughing loudly and harshly all the time. When she tried to steady his exuberant but essentially rhythmic tempo by marking time with a pencil on the edge of the piano, Slava turned on her with bared teeth, snatched the pencil from her fingers, and broke it in half. After this even Babushka couldn't teach him any new pieces, though he still played the original six from time to time, and when his mother came home from work she was always greeted by the strains of "Birdie, birdie where've you been?" and knew that behind the door of her room two smiling faces waited for her kiss. It was sweet, it was bitter, she was used to it.

By the time Slava was fifteen he could be left alone in the yard with no danger that he would stray into the street. He even earned money shoveling snow for the yard woman and hammering nails into boards outside a carpenter's workshop in the basement. The foreman soon discovered that Slava was perfectly safe with saw or hatchet, and his strength and endurance made him a valuable worker during the building season, though he couldn't be employed indoors because his chuckling laugh got on the other men's nerves. And you couldn't count on him; as soon as he was paid he was apt to stray from work till by some mysterious urge to increase his hoard he went in search of another job. He never spent his earnings, of that his mother and grandmother were sure, but for a long time nobody had any idea where he kept them, till one day Babushka, intent on mending a rent in the pocket of Slava's wadded jacket, came upon a cache of paper rubles and small change in a corner of the lining. It was decided not to risk upsetting Slava by taking it out; seeing that the amount never lessened but rather increased, the women got into a lazy habit of slipping nickels and quarters, sometimes even a silver ruble, into the slit, with a vague idea of one day buying something special for Slava.

All in all you could scarcely have found a more tranquil home in the whole of Moscow than the two rooms in the communal apartment on the ninth floor where the women lived and cherished their helpless charge. Everything went smoothly till the fatal day when Babushka was summoned to Riga, to the bedside of her daughter Galina.

The women discussed trains and timetables in writing, like people who believe there is a concealed microphone in every room; there was no time to prepare Slava, and you never knew what he took in—he had a disconcerting habit of watching lips. They packed hastily when Slava was asleep and at midnight Babushka kissed his pure forehead and tiptoed out of the room. Valentina Matveyevna, who had arranged a week's leave from the office, thought Slava looked strangely at her when she sat down to breakfast with him. It's not Sunday, his look seemed to say. (Pulling yesterday from the calendar was Slava's duty and privilege, and he always knew when it was Sunday—Sundays were red.) The only other sign that he knew something was amiss was a rapid glance over his mother's shoulder every time she came into the room. But he said nothing about Babushka, and Valentina Matveyevna said nothing. Waiting for Slava's lead had become second nature.

After breakfast Slava without a word allowed himself to be dressed for going out, and followed his mother with his usual

docility in and out of the milkshop and the bread store, then into
the vegetable store, but when she turned from the fruit counter
Slava was nowhere to be seen. Nobody in the store had noticed
him, but some little boys outside said they had seen him cross the
road and *get on a tram.*

II.

"Everywhere," Valentina Matveyevna said. "I've tried everywhere—the hospitals, the police station, the streetcar depots, the
bus parks, the railway stations. Nobody has seen him."

"You didn't try Odessa," Babushka said. Her daughter had
recovered and she had come back to Moscow as soon as she got
Valentina Matveyevna's telegram. The neighbors had advised
Valentina Matveyevna not to send for Babushka; it would only
upset her, and what could Slava's grandmother do that his mother
hadn't done? But Valentina Matveyevna had sent a telegram
just the same—she knew it was what Babushka would have
wanted her to do. And when she arrived Babushka had not
asked a single question; all she had said was, "You didn't try
Odessa."

Neighbors crowding into the hall folded their arms and shook
their heads compassionately. The poor old thing!

"He's gone to look for me," Babushka said.

Nobody believed Slava capable of finding his way to the railway station and ordering a ticket to Odessa till Babushka brought
out of the top drawer of the bureau an old candy box in which,
neatly arranged, were used tickets and a pile of "rubles" and
cardboard coins that had come with a shopping game. Playing at
"going to the dacha" had been almost a daily occupation.

"And where did he get the money?"

Valentina Matveyevna flung herself on the quilted jacket hanging from a hook in the hall and thrust her hand deep into the pocket. Her fingers groped knowingly among the loose wads of cotton but brought out nothing but a soiled lump with a two-kopeck coin sticking to it. Slava must have planned his escapade in advance; the money had been in its hiding place the night before he disappeared, Valentina Matveyevna was sure of that—she had put a paper ruble and a quarter into the slit when clearing her pocketbook after Babushka had left.

The next day Valentina Matveyevna started for Odessa, afraid that if she didn't, Babushka would go. As soon as she arrived she went straight to the little street on the outskirts where Slava was born. The house wasn't there any more, the *street* wasn't there any more, all had been swallowed up by high tenements which enclosed the original yard, with no grasses and bushes waving in the breeze, nothing but asphalt and garbage cans. Not quite nothing. In a corner of the yard was a shed Valentina Matveyevna remembered, though when she knew it there had been no iron pipe projecting through the roof to speak of a stove within. She made for it instinctively and was immediately hot on Slava's tracks. For in the doorway stood an ancient crone peering across the yard, and when Valentina Matveyevna came closer she recognized the younger of the two old ladies from upstairs in the now-vanished house she had lived in for the first ten years of Slava's life. Old Rosa told her that she had refused to go out of the yard when the street of small houses was demolished to make room for the new buildings, and they had allowed her to move into the shed and even have a stove put in. Valentina was surprised to see how snug she had made it; the shiny samovar, the Bokhara rugs on the wall, and two nineteenth-century portraits in heavy gilt frames gave it quite a prosperous, not to say aristocratic look. And there, it appeared, Slava had found her; he had always loved to play in the shed, and like his mother had gone to it instinctively in the shadow of the new houses. He stayed with her two days, Rosa said; she fed him and washed his clothes, and oh how hungry and dirty the poor lad was, and on the third day he went away with a wayfaring tinker who had just finished three days mending saucepans in the yard. She thought they went on a steamer.

The militia in Odessa were sure they would find Slava if he was anywhere on the islands, but by the time they got in touch with local authorities the scent was cold. A boy who had worked some time for a tinker on the outskirts of a kolkhoz had suddenly left; people could only remember of him that he laughed at his work. After visiting the hospitals and railway stations— even the prisons—there was nothing for Valentina Matveyevna to do but go back to Moscow.

Old Rosa had wrapped a card with his mother's name and address on it in a handkerchief and put it into Slava's pocket while he slept, and from time to time over the years news came in illiterate scrawls of a "man" who had worked three months, six months in a remote village, and gone away. Babushka and Valentina Matveyevna followed Slava's itinerary on the map as best they could by the help of the postmarks. "He's working his way back," Babushka said. "He's coming back to us."

Once a snapshot of a tall figure grasping a rake in a cornfield came; it was pale and blurred, but they recognized Slava's deep mindless eyes in the mustached and bearded face, his small neat ear flattened against the closely cropped head—and wept. Soon after, Babushka died.

Galina Vladimirovna, who had after all not died that dreadful time in Riga, came to Moscow for her mother's funeral. The sisters-in-law scarcely knew one another, but each had an intimate knowledge of the other's sad life (Galina had her own tragedy, more common but no less painful than Valentina's). The day of the funeral they talked far into the night, fascinated by a relationship made up of intimacy and strangeness. Yes, they went to bed early after a cozy supper the day they followed Babushka to the grave, and left the door open between the two rooms. "I don't remember that I ever slept in a room all to myself," Galina said. "Do you think they'll leave you the two rooms, Valya?" Valentina told her the question wouldn't even be raised; Slava's name had never been officially removed from the register, and his room was so tiny and could only be reached through her own, so that nobody could be put into it. "Couldn't they offer you one room instead of two?" Valentina didn't let this worry her. The room was Slava's and one day Slava would come back and claim it. "Valya, darling, do you still really believe Slava will come back?" Valya was sure of it, he would come back to his own home, as he had gone back to the old home in Odessa. Shuddering, Galina envisaged a Neanderthal figure plodding over plains and hills, through towns and villages, toward his mother in far-off Moscow.

"Why don't you marry again, Valya?" Galina asked on a sudden impulse. Valya sighed impatiently. "I told you. I'm waiting for Slava to come back. I can't expect a man to live in the same apartment with Slava. His own father couldn't."

"Yuri told me he never loved you more than when you refused to send Slava to a Home. It was just that he couldn't stand living with the poor boy." "I know," said Valentina. "I never blamed him."

"I think it broke his heart when you chose to give your life to Slava and not to him."

"He married again within the year," Valentina said shortly.

"And why couldn't you—after all these years?"

"Why are *you* so eager for me to get married, Galya? Have you found marriage so satisfactory? I should have thought you would envy me my freedom." "I have been unfortunate," Galya said. "Everybody doesn't have such bad luck as I had." She pushed a tear out of the corner of each eye with a sidewise action of the heels of her palms; much as she liked talking about her woes, she did not mean to be led away from the subject of her sister-in-law's life by subtle evasions on Valya's part. So she said, "I can't see what use you make of your freedom." "I do my best," Valya said. "Only I won't let any man come here. I wouldn't while Babushka was alive, and I still won't as long as there's a possibility of Slava coming back." Galya turned and looked at her sister-in-law through the open door, eyes now perfectly dry and wide open, round. "Oh, so you *do* have somebody!" she exclaimed. "I had no idea." "For goodness' sake, Galya, I'm a woman, aren't I?"

Galya went back to her own particular tragedy in Riga, nothing more was heard of Slava, and Valentina Matveyevna went to work every morning and came back every evening as usual. Even Galya, who should have known better, made a halfhearted attack on her sister-in-law's freedom. She already had three children, and a few months after her return the poor foolish woman found herself again pregnant, she who was never tired of saying how she detested and despised her deplorable husband. "Oh, Valya," she wrote, "I can hardly bear to say it, but perhaps after all you could take Natasha to live with you! She's only two, and she's such an affectionate little thing you'd soon get used to each other —I mean I wouldn't ask you to take one of the others, they're too difficult already. But I'm sure it would be no trauma for Natashka. The new baby would be much more of a trauma." (Galya had written "shock" but was happy to cross it out and use the more fashionable terminology.) "Even if Slava came back it would be all right, I mean not like him finding a man beside you, *that* I can understand would be too hard, dear Valya. Oh, Valya, you can understand how desperate I must be before I could ask this . . ." And a man who had been happy enough for years in a gentle and undemanding union with her, now felt that the occasional weekend in the country, the month in the south, were not enough; his whole happiness depended on living all the time with Valentina Matveyevna, now that this was made possible by her mother-in-law's death. He did not get his way, and as a result they drifted apart.

By now Valentina Matveyevna was beginning to think she wanted nothing more from any man. She settled down peacefully to wait for Slava.

Holiday Home

THE TRAIN STOPPED at Drozdovo, and Nina Petrovna, having not without difficulty staggered onto the platform with her suitcase, looked around for help. There was no one in sight, so she picked up the suitcase and slowly, a few steps at a time, carried it to the cloakroom. She had been told the way to the Holiday Home in advance—turn to the right when you get out of the station, skirt the covered market, and go straight on till you reached a signpost with the words TO ROSA LUXEMBURG HOLIDAY HOME painted on it.

As Nina Petrovna skirted the market, a fawn-colored dog with a tightly coiled tail snarled at her from the shelter of the fence. Farther on, a great black dog chained to a post got up on its hind legs and barked savagely; the first dog, as if suddenly reminded of its duty, now hurled itself into the road, its shrill soprano floating above the hoarse yelps of the watchdog. But as soon as Nina Petrovna turned toward the signpost at the edge of the woods, both dogs slunk away with low grumbles. She had no difficulty finding her way to a clearing in the woods where a graveled sweep encircled a bed of peonies and rosebushes on its way to a three-story house complete with pillars, balconies, and wings.

Nina Petrovna climbed a flight of stone steps to a massive door from the handle of which hung an enameled sign enjoining the public in letters three inches high to be quiet please, it was the rest hour. The door was not locked, and she entered a spacious lobby furnished with leather couches and chairs against the walls, an office desk cater-cornered at one end and a walnut radio set at the other. The sound of her steps brought into the hall a young woman in a surgeon's smock, with a white kerchief tightly knotted at the nape of her neck. There was an expression of naïve hospitality on her rosy face which she was obviously trying to change to one of official courtesy; smiling radiantly, she said the director would be in his office at five, and asked Nina Petrovna to come upstairs with her. At the first landing she turned and cried out as if Nina Petrovna were half a mile away, "Don't hurry, Babulya! It's two more flights to your room. I'll wait for you at the top—I simply can't learn to go slowly upstairs. Hold on to the railing, Babulya. Here, let me take your bag!" When Nina Petrovna did not give up her handbag the girl vanished around the turn of the staircase. She was waiting for Nina Petrovna on the top landing, and the moment her head appeared the shrill young voice rang out: "There she is. Here I am, Babulya! Don't hurry, I'm waiting for you!" "And you don't shout," said Nina Petrovna; "I thought it was supposed to be the rest hour." "Oh, I pay no attention to that," said the girl merrily. "That's for the guests, not for the staff. Besides, there's hardly anyone here yet, and they're all out in the woods —such fine weather."

Three beds stood out stiffly into the middle of the room she showed Nina Petrovna. On one of the night tables was a book; on another a glass of water, through which could be seen the tender pink and white undulations of a double set of dentures. Nina Petrovna understood that two beds were already occupied. "Can't I get a room to myself?" she asked "Surely all the rooms aren't occupied yet?"

The girl laughed heartily. "They're almost all empty. You're almost the first." "Well then, why not put me in one of the empty rooms?"

The rosy face became grave. "You'll have to ask the director." "I don't suppose he'd object, would he?" "Even if he doesn't, the matron's gone home." "But if the director allows it the matron won't object, will she?" "The sheets will have to be moved." "And is that so difficult?" "It's not that, but you see, my shift's over. I was just going home when you came."

A new idea passed through Nina Petrovna's head: "Aren't there any empty rooms on the ground floor?" "The top rooms are always allotted first." "And supposing a person's old. Or ill. Going up and down stairs is hard for such people." "Almost all our guests are old. We don't take children, so the families can't come either. You'll be one of the youngest guests." "Very well, then why put us upstairs before the downstairs rooms are filled?" "We're not ready yet—only the top rooms are ready for sleeping in." "You should have begun with the downstairs rooms and if any younger ones come later they can be put upstairs." The girl looked pityingly at Nina Petrovna. "Cleaning always begins from the top," she said, with devastating simplicity. "You'll be very comfortable here, Babulya. The other people in the room are such nice old ladies. Fanya Borisovna—those are her teeth in the glass, she only puts them in for meals—she's nice; and Maria Mikhailovna Goncharova, she's ever so nice too, though she does cough rather in the night."

Nina Petrovna sat down on the chair next to the third bed. She suddenly felt a deathly exhaustion. Her shoes reminded her of their newness by a vicious tweak. She slipped her feet out of them and felt better at once, well enough to ask the rosy maiden what her name was. "Me? I'm Katya—just Katya." "Very well, Katya, and I have a name too. My name is Nina Petrovna Orlova. People ought to use each other's names." "For me you're Babushka, Babulya, and that's what I shall call you." Nina Petrovna gave up the struggle. "Isn't there anybody who can go to the station for my suitcase?" "I'll fetch it myself. I'll bring it first thing in the morning. You can do without it just for one night, I suppose." "Indeed and I cannot. I must have it as soon as possible." Nina Petrovna had only one thought in her mind for the moment—to unpack her bedroom slippers. "You shall have it," Katya said soothingly. "Give me the receipt and I'll go for it this minute." "I don't like to think of you carrying it all that way. Isn't there a man for that sort of thing?" Katya flung out a sturdy pair of arms, and her ringing laugh was like the very voice of health and youth.

The director listened attentively to Comrade Orlova's request for a room to herself, at least till the house filled up. He didn't advise her to take a room on the ground floor; it was always noisy with comings and goings, and there was nothing to prevent guests from using the radio till midnight. On the second floor there was a consulting room and a library and a telly set. The third floor was the quietest of all. The staircase was not steep, and she could go up slowly, resting both feet on each step—the doctor actually considered this to be good for the heart muscles. He was so persuasive that Nina Petrovna left the office with a sense of satisfaction; to sleep on the third floor now seemed almost a privilege.

When she entered the dining room for supper, it seemed to her at first that there was nobody at any of the tables. But then she noticed, right at the end of the room, vague figures seated at a round table. The windows were curtained, and the only light came from a single bulb in an elaborate glass and wood chandelier. As she got nearer to the round table, she saw that the company consisted of three or four aged ladies. Later she made out two men at another table; they seemed pretty old, too. A waitress with a pleated linen tiara over a lofty hairdo approached Nina Petrovna and showed her to a seat next to the men. One of them, glancing from the newcomer to the waitress, said, "Klavochka, why are we kept in the dark like wolves?" Nina Petrovna felt that the remark was aimed more at herself than at the waitress— an old stager was apologizing for the defects of the house. She smiled into space and wished everyone a good evening. A polite laugh was heard, and the waitress, laying a place for Nina Petrovna, said loudly, as if answering for all, that the electrician would come the next day and screw in some more lamps and it would then be quite light.

After supper the guests stood about in front of the radio in the lobby, but Nina Petrovna went upstairs firmly resolved to move into an empty room. She found one that was not locked and went in. Here, too, stood three iron bedsteads, but there were not even mattresses on them. She stepped lightly to the room Katya had shown her and picked up the coat she had left on the unoccupied bed, together with blanket, sheets, and pillow; these she took to the new room and flung onto the bedstead next to the window and went back for the mattress. Hardly had she made up the bed when steps sounded in the corridor, and Katya's resonant voice filled the silence: "Petrov-na!" When she found out what Nina Petrovna had done, she put down the suitcase and whispered, "Does the director know?" "No," said Nina Petrovna. "You tell him, Katya, and see what he says." Katya was gone and back again in a few minutes. "The director says, 'All right, all right, I'll speak to Matron in the morning.'"

Nina Petrovna began unpacking her suitcase, arranging her clothes on the shelves and hangers inside the capacious closet. There would soon be claimants to some of this space, and she was determined to enjoy possession while she could. On the night table she laid out everything for what she was sure would be a sleepless night—her watch, her volume of *The Forsyte Saga*, the tube of Nembutal, the vial of digitalis drops. It was too early for her usual bedtime—the hands of her watch stood at a quarter past ten—but she was tired. The brief but intense foray she had carried out so successfully had left her pleasantly excited but at the same time exhausted, and she went straight to bed. After reading for about half an hour she switched off the light and lay down, closing her eyes. She awoke two hours later with a sense of obscure uneasiness, and it was not till she turned the light on that she remembered with a short laugh she was not in her own room at home. The degree of darkness showed her that it was still night, that this was going to be one of her bad nights—two hours of wakefulness after three or four hours of sleep, then a short doze before dawn, and waking up as if she had not slept at all. At home she would wait after a night like this till the door had opened and shut four times—after her son, her daughter-in-law, her granddaughter, and (very loud) her grandson left for work and school; then she could turn over on her side and enjoy two hours of sound, sweet sleep; the telephone and the front doorbell might ring their heads off—nothing would disturb her till she woke up with a guilty feeling of having slept while the world around was alive and working. But here in the Holiday Home the dining room would be closed at ten, and she would have to be up and dressed in time for breakfast. "And a good thing too," she told herself. "Why should I sleep the best

part of the day and miss the morning sunshine in the country?"
But the feeling of anxiety with which she had awakened returned
with still greater force.

Nina Petrovna tried to remember what was worrying her. It
was connected with home, of course, but what was it, what was
the matter? The children? Oh yes, the children. A day or two
before her departure Irochka had had a positive reaction to the
Pirquet test, and had been sent for an X-ray. The result ought to
have been ready the next day, but Sonya had not had time to go
for it, though she knew how anxious her mother-in-law was. She
told herself over and over again that it was no good worrying,
that she could send a telegram after breakfast and get an answer
by evening; she repeated, smiling, the proverb in the English
textbook: "Never trouble trouble till trouble troubles you." The
X-ray was sure to be all right, but even in this consolation there
was a drop of poison—who cared about her worrying? There
was no one to think of what *she* went through. If there was
anything wrong she might think they were trying to shield her,
but they wouldn't hurry to let her know if it was all right. The
wound to vanity was deeper than the anxiety about her grandchild's health. At last fatigue overcame worry and Nina Petrovna
slept and only just waked up in time to dress for breakfast; the
fear of missing it demanded priority over spiritual suffering.

After breakfast Nina Petrovna sat outside and gave herself up
to the calm observation of her fellow-guests, quite forgetting that
she had meant to send a telegram. Two women ran out of two
separate doors and met on the terrace. "Where have you been?"
cried one. "Why didn't you wait for me? I was beginning to get
quite nervous." The word "nervous" stung Nina Petrovna, and
she jumped up and ran into the house. In the office she was
told that telegrams were sent out when the postman brought
the day's mail, and she sat down at a table to write her mes-

sage. But when she discovered that she would get an answer in twenty-four hours at the best, she gave up the idea and bought a colored picture postcard of a Holiday Home in Odessa, on the blank space of which she jotted down in her rapid but distinct handwriting: (1) that she had arrived safely; (2) that she had managed at least for the first days to secure a room to herself; and (3) that everything would be fine if she weren't worrying about Irochka's X-ray, which prevented her from resting properly. She knew it would be at least three days before she could get an answer, four perhaps, and then only if they wrote the moment her postcard arrived, which was unlikely. People come home from work tired and hungry, perhaps they don't even have an envelope. It might be nearly a week before a letter arrived, and she had almost persuaded herself that it would be a consoling one—the writing of the postcard had done her good. She would go for a walk in the woods.

The house filled up gradually and nobody had yet been put in Nina Petrovna's room. She looked eagerly at every female new-comer, hoping each time it wouldn't be this one that would share —no, shatter—her privacy. Not this one with the empty glance, or that other with the fussy expression and flabby purplish cheeks. Not that disagreeable-looking old thing in a shawl. None took her fancy, least of all the girlish old things, well over fifty, who dyed their hair and hitched transparent stockings over pitifully veiny shins, and never stopped chattering and giggling. There were of course some who had not been prematurely overtaken by age, and at the same time did nothing to stave off its approach; these stuck to the simple clothes and hairdos they had always preferred, and their eyes showed that most of their lives had been spent in mental activities. Nina Petrovna, who had begun as a proofreader in a publishing firm, belonged to this, the smallest, group. But looking around she thought, Just the same, we're all old. Later

on, younger guests made their appearance and monopolized several tables in the dining room. A pale man who looked under
forty and his young and dressy wife attracted general attention—
he so grim in the face, she so lively and provocatively dressed and
made-up; she changed her clothes so often that there was always
somebody heard to say, "I should like to know how many suit-
cases she brought." The youngest guests were a newlywed couple,
never seen apart from one another and so closely linked that
from a short distance they looked like a single person with two
heads, and these heads were always turned toward one another,
so that it was a wonder they never stumbled; at table they hardly
spoke, ate everything placed before them, and, when there was
nothing left on their plates, started up and hastened to the door
in single file till they got to a place wide enough for them to link
up again and continue some never-finished conversation.

Nina Petrovna always looked eagerly into the pigeonholes in
the hall where the mail was put, but every day that brought no
letter seemed to bring nearer the moment when an envelope
addressed to herself would suddenly appear under the letter O
in the cubicled board hung up beside the dining room. But when
five days passed with no letter for her, anxiety and hurt feelings
took possession of her mind. And when a whole week and then
an eighth day passed and still no letter, Nina Petrovna went
about like one possessed. She set foot on the floor of the lobby
on the ninth day with a firm resolve—if there was nothing for
her today she would go straight to the post office after breakfast
and send a telegram. But as if in answer to her despair, this time
there was a telegram under the letter O. She seized the little
packet and forced herself not to tear it as she peeled off the scrap
of Scotch tape that nipped the edges together, spread it open, and
read: "Dear one, darling, everything all right, written you twice,

kisses from all, Sonya." Nina Petrovna took her place in the dining room and sat down to read the telegram once more. There was a fourth person at the table now—a brisk woman of about sixty, with small features and sparkling eyes. Nina Petrovna had already confided her worries about not getting any news to this neighbor, and she showed her the telegram and said, "I shouldn't have worried, you see." But Julia Andreyevna only glanced at the telegram and said, "It's not for you. It's for that woman over there," and she pointed to an old lady with a strong likeness to a tortoise, seated two tables behind them.

Nina Petrovna examined the telegram again—it was signed not Sonya, as she had taken for granted, but Tanya. Besides, when had Sonya ever addressed her as "Dear one, darling"? It was not the style of the house. Thin cymbals clashed in the top of Nina Petrovna's skull, but she managed to get up and take the telegram to its rightful recipient. "So far I've been the only O in the alphabet," she explained, with apologetic smiles. But in her heart she called herself an old fool.

And in the evening there really was a letter from home: Sonya wrote that everything was all right, the X-ray had shown nothing wrong, and the next Pirquet test had been negative; that they had been glad to have her postcard and only put off writing till they had good news for her, and everybody hoped she was having a good rest. And by the way, Vanya was trying to get her stay at the Holiday Home extended, so that she could be another month out of the dust and stuffiness of Moscow. Nina Petrovna was intensely relieved to hear that Irochka was not in danger, but her spirits did not rise as they ought to have; after the false reassurance of the telegram she had somehow not worried about Irochka any more.

Nina Petrovna had enjoyed the privacy of a room to herself for a whole fortnight, but she knew another contingent was expected any day, and wondered with trepidation what sort of a woman her roommate would be. There had been a moment of hope when she discovered at the very end of the corridor a tiny room—the merest closet with, however, a bed, a chair, and a small table in it; there was no wardrobe, only a few hooks on the door, and nowhere to wash—whoever lived there would have to go to the bathroom for that—but daylight streamed through a fair-sized window and Nina Petrovna cursed herself for her lack of enterprise. Why had she not looked about her instead of blundering into the first empty room? How happy she could have been in this bright closet all by herself! The bed was already made up and the mandatory carafe of water and glass stood invitingly on the table. Even now perhaps it was not too late to make a bid for the tiny room. Might there not be some woman who would prefer the conveniences in the other rooms to solitude without any conveniences whatever? Another visit to the director destroyed Nina's dream—the tiny room was being kept for a woman from Leningrad, a writer who needed a room to herself more than Nina Petrovna did, because she brought a typewriter with her. All the director could promise Nina Petrovna was to leave her room to the last; he would try to put only one woman in beside her, and would himself choose a nice quiet person. A few days after this conversation Nina Petrovna went up to her room to wash her hands before dinner, and was met in the doorway by a strong whiff of cosmetics, a kind of potpourri of face powder, scented soap, cheap perfume, and the overpowering smell of pears—nail polish, of course. She closed the door gently and sat on the side of her bed for a moment. Looking around, she saw on the table beside the third bed the upright back of a heart-shaped mirror, and knew that she no longer had a room to herself. In the dining room she tried to guess which of the newest arrivals was her roommate, but they were spread in units and couples all over the room and she gave up. After dinner she hurried back to the third floor, hoping for time to be lying down for the afternoon nap before the stranger came in. The room was empty; but a maroon-colored dressing gown hanging over the footrail of the bed at the other side of the room, and a pair of gaping felt slippers on the floor, showed that the enemy had already entrenched herself in the citadel. Nina Petrovna was sure she wouldn't be able to sleep, but she had hardly got halfway through the first chapter of *The Dark Flower* when her eyes closed. She opened them to find that she had slept for over an hour, and the sound of regular breathing told her that she was no longer alone. The mound of a body under the counterpane on the third bed, and a fluff of golden hair on the pillow (the face was hidden by the mirror on the table), helped Nina Petrovna to form an image of the sleeper. Vulgar, stout, she had to be—the drugstore smells, the mound under the counterpane pointed to that. Young she could hardly be—would a young woman come by herself to a dull, all but suburban Holiday Home and possess so frumpy and dingy a dressing gown, such squalid slippers? The sleeper moved restlessly, sat up in bed, and turned toward Nina Petrovna a short nose with capacious nostrils, densely black eyelashes, brows impeccably arched over good hazel eyes. The eyes opened wide, encompassing Nina Petrovna with a glance of almost tender kindliness. "Olga Vassilevna Smirnova," said the stranger. "We're roommates, so let's make friends." Nina Petrovna introduced herself.

The new acquaintance prattled incessantly, and Nina Petrovna had to look into her face to answer questions so good-humoredly phrased that it would have been impossible to ignore them without being ungracious. Olga Vassilevna, talking all the time and not in the least embarrassed by the presence of another person in

the room, pushed herself off the mattress and peeled a pink nylon nightdress over her head. Then, groaning heavily, she sat up
and began to stuff her feet into the disgraceful slippers. Nina
Petrovna realized what had made these lose their shape when she
saw the swollen, hammer-toed, and bunioned feet they scarcely
contained. She turned her face to the wall while the process of
washing and dressing went on, accompanied by short grunts and
sighs. When Nina Petrovna heard her roommate hobble to the
door and close it behind her, she got up herself and was ready to
go down for the tea break in a few minutes. She found Olga
Vassilevna waiting for her at the head of the stairs. Now fully
dressed she didn't look quite so fat, and Nina Petrovna connected
the grunts and sighs she had heard with the fastening up of bra
and girdle. The spreading stomach had been strapped into the
shape of a football under a tightly stretched skirt, and the floppy
breasts were lifted in firm outline beneath nylon ruffles in the
V of her jacket; the terrible feet were squeezed into high-heeled
shoes. In fact, the corpulent figure was quite trim. "We must
be friends," Olga Vassilevna said, tripping down the stairs
beside Nina Petrovna, and she added with an intimate chuckle,
"For a month at least." As if pleased with the definition, she
repeated it: "Yes. Friends for a month." Something in Nina
Petrovna's expression made her add, "Of course I mean the sort
of friendship that is only shown in mutual forbearance. Civilized
people ought to be able to share a room without interfering with
one another—as if each of us was alone." Nina Petrovna agreed
eagerly with sentiments that suited her so well, but Olga Vassilevna had something more to say that showed their ideas of
noninterference were very different. "And we need never be
bored," she said. "I brought a nice little transistor with me; we
can have as much music as we like." They had reached the lobby
and Nina Petrovna stopped on the mat at the foot of the stairs.

"What?" she cried. "In the bedroom? That's not allowed, you
know." "And who's going to raise any objections? Everybody
likes music, I think." "I am," Nina Petrovna said firmly. "Besides, next door to us—well, not exactly next door, but quite near
—there'll soon be a writer. She's sure to object." "A writer! A
woman writer! This is a Holiday Home. Let her go to a Writers'
Rest Home—you know, for creative writers—if she wants to bang
away at her typewriter. But if *you* object I won't so much as take
the transistor out of my bag. Unless of course you should want to
hear some music once in a while. I said 'mutual forbearance' and
mutual forbearance is what I mean to practice. Only I can't quite
see why it's wrong for me to do something you don't like, and
right for you to deprive me of something I like." But she
laughed cheerfully and they passed into the dining room like
old friends.

The next day the woman writer made her appearance in the
dining room—a massively built elderly woman with short iron-
gray hair, very blue eyes, and a wrinkled, weather-beaten face.
At table and on garden benches she was talked about freely, not
merely because she was the latest arrival, but because there were
people on the staff of the Holiday Home, and even a few guests,
who knew quite a lot about her. Her name was Ludmilla
Ivanovna Polenova; common Russian names, but a grave elderly
man who used the Russian language in a manner Nina Petrovna
recognized as exquisite, and—more surprisingly—an elegant
young married couple, never pronounced these names without a
kind of fervent respect. Amid the usual Holiday Home chatter
of blood pressure and the menu and the girl who changed her
clothes three times a day, a guest could be heard telling her
neighbor that the writer was a poet, none of whose verses had
been published during the last twenty years; that she had been

"sitting" (that is to say, in a camp) under the Stalin regime; and that certain influential members of the Writers' Union had managed to secure a tiny pension for her, and even hoped someday to get a discreet selection of her early poems published. Olga Vassilevna took a great interest in all this, partly because she took a great interest in practically everyone, and partly because she remembered having seen some of Polenova's poems in typescript on her son-in-law's desk, and even hearing them read aloud to an admiring circle of young people. She couldn't remember anything about them because she had been chiefly occupied in concocting a supper in the kitchen. This reminded Nina Petrovna that her daughter-in-law spent evening after evening typing out poetry after a hard day at the office. Nina Petrovna had tried to read a page or two, but it was evidently part of a long poem, and the lines didn't rhyme, and anyhow it was a long time since she had read any long poem, except for occasionally dipping into *Evgeni Onegin* and trying to get her grandchildren to listen to some of the easier passages. Olga Vassilevna broke into her reverie by wondering aloud why Polenova should make such a sight of herself—cotton stockings, sneakers, and that straight curtain of gray hair! Surely she could have afforded to get a perm before coming to a Holiday Home—everybody tried to be as smart as she could in public. It wasn't as if she were plain—she had good features, clear expressive eyes. "I always say," said Olga Vassilevna, and said it again, "I always say a woman ought to make the most of herself at all ages. You too, Nina Petrovna, you have lovely hair. Why shouldn't you—not dye it of course, it's hardly gray at all till you look close—but just have it tinted to bring out the natural shade. It would take ten years off your age if you were to have it nicely waved and buy yourself a lipstick. You don't even need to buy a lipstick—I've

got an extra one I've only used a couple of times that would just
suit your complexion, and really, Nina Petrovna, many a young
woman would envy you your complexion and your figure."

After all, living in the same room with a stranger of quite another level of culture had turned out not to be so bad as Nina
Petrovna had feared. The liveliness and imperturbable good
humor of Olga Vassilevna, and her complete freedom from affectation, acted like a tranquilizer on the suppressed but perpetual
irritability of Nina Petrovna's nerves. Besides, she had soon dis-
cerned, behind the unpromising vulgarity of her roommate's
façade, a limitless expanse of natural tact that was better than any
mere correctness. "You can't upset me," she told Nina Petrovna,
who had been afraid her bedside lamp would keep Olga Vassilevna awake in the night (Nina Petrovna could never sleep
without reading for at least an hour in bed). "Read all night if
you want to; I'll just turn my back to you and shut my eyes.
There's nobody I couldn't live with. I've lived for fifteen years
in the same room with my daughter and then with her and her
daughter both, and I may say we've never had so much as an
argument. We both know very well that people can't live so close
without getting on each other's nerves sometimes, and we made
a resolve simply never to speak when that happens." "But isn't
it hard to suppress your feelings all the time?" "It may be, but
anything's better than coming out with something you might
regret for the rest of your life." And thus two weeks passed in
Olga Vassilevna's "month of friendship." The roommates strolled
in the woods or visited the village shop, and the couple that looked
so ill-matched, like two birds of different species—a modest
brown-coated thrush and a pompous iridescent-breasted pouter
pigeon—seemed inseparable. Olga Vassilevna could somehow
talk about herself without being a bore, and Nina Petrovna

was never tired of listening to the long tale of another's life. After a while she found herself confiding sorrows to a sympathetic ear—a thing she couldn't remember ever having done before.

One day when they were resting after their morning's walk, on one of the green benches in the garden of the hostel, contentedly observing the return to the house of other walkers in twos, alone, and in small groups, Olga Vassilevna returned to what they had been talking about in the woods. A letter from home seemed to have disturbed her calm. "If I had a room of my own I'd never come to a hostel," she said bitterly. The mask of good humor slipped for a moment and Nina Petrovna caught a glimpse of the grim reality beneath it. Olga Vassilevna sighed, one of those long trembling sighs that seem to come straight from a person's heart. Then the mask settled back into place and she went on in her usual coaxing accents: "We've been lucky. Only the two of us, and we're both what you might call nice people. Sometimes you have to be stable and such disagreeable women, and try as you will to be pleasant, there's no softening them. Last year I was in with two like that, simply competing to make life unpleasant. One of them was always running to the director to complain of me—I got up early and used all the hot water, or I washed my stockings in the basin. And they each had a transistor and believe me they each tuned in to different stations at the same time—they hated each other even more than they hated me." "You could have complained about that," Nina Petrovna told her. "It's not allowed in the bedrooms." "I never complain," said Olga Vassilevna shortly. "I'm sure *you* wouldn't go running to the director if I turned mine on." "I wouldn't have to," Nina Petrovna said softly. "It was quite enough for me to tell you I didn't like it." "Ah, if everybody was like us there wouldn't be any wars," said Olga Vassilevna. "Are you sure?" Nina Petrovna asked her.

In the flood of details she was bursting to communicate, Olga Vassilevna had forgotten what it was she really wanted to tell her friend, but Nina Petrovna could see by the slightly confused and anxious expression of her face that she had not yet shaken off certain unpleasant thoughts. When Olga Vassilevna again broke the silence, her words didn't seem to have any direct connection with what had gone before. What she said was, "It'll be a relief for them when I'm gone." "You only think like that because you have to live in such unbearable proximity to one another," Nina Petrovna said. "Not only. You can't help feeling how much easier their lives will be when you're dead. One less person to have to consider." "That's natural. Everyone lives in the present. And our children have plenty of worries. Of course when we die there'll be one less." Nina Petrovna knew how it rankled with her daughter-in-law that Irochka, just entering the critical years of adolescence, had to sleep with her almost grown-up brother. She disliked it is much as Sonya could, but the question of having Irochka moved into her grandmother's room was never mentioned by either, though continually thought about by both. And the answer was that it would be altogether intolerable, not only for Nina Petrovna but for Irochka too. Irochka would have a room to herself when her grandmother was dead, a room where she could have friends in the evening, do what she liked . . .

They fell silent and took to watching the thickening procession of holiday-makers. Dinner would be ready in a quarter of an hour and most of the guests showed on their faces pleasant expectation of what was a welcome event in the long empty day.

"That's who I envy!" murmured Olga Vassilevna at the appearance in the gateway of two female figures—one tall and slender, the other dumpy. They were never seen apart and everyone knew—because the dumpy one told everyone at the first opportunity—that they had been living together nearly twenty years, that they were both teachers, though the short one was now on pension and could devote all her time and energy to one sole purpose: that of making life as smooth as possible for her friend. As they approached, a steely ray of light was reflected from objects dangling from the hands of the devoted one; these were soon perceived to be milk bottles full of clear water, which anyone who cared to listen was told triumphantly had been drawn from a distant well. "Isn't the water in the house good enough?" someone asked. At this the taller lady—who at first hung back a little, as if taking no interest in the question—moved smoothly ahead and entered the house in advance of her companion, who went on explaining that she would go every day for two bottles of water from this special well till she had accumulated enough to wash her friend's hair, which the tap water in the bedrooms did not suit. And off she scuttled on her short legs.

"Them?" Nina Petrovna asked.

"They have something to live for. They need one another, and age doesn't matter to them." "I don't think I envy them," Nina Petrovna said, but she sighed.

The newlyweds emerged from the wood, he a few steps ahead, both hands deep in his trouser pockets, she hurrying after and managing with a deft movement to slip her fingers round his arm, inside the elbow. The young man did not take his hand out of his pocket and stepped on doggedly as if he were alone.

"How soon!" said Olga Vassilevna softly. "They're bored, poor children," Nina Petrovna said. "He is, you mean," Olga Vassilevna corrected. Nina Petrovna thought they should have gone to the seaside. There was nothing for them to do here." "Except—" said Olga Vassilevna, smiling mischievously. Nina Petrovna frowned. Nobody ventured on a vulgar innuendo in her presence at the office, where she had gone straight from school, and by the time she had become the most respected member of the staff everyone respected her austerity: ribald laughter was checked at her appearance, anecdotes hung in the air unfinished, and now, though she did at first frown, she caught herself sharing a bawdy insinuation with a vulgarian. But just then another figure isolated itself from the crowd—a powerfully built woman, leaning on a stick but not bent: Ludmilla Ivanovna Polenova, the poet, whose typewriter was heard rattling almost every time the guests went out of their rooms into the corridor. In her other hand she held a little way in front of her a wild iris with three sheathed buds just beginning to part from the stem. She passed close by Nina Petrovna and Olga Vassilevna, smiled a gracious, absent-minded smile at them, and seemed to extend the flower for their admiration. "*That's* who I envy," Nina Petrovna murmured as Ludmilla Ivanovna disappeared behind a column. Olga Vassilevna was sincerely astonished. "Her? You're a hundred times better looking. You could be her daughter. If only you'd listen to me—" "She's always busy," said Nina Petrovna impatiently. "They say she's working on a sonnet cycle. She says the day isnt long enough for her." "Why doesn't she go to a Writers' Hostel?" Olga Vassilevna grumbled. "That's the place for her." "She goes to one for a month every year. But she says she doesn't like to live long among writers. She says they talk too much." "It's simply too expensive for her," Olga Vassilevna said sourly. "They give her a month free, and then she comes here." "Is it cheaper here?" "The director keeps that little closet for her gratis. They were in Leningrad during the blockade—I believe she was very kind to him. Anyhow, he seems to think the world of her." "Lots of people do, I think." "Yes, but not the right ones, or she'd be able to get her poetry published." "I'm glad I shall be able to tell my children I've seen her," Nina Petrovna said, and checked the bitter reflection that in her place

Vanya and Sonya would have done more than just *see* their poet. "I've already told mine," said Olga Vassilevna. "I wrote to them yesterday."

In two days Nina Petrovna would be leaving the Holiday Home. Olga Vassilevna was in a pitiable state. What would she do without Nina Petrovna? Worse, what sort of new roommate could she expect—nobody else would be so easy to live with as Nina Petrovna. "I think you could make anyone easy to live with," said Nina Petrovna. "Oh, don't say so! One doesn't meet tactful, pleasant people every day. I don't believe I've ever met a woman I could tell the things I've told you." "I'm sure you've told them to at least a dozen other people." "I've told you things about myself I've never told anyone else, and never expected to be able to. Most women are so narrow-minded." Nina Petrovna knew this was true—strange confidences had been exchanged. "Anyhow, you'll soon be leaving, yourself," she said. "The last fortnight passes very quickly." Olga Vassilevna burst into tears. "They've sent me an extension," she sobbed. "Always writing and saying how they miss me, and now it's worth any money and trouble to keep me away another month." Not for anything in the world could Nina Petrovna have gone over and put her arms round the weeping woman. Tears chilled her and she had to admit a mean resentment that she had been for so long cooped up with a person so far from her real interests, one with whom she could not discuss Galsworthy and Iris Murdoch, not to mention such writers as Solzhenitsyn and Paustovsky, for Olga Vassilevna never read anything but the illustrated magazines supplied to the guests of the Holiday Home. Perhaps if Nina Petrovna had not always been seen in her company she might have got to know Polenova and become one of the small circle privileged to hear her poetry read aloud once a week. But that was nonsense, of course—what was there in her to attract the attention of a poet? "My son got my time extended too, you know," she said kindly. "It's only natural. Everybody wants as much freedom as they can get. It's you who taught me to understand that."

The very next day, returning to the room after their morning walk, the friends simultaneously caught sight of traces of a stranger: on the middle bed lay a bulging net bag, beside it on the floor a battered suitcase and a pair of worn shoes. "A new person in the room!" cried Olga Vassilevna. "We're like Robinson Crusoe seeing Man Friday's footprint in the sand," said Nina Petrovna, but got no response. "I shan't have a single night to myself after you've gone." "Perhaps it'll be somebody nice," said Nina Petrovna consolingly. "Somebody very shabby, whatever else she is," said Olga Vassilevna with distaste. "Well, I'm dowdy enough, but you managed to get over it." "As if there could ever be anyone like you again," said Olga Vassilevna lugubriously, but added more cheerfully, "It's a good thing in a way—I shan't be able to cry in the night with a stranger in the room."

The newcomer made her appearance in the bedroom only after supper. She was youngish, almost girlish, pale-eyed, with a thin neck and a stringy tail of hair tied at the back of her head. All introduced themselves to one another as cheerfully as they could manage. The third inhabitant of the room named herself dejectedly as Elizavetta Matveyevna. "That's much too long," said Olga Vassilevna, "I shall call you Liza. You're young enough to be my daughter, anyhow." The girl smiled dolefully and Nina Petrovna reminded herself with satisfaction that for all their intimacy Olga Vassilevna had never ventured to call her Nina. After they were in bed, and Nina Petrovna had closed her book and switched off her light, a suppressed sob came from the middle bed. Olga Vassilevna was out of her own bed in a minute and bending over the newcomer. "Don't cry," she said. "We know how you feel, all alone with two old women. It's a shame. But don't cry. Tomorrow I'll show you where there's a tennis court, and you can make friends with people your own age. Do you play tennis?" The girl was making obvious efforts, wiping her eyes and giggling nervously, to overcome her tears. She did play tennis, but very badly, nobody would want to play with her, and she hadn't brought a racket. Olga Vassilevna assured her that rackets were to be obtained, and they'd be delighted to play with her—not many played tennis at all, partners were in great demand. "What about a little music?" Nina Petrovna said bravely. "Why not get out that transistor of yours, Olga Vassilevna?" A magic spell of kindness and jazz spread itself in the room, and Nina Petrovna actually fell asleep to the yearning strains of the blues.

The next morning she asked Olga Vassilevna if they had played long. "Till the people next door rapped on the wall," said Olga Vassilevna demurely. "But I went and asked them if they wouldn't like to come and listen, and they did, so we played Liza to sleep too." "You are a marvelous woman," said Nina Petrovna with conviction. "Liza, you're going to have a lovely holiday."

Farewell to the Dacha

TIRED OF SIEVING carrots and washing diapers, Masha bolted to Moscow with little Anton at the end of an August that looked like the end of summer. She admitted that carrots would have to be sieved and diapers washed in Moscow, too, with pram pushing added, but dreams of conviviality, of the telephone, of hot and cold water overruled all other considerations; as for fresh air for Anton, what was the good of fresh air when it rained all day? Vadim, Masha's student husband (their joint ages, including Anton, barely came to forty years), was only too cooperative; he was thankful to give up commuting. And Katenka had gone with them to be in good time for the beginning of school. But I, still believing in the forecast for September—"mild and sunny"—only went back to Moscow for a few days to pick up some warm clothes, just in case hopes turned out to be dupes.

I had gone to the dacha in May, firmly resolved to finish revising my *Twenty-nine Literary Females,* but propinquity of the most charming order had been the thief of my time. I was perpetually torn by the need for solitude and the need for stimulus, which are not to be had in the close neighborhood of one's own

family. Masha herself had come to Stepanovka determined never
to encroach upon my morning hours, but she passed my gate
every morning on her way for the milk, and how could I resist
running out to have a look at Antoshka and wheel him up the
path to the house? By the time she was back with the milk, the
kettle would be boiling, and it was I, in an access of grand-
motherly despotism that my family has not been trained to with-
stand, who insisted that Masha sit down to table, with Antoshka
beside her, lengthwise, on the seat of the old rocker.

Indeed, nothing could have been more sweet and natural; the
souls that do not mingle over new-laid eggs, tomatoes and lettuce
from the garden, homemade strawberry jam, and an all-too-
delicious baton of fresh white bread never will mingle. And after
breakfast Masha might as well pick up Antoshka and sit in the
rocker herself to feed him while I washed the dishes. The dishes
had to be washed, didn't they? (We both knew that I would have
left them indefinitely if I had been alone.) And so it would often
be twelve o'clock before I got out the blue file and took the lid
off my toilworn Hermes, only to discover that virtue had gone
out of me, only to push aside the tools of production and make
room for the box of Anagrams.

After a week in Moscow with nothing whatever to show for it
but blissful hours in the Lenin Library, browsing—or perhaps
I ought to say *wallowing*—in the pages of a vintage *Dictionary
of National Biography*, checking on Mrs. Vesey and Mrs. Trim-
mer, I threw some books and the oddest jumble of English newspapers and American magazines you can imagine (the criterion
being, have I read them long enough ago to have forgotten
them?) into a suitcase, some warm socks and a thick sweater on
top, and left for the dacha in an icy shower. My friend Em came
with me, and all through the nirvana of the hour's journey *she*
tried to finish her volume of Pepys so as to leave it with me, and

I tried to fill in the blanks somebody had left in the London *Times* crossword. I have a curious sense of communication with this man I have never met; he wonderfully knows that 6 Down, *Numerical start to a Horatian ode* (7), is *Integer*, and that 13 Across, *The lizard with the knockout finish* (5), is *Gecko*, but doesn't know that 22 Across, *The girl for James* (5), is obviously *Joyce*, and therefore fails to solve 22 Down, *A painter returns to his ship* (5), which can only be *Jason* (though why, I don't know)! Nor has he guessed that what *Saul does and David didn't* (6) is *Bellow*. We almost passed Stepanovka in our absorption, and were the last passengers to scramble out of the train onto the long platform.

The sidewalks were soggy, and we trudged down the middle of Kommunisticheski Prospekt, but when we turned into Push-kinski our shoes were almost sucked off in the deep sticky ruts. I never complain of this, because it is what keeps the road quiet.

Long before we arrived, we could hear Tyapa's shrill fierce barks. He was barking, we knew, not because he recognized our footsteps but because barking at passers-by is at once a duty and a distraction in his monotonous life. When we got near enough for him to know our voices, he was thrown into momentary confusion, not being able to switch from ferocity to joyous welcome quickly enough. The situation was further complicated by the sudden apparition of a man with a sack over his shoulder, and Tyapa, though wild with joy at our approach, felt a compulsion to rout the stranger before padding up the pathway to stand at our feet, heavy head close to the ground, veering from me to Em, tail swinging slowly in time to the enormous feelings swelling inside him. When we opened the house door, he slipped in first and stood in the middle of the room, again with that hanging head and tail, looking with obvious anxiety from me to the bed and back again. He could not have told us more clearly that he had been sleeping on my bed. At our shocked exclamations, as if they were a signal anxiously awaited, he slunk to his pad under the kneehole desk, the place he has chosen for himself as the most private and secret in the room, and curled up, one eye fixed on our movements, the tip of his tail twitching.

An incriminating layer of black hairs, sand, and pellets of damp soil showed that Tyapa had crept under the quilt and nuzzled between the sheets while I was away. "Why did they let her into the room?" Em wanted to know. (Em always calls Tyapa "her.") "She could easily have slept on the porch."

"He howled so excruciatingly they couldn't stand it. Nobody dreamed he would dare to get on my bed."

"*In*," corrected Em, and began energetically stripping the mattress and putting on clean sheets.

Tyapa stayed under the desk till he saw us sit down to tea, and then crawled out to press his side against my shin. Over his meek head we discussed the ethics of treating to delicacies from our own plates a dog so lost to decency as to have got into his mistress's bed. "Look how sad his eyes are," I said. "You can see he's sorry. He's begging us to forgive him."

"She's begging for a piece of cheese, I think," said Em, but pleasantly, not wishing to hurt Tyapa's feelings too much. "And you know what—I think she was only trying to get near you. She felt too desperately abandoned."

The thought was an amnesty in itself, and I fed Tyapa scraps of cheese and ham with a good conscience; when I was in Moscow my landlady locked him out, with his pannikin of oatmeal, before rushing off to catch the morning train, and refilled the pannikin from her own supper table in the evening. Two meals a day is supposed to be all right for dogs, but Em and I feel that life under such conditions must be a desert. "Poor doggy," I said.

"All alone these cold, wet days, waiting, waiting for somebody to come back and play with him."

"But every now and then a man with a handcart or an old woman coming back from the market to bark at," said Em. "And I bet she got under the fence sometimes to meet other dogs or chase a cat. She probably only waddled back in the evening to see if anyone had come."

Em looks at the bed complacently—so smooth, the snowy sheet turned back over the almond-green eiderdown that she had brought with her from America how many, many years ago. She picks up the old-fashioned traveling clock that has kept perfect time in so many latitudes, and winds it. Winding a clock and making a bed are among the many chores I most hate, and now Em is washing up on the porch with an unnecessary expenditure of care and precious minutes that could be so much more profitably employed playing Lexicon. Just a cigarette on the porch, and she will indulge me with a game of Riddance and then one of Twister before she is off. Or would it not be more rational for her to sit and finish the last chapter of Pepys? It would, of course, but I vote for Riddance, for Twister.

After Tyapa and I have seen Em off at the gate, we turn back to the house. Tyapa has that "You're here and I'm here, so what do *we* care?" expression in his eyes, and I no doubt look the way an old woman looks who only wants to take a pill and get into bed with a hot-water bag.

The bottle of kefir, the pottery bowl to eat it from, the favorite spoon (Mother Bear size) have been ready overnight on the kitchen table. No dishes shall be washed, no bed made, no armor buckled, and Tyapa must make do with the remains of his last night's supper till I have sat down to the typewriter beside the blue file, the optimistically numbered sheets of paper, and accomplished my morning stint. I feel no shrinking from the task; it has become the sole justification for my existence, and I have become very fond of my twenty-nine females. My two favorites are Mrs. Thrale and Mrs. Inchbald—Mrs. Thrale because she had the courage to escape from the tentacles of Dr. Johnson after her husband died, and marry an Italian opera singer against the horrified protests of her family and friends, and still had energy left to write a book of English synonyms; and Mrs. Inchbald for writing *Lovers' Vows*, the play that kicked up such a brouhaha at Mansfield Park. I even love old Mrs. Delany—Swift called her his Constant Nymph—who made still lifes of paper flowers that were a great deal more like real ones than oil paintings were.

An hour or two later, an inner voice sounds a warning I know better than to ignore. "Stop," it says, "or else . . ." I stop in the middle of a sentence. The file may only be thicker by two miserable pages, but I close it. There is no Masha to go for the milk, and Tyapa and I step out of the garden together. All the summer guests but me have gone, and many dachas have their windows boarded up, a dismal sight. Those owners who live here all the year round are busy in their back gardens, stacking hay for a cow, fetching the storm windows from a shed, or pegging out a prodigious wash. The streets have been quieter than usual this summer, because the Writers' Rest Home was emptied of writers to make room for a group of writers' children from Tashkent, made homeless by a chain of earthquakes. No lean old men and stout elderly women met on the sidewalks to stop and exchange friendly reproaches: "Why don't you ever come to see us?" The rest-home bore had taken his leonine head to the Crimean coast, and the old gentleman with the patriarchal beard and curling locks—a historical old gentleman, once a secretary of Tolstoy's— had gone to a sanatorium on the Baltic Sea and no longer roamed the streets reproving females who prefer to wear slacks in the country. (What would Tolstoy himself have thought of us, I wonder.) The children have gone back to Tashkent, their homes rebuilt. I miss them. I used to enjoy watching them through the railings of the rest home, dancing the Twist to a stately rhythm, as if it were one of their own national dances.

The sun came out and stayed a few hours, to please the child and paint the rose. But all the children were in school and the few sodden roses left over from the summer were too far gone for painting to do them any good. Only the brave morning-glory wound its hearts and trumpets round posts and palings, or cascaded triumphantly from the tops of defeated currant bushes. I can't remember ever having seen *Convolvulus arvensis* so late.

The next day I heard our tribal call outside the gate and thought it was daughter Natasha, though she never comes so early. Tyapa, who had been lying on the step since breakfast, had heard it, too, and was barking joyfully, and seconds later I looked through the window into a faunlike face peering from a thicket of dark curls, a face I had dreamed of the night before. Katenka! "How come you got away from school so early?"

Katenka smiles knowingly, but offers no explanation. "I felt like coming to see you, so I came instead of Mama." Now she is in the room beside me, unhitching her rucksack. "She gave me a darling little cauliflower, and a pullet, and a bag of grapes, and a lovely bit of smelly cheese for you."

"Little Red Ridinghood!"

"Yes, and I met the wolf. Caesar was off his chain as I passed the Smirnovs'."

"Weren't you terrified?"

"*Niskolko*. I mean, not a bit. They're only *strashniye* in their own yards. He wagged his tail at me and tried to lick my hand. He has beautiful eyes."

I told Katenka I had dreamed about her, but not that she had been quite bald in my dream. The moment we see Katenka, we begin asking her when she's going to get her hair cut, and I didn't want to tease her when she had felt like coming to see me. Besides, I don't really want Katenka to get her hair cut—only to draw it away from her forehead and cheeks, only not to hide behind it.

Katenka, who had been reading a magazine article on telepathy, considered my having dreamed about her and her impulse to visit me proof of the theory. How else could they be accounted for?

Coincidence, I said unsympathetically, and translated the new word into Russian: *sovpadenye.*

"Why can you believe in coin . . . in *sovpadenye,* and not in telepathy?"

Katenka would like to hear me say I believed in *something,* but I am as anxious to avoid an argument on insufficient premises as she is to pursue it, and I throw myself (and Katenka) into preparations for dinner.

We dined in perfect amicability off the wings of the chicken, sautéed potatoes, and baked apples with a dab of sour cream, and then Katenka had to hurry back to cover her absence by showing up at the last lesson (having skipped the one before apparently didn't matter; it was only English anyhow). I opened my Bartlett and pointed out to her the line "Like angel visits, few and far between," which Katenka liked so much that she stopped to copy it out on a piece of paper. "I'll learn it from heart in the train."

I wouldn't spoil Katenka's pleasure by pointing out a grammar mistake, and only kept her for another moment, to ask her if Natasha expected to be down soon. To my unnecessary—at any rate, useless—question "Did you take a return ticket?" Katenka replies in full flight. But what I hear is only "Ye—!" which could be either "Yes" or "*Nyet.*" Ought I to teach them to say "Yep," to avoid confusion?

On Wednesday Em came down again to make the bed, to wind the clock, to put on the kettle and go for two pails of water while it was boiling. Then, as always on Em's visits, there was just time for the inestimable comfort of tea and toast in congenial company, for one game of Riddance and two of Twister before she had to rush for the train, leaving a new (a fairly new) T.L.S. for me, for Tyapa a quite new, meaty bone.

And on Friday evening, at the very moment when a violent shower had made it too dark to go on reading at the window and I was closing my volume of Pepys on the words "And so home, bringing with me night and foul weather," Tyapa gave one joyful, sawed-off bark, and Natasha's shaggy head appeared in the transom.

She came into the room, switched on the light, and put down her brief case all in one moment, like single notes played as a chord. "Did you think I was never coming?"

"No, no, I knew you would, and the disappointment at the end of one day was compensated by the hope at the beginning of the next."

"Cousin Percy," murmured Natasha, who knew how well the discipline imposed by unrequited love at the age of seven had served me.

I showed her the sentence from Pepys.

"I've brought you something else, as well as night and foul weather," and out of the brief case came *Middlemarch* and *Daniel Deronda*! "I wonder what Jane Austen would have made of Dorothea," said Natasha, unconsciously picking up *Middlemarch* and opening it.

I took it out of her hand and opened it at another place, without looking into the pages, and put it down; it was like starting out of a trance when I remembered her last words and answered them. "Oh, just a prig! She couldn't have handled a progressive woman."

"Still, we'd give the whole of George Eliot for *Mansfield Park* or *Persuasion*, wouldn't we?"

"All except *Adam Bede*."

"I thought you hated *Adam Bede*."

"I do, I do, I meant *The Mill on the Floss*."

Natasha groped in the bottom of the brief case. "I bet you don't get through any of these," she said, coming up with *The Award Avant-Garde Reader*, and she started from her seat to go out on the porch, where I could hear her emptying water into the kettle and clattering out into the night with the pails. The kettle is on the electric ring, I know, and it is time to spread the checked cloth and get the tea things out. The top of the desk is fully occupied by the typewriter and the work in progress, and I have to toss books and papers off the table onto the bed. Good honest smells of fresh bread and sliced ham enter the room, and for the first time since Natasha and I began opening and shutting books, Tyapa is stirred.

Natasha never allows a sense of urgency to spoil the pleasures of the tea table, and she brings out her little stock of family news as if it were not getting darker and later every minute. Anton, it appears, has developed a remarkable crawling technique, the in-laws have never seen anything like it; Vadim, having (a) been half promised a book on geophysics to translate and (b) resisted the temptation to buy a new pair of skis, is feeling both rich and virtuous; Katenka has cut her hair, and it looks bushier than ever. But every word spoken sends us rattling back to literature. Speaking of Antoshka reminds us of a baby who crawled so beautifully that her aunt was quite envious—none of *her* children had crawled like that—and all because, though Tolstoy doesn't say it in so many words, Anna Karenina had an English nurse! And is there not something a little too like Mr. Micawber in Vadim's easy optimism, something a little too much like the money Richard Carstone made by *not* taking a cab in the money Vadim had *not* spent on the new skis? Even Katenka's shorn locks remind us of Maggie Tulliver—but when has not Katenka reminded us of Maggie Tulliver?

I, too, have a budget full of talking, but it is all of people in books. (Natasha's husband says Natasha and I are forever gossiping about eighteenth-century governesses and nineteenth-century clergymen's daughters.) Natasha will like to hear, I know, that Miss Talbot was upset from a canoe into the Thames, near Twickenham, with Horace Walpole. Poor girl, it really seems to be the only thing that ever happened to her; she didn't even finish any of her books, and that officious Mrs. Elizabeth Carter "edited" them and got all the cash and most of the credit after Miss Talbot's death.

When it is time for Natasha to begin to think that they'll be beginning to be nervous at home, she gets up and looks round the small room, the ravaged supper table, the cluttered bed, the chaotic-looking (but not really chaotic) desk.

"Leave everything!" I urge. "As soon as you've gone, order will be restored by one touch of my magic wand."

"I'll just . . ." says Natasha, stooping down to collect a few odds and ends of string and paper. Before she quite goes, she casts a doubtful look at the top of my desk; somehow it reminds her of the last chapter of *Alice*. It looks to her as if all the papers will suddenly fly up into the air any minute.

"They wait till I'm asleep," I tell her, "and one page will be gone forever by tomorrow morning."

Like most people, I am always ready to put aside an old book in favor of a new one; Em has been surprised to see me lay down *Roxana* and fall upon a stray number of the *Reader's Digest,* which she had expected to see me throw down the chute on sight. But it was not mere frivolity that made me pass over *Middlemarch* and *Daniel Deronda,* put Pepys on the desk, and lay the *Avant-Garde Reader* on the bed table—I really do feel a curiosity about these new young writers; I am ashamed of my imperceptiveness in their regard. But Natasha had been right; I got stuck in almost every story. How the avant-garde seems to date to the old, how easily one succumbs to the well-known illusion of *déjà lu!* But one story ended with a sentence that touched and braced me at the same time: "Lord, you were irrefragably with me when I tried." I got out of my warm bed to look up "irrefragably" before going through the story carefully a second time, in case I had missed anything. But that seemed to be all.

My neighbors think I am lonely, but I never am. In fact, this thinly peopled solitude is just what suits me. Ah, but the nights! Aren't I nervous all alone in an empty house? ("I would die!" says one; another is sure she wouldn't be able to sleep a wink.) Of course I do prefer to have my landlady and her husband next door. When the rain has kept them in town for several nights, I do not sleep so well. Fear is always lying in wait for the solitary, ready at any moment to advance out of the shadows. How easily a bush becomes a bear! But nothing will ever be worse than waiting for the tiger escaped from the menagerie to reach the top step of the nursery stairs. Pepys once woke up at three o'clock and saw by the light of the moon "my pillow which I had flung from me overnight, standing upright at the foot of the bed." At first, not bethinking himself what it might be, he was "a little afeared, but sleep overcame all." Tyapa, who is supposed to be my protector, sometimes scares me out of my wits by creeping out from under the desk and passing on rattling claws to the door between my room and the unoccupied part of the house, sitting awhile snuffling at the crack with intermittent low growls, till he rattles back to his pad with a sigh of what sounds like disappointment. I know it was only a rat in the wainscoting, or a cat under the raised floor of the house, but what, ask my nerves, if it were that more dreadful animal, man?

Once, lying awake in the small hours, I heard the unmistakable sound of a footstep in the pathway. A footstep cannot be confused with any other sound. You know it at once for what it is; it has the weight of a body on it—almost, night seems to suggest, the weight of a soul. Tyapa barked so shrilly that it was no use trying to listen for the other foot to come down. I deliberated letting him out of the house to pursue the prowler, but while I was meditating on murder and sudden death, wondering if they might not be less painful in the long run, easier on all concerned, than the oxygen tent and intravenous tube, sleep overcame all, and the next morning I had forgotten about it till I went out of the house and found Tyapa sniffing round a beautifully clear impression of a boot in the soft mud of the path, which he soon gave up to follow an invisible trail over the high grass to the wicket gate. Whoever it was must have just slipped once from the grass onto the pathway—the time I heard his single footfall. Anyway, the good Tyapa had frightened him off.

Even in the daytime there are occasional nibbles of fear. A maple presses one pale leaf against the windowpane, like a face trying to see in, and whenever this happens I feel for a moment that I am being watched. And one day I went to the market, locking up the house conscientiously, only to find when I came back that I had left the low casement window wide open. Nothing seemed amiss, and yet surely I had not left my bedroom slippers one within the other on a stool in the porch, or the drawer of the desk half open! And hadn't the mohair scarf been hanging over the footrail of the bed when I went out? Even when the scarf turned out to be in the wardrobe and there seemed nothing missing from the drawer, the remembrance of those displaced slippers, the empty place on the rail where I was so used to being welcomed by the blue scarf, left me uneasy. Tyapa had seemed infected by my anxiety, sniffing here and sniffing there as if he smelled a stranger. Still, a little loneliness, an occasional scare, is better than wasting one's substance on trivialities. It *is* bracing to let oneself into an empty house, to know there will be nobody to talk to when one is inside. And the blue file grows and grows, despite the daily process of snipping and pruning. Perhaps because of it. Like a tree.

The sun itself wakes me on Saturday, filling me with a happiness that is benevolent as well as instinctive. I am happy for my landlady and her husband—or perhaps I am only happy that I won't have to feel sorry for them if their Sunday is spoiled by bad weather. I think this must be what it is, because all day I watch the sky with that sort of anxiety one knows very well concerns nobody else but oneself. And my relief when they arrive in sunshine is really almost absurd—I refuse to take any credit for it.

Here they come, with their raincoats over their arms and their heavy shopping bags. Tyapa rushes madly to meet them, barking frantically, pretending not to know them but quickly lapsing into ingratiating poses almost under their feet. I, on the contrary, go quickly into my room and shut the door. I wait a few minutes after I hear her movements through the thin wall, to give her a chance to call a greeting or, as she sometimes does, to unlock the door on her side and poke her head into the opening. Today she does neither—you never know with Larissa Andreyevna— and I don't want to seem eager to greet her, especially as I'm not a bit, really. Still, I can't resist calling out, "That you, Larissa Andreyevna?" as if merely checking on an unidentified noise.

They are a fine-looking couple, my landlady and her husband, youngish, by which I mean around fifty. She, blue-eyed, fair-haired, with a fresh complexion, good teeth, and fine limbs, not a touch of middle-aged thickness anywhere. A knack of dressing that stops just short of style. If only I could carry her image when she is out of sight. It makes me quite ashamed that I never recognize her if I meet her outside her own terrain. Even in the garden she can make a stranger of herself by simply binding a colored kerchief over her hair or getting into slacks. Her face is a palimpsest that seems only just to have been wiped off to receive fresh marks, the imperfect blank through which the faces of innumerable other women show. Not that I ever take her for anybody else; I just don't know her.

Her husband, on the other hand, is always himself, whether the discreet civil servant in dark clothes or the suburban proprietor in faded blue jeans—always urbane and mellow, always Sergei Mikhailovich. His large melancholy face and domed head might seem top-heavy on a less massive frame. His eyes are pouched like a mastiff's, but their glance is so compelling that it is some time before you notice the thick dark nose and sunken mouth. When addressed, he stops whatever he is doing and turns his whole countenance upon you with an air of indescribable benevolence, even a touch of gallantry if it is a woman—above all, of sympathy, whoever it is. He cocks one eyebrow at me over his hands, folded on the haft of his spade, and I feel at last I have been understood. Em's severe expression melts away beneath that glance; I have seen her look positively arch in response to it. Sergei Mikhailovich himself never speaks unless he is spoken to, and not always then. Is it a pail of kitchen stuff you are not sure where to empty? Sergei Mikhailovich will straighten himself at your approach, direct that ineffable glance at your face, and jerk a seignorial thumb over his shoulder in the direction of the compost. If there is a nail sticking out of the sole of my shoe, Sergei Mikhailovich will lay down trowel or hoe without a word and will bear the shoe to the tool shed, give three sharp taps with a hammer while I stand leaning against the trunk of a cherry tree on one foot, and return it with a gesture that is, upon my word, chivalrous. Has a fuse blown? Does a can need opening? I appeal to Sergei Mikhailovich, comfortably sure that the pleasure will be his. If the tables are turned and it is I who offer a neighborly service, Sergei Mikhailovich will not waste words on superfluous expressions of gratitude. Once, I popped my head out of the window to shout to him that I could hear something boiling very hard on their kero-gas, and he only bent his nobly shaped head toward me as he strode past my window. Sometimes he *has* to answer a direct question, and then the Russian language favors his taciturnity by providing one-word replies less brusque than a bare yes or no. To the inquiry "Has the postman been?" "Been" gives complete satisfaction; if you ask a gardener, "May I have a pound of strawberries?" "May" is civil assent. And nobody exploits this convenience so skillfully as Sergei Mikhailovich. Only once did he show himself at a loss, and that was when I called him from tying up tomatoes to come and inspect Anton in his pram. He came up with his usual alacrity, glanced swiftly at the imperturbable infantile mask, nodded, smiled, since something was obviously expected of him, and hurried back to his tomatoes with obvious relief.

Larissa Andreyevna can be voluble when the spirit moves her, and she always knows the password. I have lived in her house for ten consecutive summers, in close propinquity for two days every week and for a whole month every year when she gets her vacation. I am as familiar with the whir of her sewing machine as she must be with the clack of my typewriter; she knows when I wash and when I don't wash because I have to borrow her tub; and I know she dyes her hair because she does it in the yard. Yet we both shrink instinctively from intimacy, seldom borrowing so much as a cup or a postage stamp, or asking one another the most trifling favor. We meet, greet, chat about the weather or the flower beds; in her month of vacation there have been hour-long talks when we have divulged to one another the tale of our births, deaths, and marriages, but Larissa Andreyevna's curiosity, though immense, is easily satisfied by a table of contents, and I am still longing to know what is behind her smiles and manifold masks.

Sunday wasn't the kind of morning when daylight streams into the house the moment you open the door. The air was like a wall, and if it was not actually raining, it had obviously only just stopped and would begin again very soon. But the indefatigable pair are working hard among the fruit trees and flower beds, heaping earth round the roots of an arthritic apple tree from which, last week, they had meticulously swept their natural covering of fallen leaves. Why, I wonder. Larissa Andreyevna, at her best in drab slacks and a turtleneck sweater, is digging up strawberry plants and resetting them in sparse, doleful rows. She looks up to greet me with a loud patronizing "*Good* morning!"—

flashing at me two rows of strong teeth as white and intimidating as Mr. Carker's own. I respond with a feeble imitation of her accents, but I keep my teeth to myself. Sergei Mikhailovich is winding cord round a bandaged sapling. Him I have a compulsion to greet, so I say something about the sun's having been unable to keep its promise, just to collect his slow, kind smile, his kind, deep look. "Unable," says Sergei Mikhailovich, all mellow benevolence. He waits till I have quite passed him to return to his winding.

The privy stands up tall like a sentry box between the mound of compost and a deep pool scooped out of the soil twenty-five years ago by a German bomb; the pool never seems to dry up and never scums over, and the proprietors use it as a most convenient reservoir for watering their strawberries and tomatoes. The compost is now covered with the sweepings of the garden and dead leaves, all the horrid contents of kitchen buckets out of sight; ubiquitous morning-glory has rooted itself on the ridge at the far end and begun to climb up the privy wall.

Tyapa has a go at a rat's tail hanging out of the compost; he has been trying to reach it every morning for the past week, but cannot get a foothold—the very lightness of the piled leaves defeats him. Husband and wife have moved tactfully to the other side of the garden, because the knob has fallen off the bolt on the door and you can't quite close it. The garden looks sadder and shabbier without their busy presences; the few asters and dahlias, which droop like floor mops over a tangle of undergrowth, are mournful rather than cheerful, and no birds sing. There is nothing to sing about. "Alone," "forlorn" seemed the very words for the garden and for me. But when, with fingers as stiff as its hinges, I pulled at the door, the candy-striped countenances of three morning-glories nodded at me from the dark interior, turning its darkness into light.

On my way back to the house, I stopped for a moment to listen to a few wild notes flung on the damp air. An unwise thrush, I thought pityingly; why wasn't it in Pakistan long ago? The notes were repeated, loud, unmodulated—only a boy whistling in the road.

But my heart leaped up a little, and all through the day I kept remembering the morning-glories. I knew they would have dropped and dwindled by the next day—the flower of the convolvulus has no morrow—but I had counted nine pointed buds on the spray; with a few rays of sunshine to filter through the badly aligned planks, they would last out my last days at the dacha. Every time I came upon my landlady or her husband, I wondered if they had noticed the bright visitors, but nothing was said till, no longer able to contain myself, I asked Sergei Mikhailovich, who was snipping at a few twigs and sprouts on a cherry tree he had overlooked in the morning, if he had seen them.

He straightened himself as usual and looked into my eyes. "Seen."

And the next time I went down the garden path, I opened the privy door on darkness and desolation. I put my fingers into a chink between the boards and brought away an inch of pale green stem, which had evidently been neatly clipped off on either side. Only then I remembered how the clicking had fallen silent when I passed Sergei Mikhailovich, and knew that it was I who had betrayed the convolvulus to those hungry blades. Oh, the female tongue, ever ready to tell its love! Love that never told should be.

I didn't see either of them again till Sergei Mikhailovich came out of the house in the evening, dressed for town, leaving the door open for his wife, who was still inside. "Sergei Mikhailovich," I said, "why did you destroy the convolvulus? It was company for me." In my agitation I used the English name (the

Russians adapt the Latin name and call the plant "the winder"),
but he understood me, being a gardener. Again the courteous
bend of the head, the faint smile, the quizzically cocked eyebrow,
the deep, deep look. The whole bag of tricks. But it didn't work
any longer. I felt as I suppose Jonah felt when the Lord first
prepared a gourd for a shadow for his head but the next morning
sent a worm to smite the gourd so that it withered, after which
he calmly asked Jonah, "Doest thou well to be angry for the
gourd?" Like Jonah I could have answered, "I do well to be
angry, even unto death."

Larissa Andreyevna, coming out of the house, repeated reproachfully, bolting and barring the door behind her, "It was
company for her." And smiled at me warmly. The first time ever.

"Why did he do it?" I asked.

She shrugged her shoulders. "Ask him. *Dosvidanya*, Ivy
Walterovna!"

To Be a Daniel

THE LADY WAS PROPELLED from the orbit of the four-leaved door of an Oxford Street lunch bar to a stool at the lunch counter. Sweetly imperious, she ordered a cup of coffee (black) and a cheese sandwich, laid a sumptuous pocketbook on the counter, pillowed a too-sharp elbow on the pocketbook, and dropped her too sharp chin into the palm of her hand to gaze into the street over the window display. The boy Fred, not deceived by the carefully held radiance of her smile, decided she was fifty if a day, but before he had time for a proper look she was off the stool and out in the street again. A minute later she was back, followed by a gentleman in a camel's-hair coat. The two walked up to the abandoned pocketbook, the full cup of coffee, the intact sandwich, and stood leaning against the bar, talking loudly and intimately as if, Fred thought resentfully, the place belonged to them. Fred waited, arms folded, behind his urns, but no second order was given; the gentleman hadn't a moment to spare, and they stood there giving out till everyone in the shop had to know that her name was Jane, his Dan, that they had last seen one another at the Hotel Metropole, Moscow, twenty-five—no, twenty-six years ago. The man, Dan, hurried off to the appointment he had been hurrying off to when Jane had caught sight of his head and shoulders through the window. Fred now saw that he had kind, clever eyes and slack facial muscles. Jane stayed to finish her tepid coffee, took one bite of the sandwich, paid at the desk, and clattered out of the shop.

In the street Jane stopped for a moment to look at herself in a mirror in the show window of a furniture shop: her figure was as good as ever, she thought, but her face wasn't; despite constant massage, the incipient pouch under her too-sharp chin was a mass of spider threads, and it seemed to her that her eyes and mouth were daily sinking closer to the bony structure. It was hard for her to recall her face of twenty-six years ago, though she could remember exactly what she had worn the day she met Dan in Moscow. She turned peevishly from the glass and moved on, asking herself why she was rushing off to Fortnum & Mason's to buy orange pekoe for a man who would probably have preferred coffee. And why, after all, had she asked Dan to breakfast? Wouldn't lunch have been more convenient for them both? She knew very well why—Olive came back for lunch every day, and Jane wanted Dan to herself.

The teapot, the rashers, the thin wedges of toast in the porcelain rack had been on the plate warmer nearly half an hour; Jane had been ready for over an hour—pale sweater and drab pants, youth (she hoped) replenished in skin and hair—but before her irritation had time to accumulate, the lift stopped outside and the Lincoln Imp on the door of the flat was manipulated by an awkward hand.

Dan stood just inside the door, hat in hand, looking from the blue plates on the dresser to the marigolds in the Leeds bowl, till Jane begged him to hang up his hat and put down the brief case. "Don't stand there looking at my bits and pieces, you make me nervous. Everything came to me from Suffolk after the death of my last-remaining great-aunt." "Even Ye Olde English Wallpaper?" Jane explained that the trellised and flowery wallpaper and the Lincoln Imp on the door had been an interior decorator's unhappy thought; she meant to get rid of both. "I'll have the walls painted—off-white." But Dan liked it just as it was—the Small House at Allington in Bloomsbury. "Now I know what Bloomsbury is." He didn't really, Jane told him. Handel Street wasn't the Bloomsbury he was thinking of. "No writers live here—unless you can call me a writer—Virginia certainly wouldn't have."

"I didn't know you were a writer, Jane."

"I do a women's column—syndicated, you know."

"Mrs. Lonely Hearts!"

When Jane tried to draw Dan out about his writing he became evasive—distressed, she thought. They found themselves talking about Scrabble: Dan, it appeared, always found room for the folding board in suitcase or rucksack and often played his right hand against his left far into the night in hotel bedrooms; Jane had gone over to Anagrams—she found it more relaxing than Scrabble, no groping for a pencil, no tiresome columns of figures. She produced a cardboard box with the word Anagrams in commercial Gothic on the lid; Dan was struck by the maniacal agility with which she let down the hinged flap of an eighteenth-century *secrétaire* and reached for a loosely filled velvet bag from a pigeonhole. The harsh rattle as she emptied the bag on the flap reminded country-bred Dan of a sack of nuts being emptied on the floor of a barn. Jane expounded the simple rules of Anagrams, but Dan did not find spelling out words upside down particularly relaxing. One round led to another till the door opened and a sturdily built young woman burst into the room with shopping bag dangling from one hand and a potted lily held against her chest. "Olive!" cried Jane. "Come and say how d'you do to Dan." The young woman passed Dan on her way to a narrow un-paneled door behind his chair, and his gallant attempt to take the shopping bag from her remained a mere sketch in the air. She dumped the bag on the other side of the door and came back into the room holding the flowerpot with both hands at arms' length. The lily's silvery trumpet quivered with each of her abrupt move-ments, and its thick glistening calyx threw a greenish tinge on her broad, lined face—*not so young, after all.* "Come and say hullo to Dan," repeated Jane rather less suavely. Without even looking up, Olive moved magazines and newspapers from a table in the bow window and placed the pot in the middle. "Olive's a great admirer of *Red Pastures*," Jane said. There was a shade of admonition in the words obviously intended for Olive, who now said: "Oh, hullo!" and thrust a blunt hand toward the visitor, withdrawing it before Dan could practice the charm of a warm pressure. "Isn't that lovely, Jane?" she said. "Don't say it isn't absolute perfection!" Jane studied the arrangement through narrowed eyes. "Bit obvious, isn't it?" Olive flushed to the ears and lifted the flowerpot, causing the heavy glistening head to sway violently and the narrow stepped leaves to tremble. "Where shall I put it?" she barked. "Down the chute? Out the window?" "Put it anywhere you like," barked Jane.

Dan was beginning to feel like the Invisible Man, and won-dered if he should steal away, when Jane suddenly remembered her manners. "Where's the Scrabble board?" she said. "Dan doesn't *take* to Anagrams." Unheeding Dan's deprecatory assur-ances that he really must go, Olive strode to the dresser, raised the lid of an immense silver tureen standing on it, and plunged her hand into its depths. Out came a shallow gun-metal box. "Travel Scrabble!" cried Dan. Olive's hand went back into the tureen for a wash-leather pouch that she tossed to Jane. Jane fielded it deftly and handed it to Dan. "What about my book?" he said faintly, but even as he protested he was loosening the drawstring of the pouch and fingering at the tiny slabs inside like a pilgrim telling his beads inside his scrip.

"Oh, are you writing another book?" said Olive, and snatched the pouch from his hand. "Then of course you must go home." She swept pouch and box back into the tureen, but Jane was busy setting out a tall black bottle and wineglasses. "Seven other devils worse than the first," Dan said. Jane was now filling the glasses from the bottle, watched in unconscious intensity by the other two.

Dan was no match for two women and a bottle. He settled back in his chair and told them his dilemma. He had been unable to fulfill the great expectations raised by the success of *Red Pastures*. Writer's block.

"We needn't ask if you have been analyzed." The words were Jane's, but Dan looked from one to the other, as if both had spoken. He told them he had tried everything from hypnotism to group therapy; he had tried living alone and he had tried not living alone. They wanted to know if not living alone meant being married. Not necessarily, he said. An American friend had invited him to stay at her ranch in Arizona for the duration of work on his book. She had allotted him a long room with walls and ceiling of polished brown planks, like the inside of a Swiss ski hut. "Or a private compartment in an express train," suggested Olive. "Sometimes I felt as if I were the last cigar in the box with the lid shut." The women laughed at this a little over-heartily. "Doesn't sound a very stimulating background," Jane said hastily, feeling the laughter had been tactless. "Pictures and bookshelves and things must have looked awful against all those vertical seams."

There hadn't been any pictures on the walls, except for a portrait of Brenda over the writing table. Brenda thought it might
be a stimulus—her spirit willing him to work.

"And was it?"

No. The only time Dan had had a creative spurt was when he
was banished to a room in the local bar to make room for a
celebrated composer who stayed for a fortnight without writing
a note. Dan had been sorry to come back to his ideal study, hadn't
minded a bit the garage under his room at the bar, where cars
kept coming and going all day long. He had preferred it to the
discreet perfection of the study which Brenda had created for him.

"Like the roof study Jane Carlyle made for Thomas," Jane
observed.

"I thought of the studio Mary Hemingway made for Ernest,"
Dan said. And Olive: "Me it reminds of *The Lesson of the
Master.*"

Jane quite understood; some of her best work had been done
seated on her bed with her typewriter on the bedside table in
small-town hotels right on a busy High Street. "You can write
anywhere if you have a deadline."

Olive had read in the *Reader's Digest* or somewhere that
writers ought not to type: the rattle of the keys set up antithought
vibrations in the brain cells. "Don't interrupt," said Jane. "You
began it," said Olive, and again Dan felt as if he ought not to
be there. But they both recovered their tempers at the same time
and begged him to go on with his story. They said it was fright-
fully interesting—hypnotizing.

He told them of sitting at the spacious writing table morning
after morning, day after day, week after week—"Month after
month," said Olive briskly. "Go on, tell us about your writing."

There wasn't much to tell. What was written one day was
destroyed the next, new beginnings were made and rejected.

Some mornings he had hardly had strength enough to take the
cover off the typewriter; he would go for a stroll, come back for
another go, play a contraband game of Scrabble. The great difficulty was to hide the Scrabble board from Brenda, who would
have been mighty in her wrath. He was often too languid even
to get up and pour himself a drink of orange juice; it was sur-
prising how little one seemed to want orange juice when all that
was required was to take a pitcher out of the fridge. No treat
at all.

"The bruit went forth at one time that you had gone to the
Spanish war," Jane said, and filled up his glass. "I was going to,
I even began learning Spanish, but Brenda thought it would be
desertion not to finish my book after so many sacrifices had been
made."

"Sacrifices?"

"Well, you know, her living at the ranch all the year round
for my sake, and all the trouble and expense she went to."

"Didn't you ever finish it?" asked Olive, and both were surprised to hear Dan say that yes, he had finished it. He had gone
back to the Soviet Union and seen more kolkhozi and industrial
plants, finding in the experience an impulse that carried him to
the end of his manuscript. But his agent would have nothing to
do with it; times had changed and there was no longer a demand
for enthusiastic descriptions of life under collectivization. Everybody wanted him to write his autobiography—look at the adven-
tures he had had, the celebrities he had hobnobbed with! But Dan
had never been able to get further than: "I was born in the city
of Duluth in 1902, but so were a whole lot of other people."

Jane and Olive thought it a very nice beginning for a book.
Others had too, Dan said, and last year he had come across an
English publisher visiting New York who was a great admirer
of *Red Pastures* and offered him a job in his American Depart-

ment and a contract for his next book. That was how he came to be in London now.

"And how did you come to be in New York last year?" Olive asked. "I thought the idea was that you were to stay put in Arizona till you'd finished your book." "It was, but as it didn't seem to be a success Brenda thought a little squalor might be more helpful."

Dan went away without leaving his telephone number, because the telephone was in Selina's room, and Selina had begged him not to give it to anyone. Selina, they gathered, was his present landlady, in a street off the Fulham Road. He promised to give them a call in a few days and let them know how the book was going.

As soon as the click of the lift announced that the visitor was on his way down, the women leaped to tidy their room like ants after routing an intruder. Bottle, glasses, breakfast dishes were carried out as if they were so many dogs who had misbehaved, the rug was vacuumed till not a crumb lingered on its pile, and in no time the room was back in its original state of chilly coziness. Jane draped herself against the back of a kidney-shaped couch from which she could see a reflection in a wall mirror more flattering than the one she had studied in the furniture-shop window. The elegant anachronism of slacks and sweater against pale brocade soothed her, the cigarette she plucked from a mustache cup on the brass fender struck no jarring note, the latest issue of *Vogue* was perfectly at home on a bandy-legged console table. "Leave the washing for Mrs. Kew!" Jane called toward a clatter of dishes in the sink. Calling back that she had just finished, Olive came out of the kitchen wiping her hands on a striped dishcloth which she flung neatly onto the back of a chair in passing. She made a place for herself at the end of the couch by lifting Jane's crossed ankles, then lowering Jane's feet gently on her lap as soon as she was seated. Jane handed her a cigarette and they sat smoking in silence a few minutes. "Was Dan like what you thought he'd be?" Jane asked, after giving Olive every chance to begin. "I never thought about him," Olive said viciously. "Well, from what I told you about him." "You only told me you typed his manuscript in the Hotel Metropole, and when *Red Pastures* came out he never even sent you a copy. You were in love with him and you still are." "I am not," Jane said steadily, "but I'd like to help him finish his book. Don't you think *we* might be able to create the right background for Dan? I'm sure Selina's no good; that room off the Fulham Road sounds too slummy for words. Couldn't he work in your room while you're at the office? I could leave breakfast ready for him before going out." "Following in the footsteps of Brenda and Selina." "I came first," Jane said. "I was the one who typed *Red Pastures*." "All women are like the Shulamite woman who made a little chamber in the wall for the prophet and put a bed and a table and stool and candlestick in it." "And the prophet was very glad of it—he stayed there." "He was soon off again. You might at least give him your picture to hang over his desk in Fulham Road, only I suppose Selina would be jealous."

As a matter of fact this was just what Jane had done while Olive's back was turned: she had torn off its mount a photograph of herself that she thought did her justice, and taped it to the inside of the Anagrams box.

One day Olive came across a woman who knew a great deal more about Dan than the friends did. Her name was Patricia Harris and she ran a literary agency with a new slant: she was to write celebrities' autobiographies for them and go halves if she managed to sell them to a publisher. Jane remembered a Pat and

Harris agency. "I knew Harris, but I never saw Pat." "Well, now she calls herself Patricia Harris, and Harris doesn't seem to be around any more. It wasn't quite the way Dan told us. It seems Pat was staying at a ranch not so very far (by Arizona standards) from Brenda's ranch, doing the life of a bottle-top king, and Brenda thought it would be a good idea for Patricia to help Dan write his autobiography." "The insult! No wonder he ran away!"

"Not at all, he quite cottoned to the idea—it was Brenda who couldn't stand it."

"You mean she was jealous?"

"Of course she was jealous." "And she gave Patricia the sack, I suppose?" "By no means. She said she thought it was time for Dan to work on his own. Patricia could start doing *Brenda's* autobiography. And of course the only suitable place for them to work in was Dan's study. Brenda had been quite ready to help Dan settle down somewhere else, preferably in New York, where he could establish contacts with a publisher. And it came out the way Dan told us—he couldn't get anybody to *look* at his manuscript in New York, so he went to London with this English publisher."

A week later Jane, coming back from a party at the Women Writers' Club, was greeted by Olive with the words, "You'll never guess who's been!" "Who?" Jane said coldly, though she guessed from the triumphant gleam in Olive's eye that it was Dan. "*Thing!* He asked for you, but I offered myself as a substitute and he didn't seem to object." "Who 'Thing,' for goodness' sake?"

"As if you didn't know! He brought back the Anagrams box. All wrapped up the way you gave it him. He says he'll be leaving England in a week or two and hates carrying things about with him. I don't believe he ever opened it." "Is he going back to Arizona?" "I asked him but he said, 'No, no!' very decidedly. Just leaving England. I think he's lost his job."

Jane was longing to know if her photograph was still inside the lid of the Anagrams box, but she tossed the parcel carelessly into the *secrétaire* and waited for Olive to go out to get something for supper before she retrieved it. She had it unwrapped in a few seconds and made the string into a neat coil before removing the lid. There was nothing inside it but four glistening patches where the Scotch tape had been. Dan must, after all, have opened the parcel; he had taken out her photograph. What had he done with it, she wondered . . .

Dan disappeared like a stone dropped into a well. Jane picked up rumors of him at parties and literary weekends, none of them very convincing. Some people said he had gone back to Arizona, but Olive had met Pat Harris again and Pat had told her that Brenda was now interested in a young abstract sculptor. Others had heard that Dan was in Moscow teaching Basic English in a Workers' University, but Jane knew Basic English was regarded as a branch of imperialist propaganda in the Soviet Union, and you had to have a college diploma and a thorough knowledge of the Six Forms of the Infinitive to teach there nowadays. She was sure Dan had neither of these qualifications. The rumor that he had accepted a call to Duluth after his father's death seemed more credible. Jane thought Dan would make a lovely minister; so many people would go to him for help and stay to help *him*, and helping others made Americans feel so good, which, Jane supposed— next to making them feel miserable sinners—was what ministers were for.

The friends almost stopped talking about Dan after Jane got round to an idea that concerned them both closely—the stripping of the wallpaper in the sitting room and the return to a painted surface (off-white, of course). There had been a certain coolness between them ever since Jane, going to look for a clean handkerchief in Olive's chest of drawers, had come upon the photograph she had sent to Dan. She had once or twice before been struck in the watches of the night by the horrid thought that Olive (not Dan) had opened the parcel and taken out her photograph, and now she knew she was right. But any change in the interior of their nest was of such prime interest to both that antagonisms were allowed to sink below the surface.

Jane had heard of a marvelous little woman who came and sat all day in your room absorbing the atmosphere before she diagnosed for the walls; she mixed the colors herself and had her own plasterer and was said to be very reasonable. Olive thought they should put the job in the hands of one of the big firms; it wasn't worth chasing after some amateur in the sticks (the marvelous little woman lived on one of the new housing estates outside London), and after all they only wanted white walls. Jane knew the little woman was no amateur, she had done a marvelous job for people she knew; and white was one of the trickiest colors: the big firms would make the room look like an Ideal Home, and the local men always put too much blue in when you weren't looking and it came out like a hospital ward. The walls— as Jane often had occasion to tell her readers, when some new paint or paper came on the market—are the most important feature of a room, and she half hoped to get some copy for her column out of the Little Woman (you never knew).

In the end it was Olive who drove outside town in search of the Little Woman, but nobody was at home—a fact which had not prevented Olive from bringing home a budget full of gossip: getting no answer to her ring, she had peered into a downstairs window and obtained a clear view of a comfortable sitting room: Chelsea figures on the mantelpiece, a grandfather clock in the corner, a rug that looked as if it might be really good, a huge ebony vase filled with teasels in a corner. There were two tables—

one against the wall with a closed typewriter and a spread of papers on it; the other right under the window through which, by standing on tiptoe, Olive had been able to make out a flat gun-metal box and a droop-necked chamois-leather bag. Besides these familiar objects, Olive was sure there was a man's camel's-hair overcoat hanging in the passage, just visible through an open door.

"Is that all?" Jane asked.

"Not quite. In the hall, next to the hatstand, I'm certain I saw the handle of a pram." "Oh, come off it, Olive!" "You mean you don't believe me?" "I believed in the jar of teasels and the Chelsea porcelain, but I didn't for a moment believe in the Scrabble box; after that I knew you'd go too far and give yourself away." "I was only trying to amuse you." "You tried too hard. I knew the pram was a lie." "How did you know?" "I know Dan." "One day some woman will show you you don't." "Perhaps it'll be you. It'll be worth waiting another twenty-five years to see you pushing a pram in Kensington Gardens." "In another twenty-five years we shall be seventy-five." The words meant no more to these fifty-year-old women than they would have to a girl of seventeen. They just couldn't imagine themselves at seventy-five any more than people can imagine themselves dead.

Change and decay were less evident in the quiet Bloomsbury backwater than in some other parts of London. Hoardings plastered with recommendations to drink anything from a Cuppa Tea to a Glass of Guinness screened the occasional bombed-sites and wild convolvulus groped for nourishment among the rubble behind them till the day men came with bulldozers and cranes to topple the hoardings and fling the convolvulus out with the rubble in a single day. Only the nettles kept springing up in obstinate patches all through building operations; ladies no longer came in from the suburbs to change their novels at Mudie's,

which had at last succumbed to the competition from more
modern libraries with branches all over England. The Austrian
waiters at the Vienna Café no longer rose reluctantly from a
game of draughts at the back of the room to serve customers
from the British Museum—they had all been interned in the First
World War, naïvely referred to at the time as the Great War.
But the lunch bar in Oxford Street from the window of which
Jane had caught sight of Dan's head and shoulders over the
window display, stood firm, merely bowing to the spirit of the
age by going plastic in a rather swooping manner.

The years brought wildly accelerating development into the
lives of Jane and Olive. First Olive had a Nervous Breakdown
and spent ten months in hospital. As soon as she recovered, Jane
took her to spend her convalescence at her bachelor brother
Hilary's vicarage in Devonshire. From there, since wonders never
cease, Olive returned engaged to Hilary. No pram was pushed
through the Devonshire lanes, but the union presented a normal
picture of conjugal life, and Hilary was better fed and better
dressed than he had ever been before.

Olive had always been *the one* who saw to the mechanical
details of life, renewing subscriptions to the Times Library and
the Book of the Month Club, making appointments for Jane at
the beauty shop; after her defection Jane took skin treatments
less regularly, washed her hair at home, and only went to her
manicurist when her nails began to break under the strain of
typing. Now when she wanted something to read in bed she
turned to the shelves where the books she had brought with her
from home—and the smaller contingent she had bought off
secondhand bookstalls when she first came to London—had been
patiently biding their time. Stealthily the nineteenth century
closed in on her mind, and now when unknown women wrote to

her for help and advice (really, she knew, to unburden themselves), she compared them to the dissatisfied heroines of nineteenth-century fiction and memoirs. If Dan had not been Dan,
might not she herself have become another Jane Carlyle, nursing
a perpetual grievance against the disgruntled sage to whom she
had devoted her life?

Years later Dan's book came out, a thin volume with wide
margins; most of it contained whimsical descriptions of eccentric
relatives—"My Father," "Poor Old Uncle Jo Who Played the
Flute," "Cousin Izzy," stately Grandmother Perkins who wore
a wig and rouged under her eyes to the last day of her life; the
rest amounted to little but a rehash of *Red Pastures*. It was the
Book of the Month's Alternate Choice; reviewers struggled vainly
to conceal their yawns, and the publishers did their best with:
"Sensitive piece of writing"—*Scot's National Observer*; "evoca-
tive"—*Glasgow Herald*; "vivid reminiscences of the beginning of
Collectivization in the Soviet Union"—*New Republic*.

Jane saw Dan a year later at a party to launch an autobiography by a new author. As she moved into the room she heard one
woman say to another, "If one could only create the proper
conditions for him . . ." Jane looked where the speaker was
looking, toward a low table covered with bottles and glasses in
the bow window of the publisher's drawing room. Two figures
were conspicuous in the group around the table: one, obviously
the hero of the day, had a youngish but ravaged face, with anxious
eyes under shaggy brows; the other was Dan, sprawled, almost
slumped, in a deep armchair. A twinkle from the pendant of a
crystal chandelier in the middle of the ceiling was unkindly
repeated in the watery corners of his eyes. As she watched, a
hearty-looking gentleman stepped up to the bow window and
put a hand on one shoulder of each man. "When's the next book

coming out, boys?" "'Follow up, follow up, follow up, till the field ring again and again!' That's the secret of success, boys!"

The sick smiles of the writers went to Jane's heart. She tiptoed from the room. She had an appointment at home with an interior decorator, having at last decided to have the Lincoln Imp unscrewed and the door repainted.

Sowing Asphodel

A MABEL LOOKED from the magazine propped against the toaster to the faces round the table. It was Sunday morning, in London. Everyone was peacefully eating or drinking, and she thought they didn't look altogether unreceptive. So, tapping the point of a knuckle against the doubled-back page, she announced, "It says here people are always talking to themselves when they're not talking to someone else."

Charles raised one eyebrow at his mother, with an effect of amiable response. Dorothy put down her cup and said with un-expected energy that it was perfectly true as far as she herself was concerned; she sometimes wished she could stop. Their fifteen-year-old daughter Cynthia said, "Gammer always talks to herself when she's alone. You do, Gammer. Your door was open this morning when I passed, and I heard you say, 'Now, wherever have you got to this time, I wonder.'"

"I wasn't talking to myself. I was talking to my shoes," Amabel said. She turned to Charles. "It says here that everybody keeps up an incessant discourse with themselves."

"Like Mrs. Bloom," Dorothy said.

Amabel thought it was more desultory than Mrs. Bloom's unpunctuated reminiscences. "More like Mr. Bloom, I think."

"I refuse to identify myself with either of the Blooms," said Frances Liddell, who had come to give Cynthia a music lesson and had been persuaded to sit down for a cup of coffee first. "And how does a writer in the *Scientific American* know what's going on inside other people?"

" 'The isle is full of voices,' " Amabel suggested, as if in tentative explanation.

" 'Noises,' " Frances corrected.

Amabel sighed. " 'Voices' would have been nicer." She nipped a corner of the page between her finger and thumb, tilting it toward the others as if she were Counsel for the Defense displaying Exhibit One to the jury. "The article's called 'Internal Speech,' but it's mostly about reading. It used to be considered the thing to stress the sound element in teaching children—more dynamic, or something—but modern psychologists . . ." Here Amabel began reading boldly from the printed page. " 'Modern psychologists incline to the opinion that emphasis on aural reception may inhibit visual perception.' "

Dorothy looked vague, Frances repeated injuriously, "Modern psychologists!" and Cynthia jumped up from the table, saying it was time to take the poor Wogs out. At the sound of his name, a grizzled Scotty emerged from somewhere near Charles's feet and ambled cautiously round the corner of the swing door, which Cynthia was holding for him.

An alert look had come into Charles's eyes while his mother was reading, and he now said, "Aural reception is not essential. The deaf can be taught to read."

"Perhaps children should be taught to read as if they *were* deaf," Amabel proposed brightly, but Frances reminded her that the Americans had tried this, with disastrous results: "You said yourself they were bringing up a generation of illiterates."

"Did I?" said Amabel, pleased.

"Nobody knows exactly how we recognize symbols," Charles said. "It's one of the things that make it so hard to teach machines to read."

"Children aren't machines," Frances said, and Dorothy sprang to her husband's defense.

"Charles never said they were."

"I don't know about machines," Amabel said, "but I'm sure *my* memory is purely visual."

All three women were eager to stake their claims in the field of visual memory. Frances, playing recklessly into the hands of modern psychologists, could never remember how many c's and s's there were in "vicissitudes" till she saw it written down. Dorothy said that she had been forced to try out "psychiatry" and "schizophrenia" on a scratch pad when sitting for her medicals. Amabel always wanted to put a t in "bachelor," but realizing that this was hardly an argument for visual memory, checked herself. Each had a tale of its uncanny workings. Dorothy had recognized the merest acquaintance after the lapse of thirty years in a crowded railway terminus; Frances had spotted her former kindergarten teacher sun-bathing on the beach at Brighton. And Amabel was ready with a story of much greater entertainment value, though perhaps less cogency. She cleared her throat for a brilliant beginning. "When I was in Geneva—"

Charles, who had half risen from the table, waiting for a convenient pause to escape to the news broadcast, sat down again. When it appeared from Amabel's next words that this was only going to be another story of instantaneous recognition, he straightened himself and made for the door, pushing it as far as the hinges would allow but checking its backward swing with his foot. "Try not to use the telephone while the broadcast's going on," he begged, looking from his wife to his mother.

"And if Tom rings up?" Dorothy said, low-voiced.

"Much more likely to be somebody trying to get hold of Tom." Charles's voice was not as urbane as usual.

No one spoke for some seconds, and when the front-door bell rang all except Amabel, who did not hear it, started. It was only Cynthia and the Wogs back from their walk, but Amabel could see from the expression on her daughter-in-law's face that she was thinking of nineteen-year-old Tom, who had flung out of the house three days before and not been seen or heard of since. Charles sent his wife a keen, steady look before removing his foot to step out of the door's orbit into the hall.

Frances pushed herself from the table and stood up. "Time for Cynthia's music lesson, for which we shall both require all that aural and visual memory can do for us."

Plus a little something that Cynthia hasn't got, said the imp inside Amabel. But a no less watchful imp prevented the words from escaping into the public domain. Now Amabel was alone with her daughter-in-law. She shoved her plate, cup, and saucer toward the end of the table for Dorothy's greater convenience, but knew better than to offer help with the washing up. "What was I saying?" she asked. "Oh, yes, Geneva. The only person I made friends with there, strange to say, was the wife of the German delegate."

Just then Frances came back into the kitchen to pick up her glasses. "The Germans weren't in the League of Nations," she rapped out and was gone again.

"Did I say they were?" Amabel moaned to the imperturbably swinging door. "It was the Preparatory Commission for the Disarmament Conference."

Dorothy gave a short laugh and turned a stream of scalding water on the dishes.

"Where did I get to?" Amabel said. "Oh, yes. Frau von Bernsdorff. She spoke English perfectly; some people thought she *was* English. She wore English tailor-mades and pale billowy scarves, and she was madly well-read. We often met in bookshops, and I can remember her surprise when she discovered I hadn't read Rousseau's *Confessions*. She thought I was very lucky to be reading it for the first time in Geneva. We met like old friends at the second session, and the only thing that induced me to go to the third was the hope of meeting Frau von Bernsdorff again."

"You mean you didn't *want* to go?"

"By that time I was bored to death with Geneva—stony, drony Geneva. Frau von Bernsdorff and the heavenly bookshops were the two bright spots."

"But the Alps! You can look at bookshops in London, but you can't see Alps every time you look out of the window."

"You can't in Geneva, either. Sometimes you don't see an Alp for weeks. One evening I went out in a Scotch mist that suddenly rolled away, and there was Mont Blanc, pink all the way up in the sunset. And another time—but never mind scenery. When we arrived for the third session, I was disgusted not to see Frau von Bernsdorff anywhere. At first I thought the delegation hadn't yet come, but the Graf was in his place at the opening, and when I asked one of their interpreters after Frau von Bernsdorff she said she thought she wasn't coming. The next day I had an appointment for a perm—"

"You went in for perms, Amabel?" Dorothy could not imagine her mother-in-law's smooth head plowed into symmetrical ridges.

"I did, poor fool, and to general acclaim. I got the girl who al-

ways set Frau von Bernsdorff's hair, and she told me she had
heard the Frau had just had a stroke. At once it seemed to me
that there had been something strange about the interpreter's
expression. I kept catching sight of the Graf in the corridors, but
he was never alone and I didn't like to go up to him."

Dorothy interrupted to ask how old the countess was, but
Amabel didn't know. "She was older than me, of course. Everybody seemed to be older than me then."

The interruption had altered the course of her thoughts, and
she had to pick up her story a little further on. "The last day of
the session, our Miss Oliver and I went to have chocolate *Schlagobers* at the principal café in Geneva—I can't remember its name.
I have a haunting vision of 'Café Royal' in gilt flourishes on a
plate-glass window, but on second thought surely not! Could it
have been 'Majestic'? Even that . . ."

"What does it matter?" Dorothy said.

"What does anything matter?" Amabel said. "Oh, I believe it
was 'Café des Alpes.' Yes, that was it. There was a splendid view
of the lake out of the window, but people mostly watched the
door for celebrities. While we were waiting for our *Schlagobers,*
somebody came into the café and stood holding the door for an
old lady leaning on the arm of a young girl. They looked like
Death and the Maiden. I don't think there was a soul in the café
who didn't look up for a moment. The girl at the pay desk pulled
back the little green curtain on her side window to watch them
walk slowly to a table in the middle of the floor, and none of the
waitresses moved till they reached it. When they were settled, the
old one turned and looked across the room, and I saw her face
clearly. It was Frau von Bernsdorff, but changed into an old
witch. There was still something of her former self left that could
have been nobody else. Miss Oliver saw the likeness as soon as I
pointed it out, but at first she couldn't believe her eyes. She took

another look and said she supposed I was right. And when the poor old thing tugged impatiently to free her lorgnette from the mauve chiffon scarf she was wearing, Miss Oliver and I exchanged glances—we had so often seen her raking the tables at a sitting of the Commission. That and the mauve scarf convinced us, and from that moment neither of us had any more doubts. Miss Oliver still thought it almost incredible that a woman who had been so full of life and energy a few months before could have collapsed so utterly after a single stroke."

"We get cases like that every week," Dorothy said. "Why, Amabel, it could happen to—" She broke off and began again with an inept "It's fairly common."

Amabel hurried back to her story, feeling a little guilty at having embarrassed her daughter-in-law. But the life had evaporated from her voice; she became unnecessarily descriptive, hopelessly discursive. When at last she allowed herself to look toward the sink, she discovered that she was alone and—judging by the absolute immobility of the door—must have been talking to herself for at least a minute. Dorothy had probably rushed to answer the telephone, with an apology that had fallen short of her mother-in-law's zone of hearing. "I'm an old bore," Amabel told herself tolerantly. "I'll go to my room and stay there."

A backward glance from the door sent her to the table to wind the cord of the toaster round its base and set it on the shelf beside the upended electric iron. It was a point of honor with them all, even the slapdash Cynthia, to keep the kitchen tidy. It was easy, really; you only had to make sure there was nothing in the sink or on the table, to hang mops and towels on their hooks, and stow leftovers in the icebox.

Out in the hall Amabel almost collided with Dorothy. "Was it Tom?" she asked, though Dorothy's bright eyes had already told her it was. "Is he coming?"

Dorothy tried to sound indifferent—indeed, severe. "And without a word of apology! Just says he'll be back for dinner. And we're all supposed to be delighted."

"As we all are," Amabel said.

"I told him if he wasn't in time there wouldn't *be* any dinner, but I doubt if it registered." Dorothy passed on, smiling and humming, and through two swings of the kitchen door Amabel heard her break into song.

Amabel decided to call Deborah, but before lifting the receiver she opened the door next to the telephone and discovered Charles crouched in front of his set, a pipe stuck in the side of his mouth. "Could you bear it if I rang up Debbie?" she asked.

Without removing the pipe, Charles said he hoped she wouldn't take half an hour over it. As it was, there was a music lesson going on in the next room.

Now that he mentioned it, Amabel's dull ear caught the perky melody of a Kuhlau sonatina played with hatred and exasperation. She handed the *Scientific American* to Charles and promised not to be long at the telephone.

He took the magazine with a deprecating smile intended to soften any bearishness.

"I'll just . . ." Amabel said, as she closed his door. She began dialing, but set herself back by calling out, "I hear Tom's coming home!" Wondering if he had heard her through the closed door, she put back the receiver and then had to start dialing all over again.

A dull "Hullo!" thudded against her eardrum.

"Good morning, Grannie Butts!" she cried brightly, but the voice that answered her was now cool and clear.

"It's Susan. I'll call Mother."

Cursing her clumsiness, Amabel forced a laugh into the re-

ceiver and was relieved when Debbie's voice—mellow, noncom-
mittally cordial—carried everything onto another plane. "Hullo!
Oh, hullo, Am!"

"Oh dear, I took Sue for Grannie Butts again!"

Deborah's voice came back a little dry. "Sue's in the sulks.
. . . Oh, nothing special. Sunday morning. Daughter late for
breakfast. Father nags. Daughter answers back."

"And Grannie Butts smiling into her plate, I suppose."

Grannie Butts, it appeared, was away for the weekend.

"Well, cheers! I mean that's something, at any rate. And what's
Ianthe up to?"

Ianthe wasn't up to anything. In fact, Ianthe wasn't up.

There was a slight pause for readjustment of nerves, and
Amabel remembered that she had news. "Tom called up. He's
coming home."

A few caustic remarks were exchanged on this subject, Deborah
asked her mother how she had slept, Amabel reciprocated, and
they hung up almost simultaneously, but not before Amabel had
caught the end of a sharp, short sigh. "How often when you go to
the telephone for distraction," she told herself, "you leave it with
chagrin as your only reward."

Just inside her room, Amabel stubbed her toe on a brass mortar
and pestle sometimes used to prop the kitchen door. Swearing
innocuously, she shoved them into the hall with the foot that
didn't hurt.

The cluttered interior of her room offered no refreshment to
her spirits. It was not so easy to keep a room used only by oneself as tidy as a room used by the whole family. The old portable
Remington on her desk attracted her attention no longer than
it took to pick up the lid from the floor and replace it. She had
allowed herself to be upset, and it would be no good attempting
to finish the long letter to a woman friend begun a few days

before, still less to add a passage to the memoirs. Amabel yawned. She wished there was a box of chocolates in the drawer of her desk, and then was glad there wasn't. She could have given herself to a game or two of Anagrams, but everybody was home; at any moment a member of the family, or Frances, might catch her at it and receive the undesirable impression that Amabel did nothing from morning to night but play Anagrams. Or the detestable suggestion "Why not go for a little stroll to get an appetite for dinner?" might be made. Most of all she longed to lie down, though she had been up only a few hours after a tolerable night. "And that is what I will do," she said.

Just then the door opened and a grave, ingratiating face appeared in the opening. Dorothy wanted to borrow five shillings till Thursday; Charles had no more penicillin left. She came right into the room to help Amabel search for her pocketbook, which was so slim and dark as to be almost invisible, though Amabel was sure she always kept it on top of a row of books. But which row, Dorothy asked, and Amabel had to admit she did not always use the same row, sometimes choosing the top of tall volumes on the bottom shelf, sometimes the line of Trollopes. This time the pocketbook was found lying across dictionaries and reference books.

"And why on earth I keep my father's Sanskrit dictionary is a thing I should like to know," Amabel said.

"To hide your pocketbook on the top of," Dorothy told her.

Amabel dropped assorted coins into the palm of her daughter-in-law's hand. "No better?"

"The minute one heals, another starts," Dorothy said plaintively. Charles' furunculosis was a kind of shared secret among his womenfolk, never referred to in his hearing.

Dorothy went away, closing the door with gentle firmness, and Amabel was sure she would be alone till dinnertime now. She went to her bookshelves to find something she had read un-counted times, but not too recently. Beginning with A, her right hand hovered from the *Arabian Nights* to *Persuasion* and stopped for a moment to take *Mansfield Park* from its place and transfer it to her left hand. Then the right hand traveled on, paused for a moment at *Corduroy*, at *Boswell's London Journal*, at *The Unquiet Grave*—all, all, too familiar. *The Egoist* had got among the E's and she put it in its place three shelves down. Feeling she had been a little harsh, she stroked the spine compunctiously before skipping the great line of D's, and quite ignoring Freud and Flaubert, she stopped again at G. *Loving? Back?* Not for reading in bed. The exploring hand fell to her side. *Mansfield Park* would have to do.

Amabel's great mahogany bed fitted nicely into the oblong recess that made such a good bed-sitter of the room—you had only to draw the voluminous blue curtains together for bed and clothespress to disappear. She drew them now, and, pulling aside the heavy counterpane (*when had Dorothy found the spare minutes to do the bed?*), let herself down on the blanket without taking off her dressing gown, and pulled the eiderdown up to her shoulders. It was quite dark behind the curtains, and she switched on her table lamp before dropping her head onto the piled pillows and opening her book at Chapter 1. "About thirty years ago," Amabel read, "Miss Maria Ward of Huntingdon, with only seven thousand pounds, had the good luck to captivate Sir Thomas Bertram, of Mansfield Park, in the county of North-ampton, and to be thereby raised to the rank of a baronet's lady, with all the comforts and consequences of a handsome house and large income."

A scratching at the door, a faint, short whine made Amabel look up. She might not hear electric bells, but she never failed to hear the Wogs' humble plea for admission. When she opened to him, he hesitated in the doorway, looked up appealingly, down deprecatingly, and at last, heavy head drooped, shortish fringed tail swinging, came into the room as far as the edge of the carpet, and waited for Amabel to shut the door behind him and receive him into her presence before he ventured to waddle to the armchair at the other end of the room. There he again stood waiting, till told to jump up. The short spring seemed an effort, and once on the cushioned seat he sank onto his side, front paws limply curved, hind paws sloping to meet them. The edge of a crimson tongue, the gleam of an eyetooth were the only points of light in the dense black hulk. Amabel wooed it with fond and foolish words, but nothing gleamed from the slit under beetling brows; only the tip of the tail twitched, once. The Wogs slept. "And I will, too," Amabel said.

Opening her eyes to heavy darkness, Amabel switched on her bedside lamp and was astonished to find it was half past twelve. She could not remember exactly when she had turned off the light, but it was clear that half a day and half a night had been slept away. This was good news in one way, but how on earth was she to get through the hours till daylight? She pushed back the eiderdown and put a foot out of bed, and the moment she parted the curtains she stepped into broad daylight and understood that she had slept an hour and a half at the most. The Wogs was bolt upright on the seat of the armchair, his ears standing up like distant turrets. When he saw Amabel, he dropped to the carpet and thudded to the door, evidently excited by confused sounds from the hall. Amabel listened for a moment—Tom, of course. Releasing the Wogs through the narrowest possible crack, she closed the door softly behind him, without looking out. Partly, she did not wish to be seen rumpled and creased from her nap, but also she was determined not to make a "thing" of Tom's return. Prolonged growls and hysterical yelps told her that the Wogs was groveling at the feet of the returned prodigal. (He had not greeted *her* so exuberantly when she came back from her summer holiday.)

Now Tom was home, the next thing would be dinner, and it was time for Amabel to dress. Instead, she sat on the side of the mattress in her dressing gown, trying to remember her dream. Her sleep had not refreshed her; in fact, she felt a fit of depression coming on. Like an invalid who doesn't know which pill to take till he has discovered whether the pain comes from heart or liver, she tried to trace the trouble to its source. *What can ail thee, knight at arms?* The mounting anxiety was too intense to be accounted for by habitual worries. Experience had taught her that intolerable anxiety was always tied up with feelings of guilt, and her thoughts, traveling backward, arrived quickly at the story she had been prevented from finishing. It was a story she had told once before up to the same point, to her own mother, at a time when she had not known its sequel. Now, sensing again the chill of Dorothy's careless "It could happen to—," she was compelled by the integrity of memory to recall the look of distress her story had brought to her mother's eyes. Her mother needn't have worried, poor darling. The lingering illness, the devastating stroke she feared, had not come; she had died without the slightest warning, peacefully (*how does anyone know?*) in her sleep. Amabel had not seen her for over a year, so there had been no moment of shock, no sense of loss, even. But the dead are patient; they wait for us to understand what we were unable to understand while they were with us, and Amabel was forced now to remember her mother with grief and remorse.

Amabel had accompanied her husband to Berlin just after the burning of the Reichstag. Diplomatic receptions were less frequent than before, but they still occurred, and at one of them a

Swedish lady whom Amabel had met at Geneva and not seen since came up to her to say, "A friend of yours wants to know if you remember her." Then Amabel realized that there was something special about a figure standing a few paces behind the Swedish lady—the aura that surrounds an unrecognized individual who has recognized oneself. The aura thickened for a moment and dispersed completely when Amabel identified Frau von Bernsdorff. It was her very self, the brisk and elegant Frau von Bernsdorff of Geneva—not the wreck who had been towed into the Café des Alpes. Her hair was quite white, but still set in rigid waves already a little old-fashioned; she wore horn-rimmed glasses instead of carrying a lorgnette, and a strip of orange tulle was tucked into the opening of her tailored suit instead of the exuberant folds of pastel-hued chiffon that Amabel remembered. The folds of flesh in her face, on the contrary, had broadened and paled, but the features were notably firm and symmetrical; there was no trace of their ever having been knocked sidewise by a paralytic stroke.

Amabel faltered something that she felt to be not quite tactful about the third session of the Disarmament Commission, when her friend had had such a terrible illness. Frau von Bernsdorff raised her eyebrows. She had never been to Geneva after the second session, she said with a touch of asperity. And had never had a serious illness in her life. Almost at once, she had walked away with the Swedish lady. Perhaps she had put Amabel's embarrassment down to political causes. "And bang goes visual memory," Amabel said.

Certain comings and goings in the hall, the rattle of dishes on a tray, Cynthia's high, defensive voice, a gruff remark and a guffaw from Tom, the closing of a door, and profound silence suggested to Amabel that all were seated round the dining-room table. They've forgotten all about me, or perhaps they think I'm asleep, she thought. But there came a careless thump on her door, and, hardly giving her time to huddle her dressing gown over her nylon slip, Tom was in the room. "Dinner's ready," he said.

"Hullo, Tom!" Amabel moved toward him and he took a step to meet her, stooping to kiss her forehead—the last few years in which Tom had been shooting upward, Amabel's frame had spent in settling on its roots. Amabel kissed him on his glowing cheek, turning her own to rest against his full, childish lips. His return kiss was warm and impetuous. "That's better," Amabel said. "I hate unilateral kisses. Say I'm just coming."

She brushed her hair in front of the mirror over the bathroom basin, pinned it in a coil to the back of her head, and splashed her face with silky, tepid water. A glance into the mirror was enough to direct the mechanical thrusts of the hairpins, but as she scrubbed her knuckles under the tap she examined her reflection closely, trying to preserve for the benefit of the assembled family the mellow liveliness that the encounter with Tom had brought to her face.

All looked up as she came into the room, and Cynthia started from "Gammer's place" and slid into the empty chair next to Tom. Gammer hated this, and they all knew she hated it. Would she have liked them to keep the seat by the window inviolate, even when she was not there? Yes.

"Where's Frances?" Amabel asked, unfolding her napkin.

"She went home to get John's dinner," Dorothy said. "She promised they'd be back by three for bridge."

The eating part of dinner, as Cynthia called it, was over by half past two, and Dorothy wanted to know why Amabel shouldn't get in a little nap before her guests arrived. "Charles and I will hold them in parley till you wake."

"I've had a nap," Amabel said. "I don't want to sleep my life away." *Why not?*

"I'll bring the bridge table," Charles said. "I took it for drying negatives. Shall I get the bathroom stool for the Freak?"

"No," Amabel said, "the encyclopedia's better, really." Tiny Mr. Carruthers was the fourth member of the bridge group. Amabel, who believed it was less painful to accept another's deformity than to ignore it, always called with loud cheerfulness for a volume of the Encyclopædia Britannica to put on Mr. Carruthers' chair when he approached the table.

An hour later the flat was as silent as a sea shell on the mantelpiece. In Amabel's room, the bridge players hardly spoke; Charles and Dorothy dozed on their beds, the Wogs snoring lightly on the mat between them; Cynthia had made a getaway before her mother could catch her; and Tom was sleeping off what had perhaps been his first solid meal for three days, curled up on the dining-room sofa with his shoes on.

"Everybody vulnerable," John Liddell announced.

"Telephone!" Frances said.

"I'll go," said Amabel, who happened to be dummy. "I don't want anybody waking the children."

The call was for her. From Deborah. "No. It's all right," Amabel said. "I'm dummy. Frances and John and the darling Freak have come to help me abridge my doleful days. . . . Did I? And did you look it up? Look under 'doleful,' 'death,' or 'days.' "

Amabel had left the door of her room open, and every word she said could be heard by the bridge players, so when she strolled back it was to a set of smiling faces. Nobody showed the slightest sign of embarrassment. Mr. Carruthers had long ago discovered that he was known to them all as the Freak. He minded the title no more (perhaps no less) than court jesters of old were supposed to mind being mocked at as dwarfs and hunchbacks. "And how is my friend Deborah?" he asked now, with his usual courtliness.

Amabel yawned and took her place at the bridge table. "Same old round of poverty, hunger, and dirt."

Frances made indistinguishable sounds of indignation.

"What did you say?" Amabel asked sweetly.

"Nothing. I didn't say anything."

Again John Liddell reminded them that everyone was vulnerable.

Sounds in the hall told of Cynthia's return. More complicated sounds followed. Steps passing and repassing, a sour exchange of admonitions and defense between Dorothy and Cynthia—the unwashed dishes. Charles spoke once with calm authority; the sound of rushing waters between the opening and shutting of a door; a deep growl from Tom. The front door slammed. The silence that followed was soon broken again by a muted whine in the hall.

Frances, now dummy, got up and stretched her arms. "I'll go and put the coffee on," she said, and, not allowing the Wogs time for his ceremonial hesitations, she bundled him into the room with a kindly push from behind. Frustrated, he stood at the edge of the carpet twitching all over, then wriggled up to Amabel, wagging his tail and nuzzling at her ankles.

"Yes, you love me very much when there's no one else at home," Amabel said.

The rubber was over and had been hotly discussed by the time Frances came in with the tray.

"What have you been doing?" Amabel asked suspiciously. "Not washing up, I hope. Dorothy'll be furious."

"I had to do a little to get at the tap," Frances said pacifically. "There's plenty left."

Coffee was drunk in relaxed silence, as if everyone was suddenly tired. Afterward there was time for one more rubber, in the middle of which the family could be heard returning. Amabel was longing to know what they had seen, but she knew they wouldn't come into her room; they never did when she had friends. But somebody opened the door a crack to let the Wogs out for his bedtime walk.

The last rubber came to an end, and good-bys were said in the room. John Liddell stood looking at Amabel as if he were again going to say, "Everybody vulnerable," but he only gave a stiff half bow over her hand and thanked her for a pleasant evening. Mr. Carruthers bowed over her hand as if he were going to kiss it, but he didn't. Frances and Amabel exchanged faintly conspiratorial glances and nodded to one another.

When she heard the front door close gently behind them, Amabel went into the hall to put out the light. And if Charles has forgotten to leave me the paper, he's a bastard, she thought. He wouldn't, of course; he never does. But it would be just like that Tom to have quietly snitched it without a thought of his poor old grandmother lying awake with nothing to read. If he has, I'll drag it from under his very pillow, whether I wake him or not—as if anybody could.

But there was the *Observer*, folded lengthwise on the telephone table. Why does one always prepare for the worst, she wondered. So as not to be let down, I suppose—insurance against disappointment.

Amabel remembered, as she had to remember every Sunday evening, how her husband began the difficult crossword with the Greek name at home and took it to the F.O. to finish—*in collegium*, he said—and brought the paper back on Monday for her to do the Everyman with her mother. She could never quite finish them now; her mother had been better at them than she.

Amabel undressed, glancing the while at the front page, but as soon as she was in bed turned to the book section. An article about Meredith seemed to start out of the page as if there was nothing else on it, and Amabel suddenly remembered her dream. She had dreamed that Meredith was dead and it was all her fault. For ten minutes she lay on her back with closed eyes, searching for associations. None came, but the depression returned in full force. She knew the thing to do was to recall the pleasant things that had happened during the day—the talk over the breakfast table had been nice; Tom was back; the dinner had been good, the bridge party a success; Charles, the Wogs had been darlings, as usual, Dorothy affectionate. But what was the good when Meredith was lying in wait for her at the end?

It was a clear case for the golden capsule that put you to sleep for three hours and the green capsule that took over for the rest of the night. Amabel struggled out of bed to go for a glass of water—lukewarm was supposed to be best; it dissolved the capsules quicker. *Meredith.*